Outlaws of Ravenhurst
Study Edition

Outlaws of Ravenhurst
Study Edition

Text by
Sister M. Imelda Wallace, S.L.

Illustrations by
Louis A. Schuster, S.M.

Aids to Appreciation by
Janet P. McKenzie

A RACE for Heaven Product

Biblio Resource Publications
108½ South Moore Street
Bessemer, MI 49911
2009

Published by
Biblio Resource Publications, Inc.
108½ South Moore Street
Bessemer, MI 49911
inquiries@biblioresource.com
www.BiblioResource.com

ISBN 978-1-934185-23-0

Library of Congress Control Number: 2009923824

With the exception of pronouns referring to God, rules of capitalization of religious and doctrinal terms follow the *Style Guide* of the United States Conference of Catholic Bishops, 2008.

A **R**ead **A**loud **C**urriculum **E**nrichment Product
www.RACEforHeaven.com

Printed in the United States of America

1.0

Table of Contents

Table of Contents

Preface

L.M. Wallace wrote and illustrated *Outlaws of Ravenhurst* in 1923 for publication by Franciscan Herald Press. After undergoing considerable editing, Catholic Authors Press republished *Outlaws* in 1950, attributing authorship to the religious name of Sr. M. Imelda Wallace and adding illustrations created by Louis A. Schuster. Subsequently reprinted by several publishers, this exciting work of Catholic historical fiction has become a Catholic children's classic.

This new edition contains the revised story of 1950 in addition to chapter-by-chapter aids designed to assist readers in assimilating the book's strong Catholic elements into their own daily lives. The "Aids to Appreciation" section focuses on critical thinking, integration of Biblical teachings, and the study of the virtuous life to which Christ calls us as mature, confirmed Catholics. With its emphasis on the virtues (theological and moral plus the gifts and fruits of the Holy Spirit), the spiritual and the corporal works of mercy, and the Beatitudes, this study edition of *Outlaws of Ravenhurst* is an excellent catechetical tool for those preparing to receive the Sacrament of Confirmation. Use this exciting story as a living book to better understand the personality traits Christ wants us to develop and how we can live the "authentic Christian life" (*Compendium* of the *Catholic Church* ¶360) that the life and teachings of our Lord Jesus model for us.

About the Authors

LORABEL MARIE WALLACE was born near Forester, Michigan, on September 6, 1884. She graduated from Northern Arizona Teachers College in 1903 and taught in the mining camps of Arizona until joining the Sisters of Loretto in Nerinx, Kentucky, on July 4, 1908. Thereafter, Sr. Mary Imelda taught in various parish schools in Missouri, Nebraska, Colorado, and Kentucky. Sr. Mary Imelda received her B.A. degree from Loretto Heights College, Colorado, in 1934. She is the author of *Outlaws of Ravenhurst*, a well-researched historical fiction account of Scottish Catholics in the seventeenth century, and *The Lure of the West*, a western romance published in 1924. She collaborated for eleven years in writing the five-volume *Living My Religion* series for Benziger Brothers in 1942-1951.

JANET P. MCKENZIE graduated from Michigan State University with a B.A. in 1976, majoring in social work. A convert to the Faith in 1981, Janet has over twenty-five years experience in parish religious education. Happily married for over thirty years, she and her husband have five children and five grandchildren. They home educated for twelve years. In 2001, Janet began writing Catholic resources for home educators and has authored thirteen books including study guides for the Mary Fabyan Windeatt biographies, a family First Holy Communion preparation program, *The King of the Golden City Study Edition*, and *Reading the Saints*. A secular Carmelite since 2003, she is a member of the Carmel of the Holy Cross in Iron Mountain, Michigan. In 2008, she obtained her master's degree in religious education from Loyola University, New Orleans. She is currently working on a family preparation program for the Sacrament of Confirmation.

1

THE GRAY-CLOAKED STRANGER

Night lay on the long swelling waves of the Chesapeake Bay: no wind, no star, a murky darkness. The spars[1] of an unlighted ship loomed through the fog and sank into fog again. Stealthily, from the bulky gloom of the deck, a dory[2] slid on oiled ropes to the somber waters. Two seamen followed. Then down the ropes came an object that seemed to be a man with a bundle, wrapped in a long gray cloak. The dory pulled off and was swallowed by the fog.

For an hour, the ship swung at anchor, still no light aloft or alow, and no sound save the dull lapping of the waves. Then from the stern, a bell began to toll. One slow, booming tone rolled off and died away before the next followed. As if drawn out of the fog by the bell's deep calling, the dory came gliding back again. Two seamen were at the oars. The anchor sobbed up from the sea's grip. The tide

---

[1] Long poles to which sails are fastened; masts
[2] Flat-bottomed boat

was offshore and the ship floated out with the current, unlighted, silent, back into the white smother[3] from which it had come.

Keen and marrow-searching, the morning wind rose along the shore of Maryland. Dense fog became a fine, drizzling rain turning to sleet. Breasting it along lonely ways among the sand dunes, hurried a lean, bent man carrying a bundle under his cloak—a long, muddied, thread-bare garment as gray as rain-soaked ashes.

The bundle was hard to manage. It seemed to move of its own accord. Once in a while, a sound came out of it, a wailing cry, "Dunkie Teewee! Take Dordie out."

"Sh!" the man would whisper. His tone was a stern command, but his eyes glowed with great love. The bundle would sniffle a moment or two, then grow quiet.

After hours of tramping, the man found a nook where the forest met the last sand dunes. Here, crouched between a low bank and a tree, with his own body shielding the bundle from the sleet, the man opened his cloak and loosened the sailcloth and the plaid shawl within. A fat fist slipped out of the opening, then a tousle of brown curls, a gurgling laugh, and a piping voice, "Dood Dunkie Tee-wee! Take it all off!"

"Hush!" came the man's low command in a tone that would have been menacing except that it was so deeply kind. "Drink." He drew a flask from his cloak.

The child drank, but all the while he stared over the bottle's rim at the man—a wise, wide, baby stare. His eyes were blue and deep as the sea, with a flash in their depths that in the turning of an instant might be fun or fury; just now the eyes shone with a puzzled and half-angry trust.

---

[3] A confused multitude of things

Even in this short time the little fist which guided the flask was growing blue though it gripped with deft strength—a swordsman's right hand still in the making. The stranger hastened to enclose the baby in his warm coverings. He wound the cloak about himself and his bundle, left the shelter, and hurried on through the stinging sleet.

By midafternoon, they had reached the top of a rough knob. Here the man seemed to be expecting someone. Placing himself in a spot well screened by the underbrush, he kept a constant eye on a little path that wound around the base of the hill.

It was almost sundown before the expected one arrived, a gentle old man on a steady-going bay horse. His round, low-crowned hat, sober clothing, and great saddlebags gave him the appearance of a missionary passing from one Mass station to another. If the man of the gray cloak was expecting the meeting, this other person evidently was not; yet the stranger studied the missionary's face with a look of recognition and relief. Then, turning sharply, he slipped off in an opposite direction across the hill and down the other side until he reached the path at a point where the horseman must soon pass.

Here the stranger took his queer bundle from beneath his cloak and propped it up against a stump. He loosened the wrappings from the baby's face and pressed upon the little brow one long, long kiss. The child awoke and cried out to him. The gray-cloaked figure whirled and darted up the hill into a thicket. Perhaps he feared the horseman would come before time. Perhaps he could not trust himself further lest he fail to carry out his plan.

The child, left suddenly alone, cried out at first as if it were some game; then, cross from weariness, he screamed and struggled with his coverings. At last, as if too weary to battle longer, his voice dropped to a convulsed sobbing, "Dunkie! Dunkie Teewee!"

Far up the slope, the stranger knelt between a ledge and a twisted mass of brush and vine. His clenched hands were outstretched on the rock, gripped upon each other till the fingernails bit into the lean flesh. His hollow, weather-furrowed face was set by the clenched will behind it, but his eyes were wet with an agony of love and longing.

4

2

BROWN-HEAD GOES FISHING

Two boys trotted along an old Maryland path. The brown-headed one carried poles and bait. The red-headed one held an old flintlock gun[4].

"Joel," grumbled the brown-head, "look at this bait. Not a blessed thing but cabbage worms! We won't get a fish till the owl knows when."

"What's bitin' on you, George? That's the best kind. A fish can have white worms any time he wants to nose along the bank, but he doesn't get green ones every day. Anyhow, I had to clean the cabbage pit this morning."

"Yah! I thought you had lazy man's reason."

"'Tisn't either lazy man's reason."

"Redhead's temper's red. Better run or he'll kill me dead," mocked George, leaping over a log and racing downhill.

---

[4] A type of gun that has a flint in the hammer to strike a metal plate, causing a spark to ignite the gunpowder

"You'll take that back!" panted Joel, scrambling after him with the old gun bouncing up and down on his shoulder.

"Like to see you make me!" But George's foot caught in a vine and down he went.

Joel sprang astride his back and began bouncing up and down, singing, "Take it back!"

"N-n-n-o-ooo-o, I won't!"

"Take it back!"

"I-ii-ee-ii-wo-wwo-ww—wo won't!"

"You've got to! I'll bounce till you do! Ouch! Oh, my foot!" Joel caught his big toe in both hands.

With a wiggle, George was free. "Have to take it back, do I?" He sprang over a log, then paused, for Joel was still hugging his toe. "What's up?"

"Got a splinter in my toe!"

"Cryin' for a splinter! Baby!"

"You'd cry if you had it!"

"Let's see. . . . That's a bee's stinger. Sure it hurts. Here, I'll pull it out for you."

"Ouch!"

"Mud'll take the sting out. Here's some."

"Was it a honeybee or just an old bumble?"

"Honeybee! See him under the violet? Maybe Daddy will hunt for the bee tree Sunday."

"Look, I must have stepped right on him. His wing is broken, and a couple of legs. I don't wonder you stung me back, old buzzer."

"Say, we'd better be going, or we'll get what Paddy gave the drum. You know Mother said she didn't send us to go gallivantin' in the woods. She sent us to fish." Then away they went, jumping over logs, dodging under bushes, setting all the blossoming sprays of May dancing in their wake.

They paused, out of breath, on the bank of the stream and dropped down on the moss to watch the fish slipping from stone to stone in the pool below.

"Look at that oriole," whispered George. "He is making a twin for himself in the water."

"The pool is a good looking glass to make doubles in," agreed Joel. "Whee, but your face is dirty!"

"So is yours!"

"Nothing else is the same, though. We are the least alike for a pair of twins—"

"Our eyes are the same color."

"Now, look again. Our eyes are blue, but yours are almost black, and mine are like skim milk. Your nose is long and there is a hump in it. Mine turns up at the end. Your jaws are as square as old Dick's bulldog's. Mine—"

"Quack, quack says the crazy duck! I'll pitch you in the creek for callin' me a bulldog." George sat up sharply, turned, and began digging for bait. The subject seemed to irritate him; yet, Brown-head, hunting by a rotted stump for worms, could not have remembered the baby Brown-head propped against that same stump by the gray-cloaked stranger some eight years before.

"I'm glad we're not as much alike as Which and Tother are. I found Which out behind the woodpile crying this morning. Tother stole the cream to feed his cat. Along came Mother and spanked Which for it. If we were alike, I might get a switchin' every time you need it."

"Would you get a lick amiss?" But Joel suddenly had a greater interest. His eyes were on his wooden bob. Under it went. He jerked the line, then drew in. "Quack yourself, old know-it-all! Cabbage worms won't catch fish! Look at this one, will you? Half as long as my arm!"

"Hsst! What's over there in those bushes?"

7

"Where?"

"The big ones on the other side of those cattails. Watch 'em wiggle! I bet it's that old fox. Daddy said to keep an eye out for him." George reached for the gun. "You won't steal any more of our chickens, old boy."

"Ready?" Joel was picking up a stone. "I'll bring him out for you."

"Let it fly!"

The stone hit the bushes squarely. There was a snarl. The branches parted and out sprang, not a fox, but a large brown bear. She looked up at them, growled, and put one foot in the water. The boys waited for no more but dashed up the bank.

Joel gave a sharp cry. George turned. "What's the matter with you? Quick! She's swimming!"

"I stepped on my fishhook!"

"Pull it out! She's comin'!"

"Can't! It's all the way in!"

"Here! Let me get hold of it!"

"Ow! Don't!"

"You got to stand it! She's halfway over! There, it's out! Come on now!"

"Oh! I can't step! Ow!"

"You've turned your ankle! Lean on me! Hop! She's almost here! Hop! I'll help you!"

"Go on, George, save yourself!"

"Do you think I'd leave you? Here, try to climb this tree."

"Too little! She can climb. Go on! You can run. Go on, George, quick!"

"Quit cryin'! Climb! I'll boost you!"

At last, Joel was astride a crotch in the tree.

George looked at his white face, jerked off both their belts, buckled them together, slipped one end of the strap around Joel's waist, twisted the rest around the limb a couple of times, and fastened it securely. "You can't fall now. Take the gun. You reload it. Fox-shot won't kill bears. Put in all we've got." The gun was a muzzle-loader[5]. One could put in as much powder and shot as needed.

"The bear hasn't come up the bank yet," whispered Joel. "Maybe she'll go downstream."

"No such luck! I've made a mess of it. There's a cub out on that limb."

"Whee! She'll come all right!"

George cut a branch, lopped off the twigs, and tied his knife to it. Then, reaching out, he poked at the cub's feet. The woolly baby whined, snarled, and backed farther out on the branch.

"His mammy hears him. Wow! She's mad!" warned Joel. "Get him down quick."

George gave a swift jab. The cub sprang back, and down he went squalling as he fell from bough to bough and shaking the branches wildly.

George plunged forward, lost his balance, caught himself again, and climbed into the main fork of the tree.

"She's climbed the bank," whispered Joel. "Do you want the gun?"

"No, wait till she's nearer. I might miss."

"Here she comes!"

The old bear came lumbering toward the tree. Her cub began to crawl to meet her but whimpered and sat down on its woolly haunches. Mother Bruin hurried forward and licked its bruises.

"Maybe she'll go off now."

"No, she won't."

_____

[5] A gun that is loaded through the open end of the barrel

"Hang on tight. Here she comes."

The bear charged the tree with all her force, retreated, and lunged again.

George clung desperately. Joel's wrenched ankle banged back and forth against the trunk until he moaned with pain, but he held the gun tightly and kept the muzzle pointed away from his brother.

Three times the old bear charged the tree. Then she began to climb.

"Quick, Joel! The gun!"

"Good! I've got it."

"Shoot quick! Look how high she is!"

"Might miss."

"Shoot, will you! She's almost up to you!"

"Might miss."

"She'll get your foot! Shoot!"

George was very still. He was looking straight into that great red mouth. He thrust the muzzle against the shining teeth and fired.

There was a roar, a snapping and recoil of branches, and a great thud at the base of the tree. Clutching the swaying branches, Joel twisted in his strap to see down through the leaves.

"George! O George!"

No sound came from below.

"Are you hurt?"

Then Joel saw the bleeding pile at the foot of the tree. The bear was on top of George. Both were still.

"George! Wiggle your foot if you hear me."

The bare foot lay still.

"He's dead!" sobbed Joel in helpless misery: the rebound of the tree had left him almost suspended by the straps, and the strain on his waist was making him faint. He struggled

back into the crotch again and began searching for the buckles, but they were out of his reach and behind the limb.

"George!" he pleaded. "Wiggle your foot, even your toes, just a little bit."

No movement below.

The silence of the forest closed in upon him, that silence which the noises of the wood-folk make only the more intense: a catbird calling his mate, a woodpecker tapping somewhere across the creek.

Joel struggled with the strap, trying to break it, but the rawhide was too tough.

Helplessness began to numb him. Would help . . . could help ever come? The folks at home would not think of searching till after supper, and by then. . ..

"O George, wiggle! Kick! Do anything! I can't stand this. You're dead and I'm a-dyin'! I know I am.

"Things are so black and swimmy and I'm so queer inside. There is no one to help us. No one can even hear us. But God, God can hear us. I forgot."

Then he prayed as he had never dreamed of praying. There was a strange, sweet sense of One unseen but very near. The numbing loneliness was gone.

"That woodpecker keeps tapping all the time. It's such a queer one, too. It goes click-a-clack. Maybe it's a cricket. No. A frog? They don't go like that either. It sounds like chopping. Could it be Daddy out in the new clearing?"

Joel made a horn of his hands and called, "Dad! O Daddy!" His voice was pitiful and weak.

The sound of the chopping went on steadily.

"He can't hear me." The boy drew a long breath. "O D-a-a-a-d!"

The chopping ceased for a moment, then went on.

12

"Dad! O-o-o Dad!"

Clear above the voices of the woodland came an answering hello. There was silence a while, then a call somewhat nearer. Another call, and then a giant, red-bearded horseman came in sight on the bank beyond the creek.

"Who's there? What's wrong?"

"A bear. It's killed George."

There was a splashing in the creek bottom, a rattle of stones on the bank, and John Abell came crashing through the alders[6]. He sprang from the saddle, threw the body of the bear backward, and passed his hand over the boy's body.

"Heart's still beating! Thank God! No bones broken.

"Just stunned, I think. Small thanks to you, Joel. Why didn't you pull the bear off? He's nearly smothered."

"I couldn't, Daddy," came Joel's voice weakly. "I couldn't reach the buckles."

John Abell looked up and saw the swollen, blood-stained foot and the white face. "Well, Son, are you hurt, too? Did the bear bite you?"

"No, Daddy, I hurt my foot."

"Well, you'll have to be a man and stand it a while longer. George needs me more." There was nothing in his tone to show which boy was his son.

Abell lifted Brown-head in his powerful arms and carried him to the pool. As he plunged him into the water, the lad gasped and opened his eyes.

"O Dad!" he cried as he caught sight of the red-bearded face. "The bear! She'll get Joel. He can't run."

"That bear won't hurt anybody now."

"Is she dead? Did I hit her?"

---

[6] Small, rapidly growing trees; members of the birch family

"Hit her? You about blew the gizzard out of her. You don't need to fill a gun chockfull even to kill a bear. You blew the gun up, boy."

"Oh, did I break it? And they cost so much!"

"Never mind the cost this time, Son. It's the boy I'm thinking about. 'Twas by the mercy of the Lord you didn't blow your own head off, but there's only a small powder burn. We'll say a rosary this night in thanksgiving."

Abell laid the boy on the moss. "I am going back to get Joel now," he said.

The wounded foot and wrenched ankle were soon bathed and bound.

"What is your old daddy going to do?" laughed Abell. "One dead bear, one live cub, one wounded hunter, and one dead one—they must go home right now. There is only one horse. We'll put the bear across the saddle. Joel can ride behind. Maybe the cub will follow. I'll carry George."

"No, no, Daddy, I can walk," announced the "dead" hunter, suddenly sitting up. "I'm not hurt, I just feel shaky inside."

"All the same, I'm going to carry you for a piece. Sure, you think you're as big as a man since you killed a bear all by yourself. I'll carry you with small trouble, but next time you go hunting I'll send to the fort for the army surgeon and the hospital corps to care for the dead and the wounded."

3

UNCLE ROGER

T here is Mother at the edge of the clearing," called Joel from his perch on the horse's back. "I wonder what brought her away out here?"

"Well, if the little twins have let their mother bring in the cows, they'll hear from me right now," said John Abell sternly.

"I don't think she's after the cows. It looks to me as if she's crying."

"Crying! Are you sure of it? Something is wrong then. Slip down, George, you'll have to walk now," and John Abell hurried through the woods.

"Mary!" he called as soon as they were within speaking distance. "What has gone wrong? Whatever it is, don't cry that way. We'll get through somehow, for sure and God's good."

"They've come for George!" she sobbed.

"Don't be taking that to heart now. It's one thing to come for him, and another to get him. I've had that boy too long to give him up at a minute's notice. They will prove their right before they take him, and we won't cross that bridge until we come to it. What do they say?"

"It's proof enough they have, and more's the pity. The minute I saw the gentleman, I knew he must be kin to George. He is like enough to the boy to be his father, but he is only an uncle. There are letters, too: one from His Excellency, Cecil Calvert[7], and one with the King's own hand and seal. They be great folk, John, and no mistake. The squire[8], too, is with them. They took Jim and Johnny till we deliver the boy. Oh, there's no way at all. We'll have to give George up."

"Calvert and the King and the squire, too?" said Abell slowly. "We've come to the bridge after all. I've no right to keep another man's son. No man would have the right to keep mine. But it's hard, bitter hard. I love the boy."

"Mother," broke in George, "they can't take us away from you? You won't let them take us, will you, Daddy?"

Mary Abell drew the boy into her arms. "You tell him, John," she sobbed. "I can't do it."

"Well, there is nothing else to do but say out straight and blunt a thing I never meant that you should know. George, you are not one of the Abells. You are not Joel's twin. You are not my son, though God knows there is not one of my own that I love more than I love you, child. Father Cornwall found you sitting by the roadside and brought you to us. I set you on Mary's knee beside Joel, and so far as love and care go, you have been ours ever since. It is a bitter thing to me to give you up. Still, I have

---

[7] Second Lord Baltimore; obtained a charter from England's King Charles I for the colony of Maryland, established as a Catholic refuge; Lord Proprietor of Maryland from 1632-1675
[8] Judge

no right to keep you from your people."

"Oh, you were so sweet that night," sobbed the woman. "I asked you your name. You put one arm around wee Joel and up you looked with your big blue eyes for all the world like a robin. 'Me's Dordie!' says you. 'Me wants Dunkie Teewee, me do!' We thought by that your name was George, but the gentleman called you Gordon. For many a day you cried for 'Dunkie Teewee!' But, John," Mrs. Abell turned toward her husband, "there is worse than the taking of him. I don't like the looks of that uncle. Oh, how he did curse when he saw the image of our Lady on the mantel! Perhaps he will lead our lad astray."

"As for leading our lad astray," said Abell, putting one great hairy hand on the boy's shoulder, "no man can lead you into sin if you don't follow him. You will have to stand on your own two feet and be a man. Remember one thing: there is nothing worth buying, not fast horses nor fine hous-es, not even a place in the King's court, if the price you pay for it is the fire of hell forevermore." There was a clatter of hoofs on the bridge in the hollow. "Here they come now! Good-by, lad! We'll say the beads[9] every day till we know that you are safe." Abell's deep voice trembled. "Good-by, boy, and God bless you."

"The one on the gray horse is his uncle," said Mary, pointing one roughened, toilworn hand. "You can see the likeness yourself, John."

"The boy's face is brown and his jaw is more square," said Abell, "though they are indeed alike, but God grant the boy's face may never be like the man's. It is bitter hard to trust our boy to such a keeper—bitter hard."

The horsemen galloped toward them, straight across

---

[9] Rosary

the sprouting corn. The gentleman sprang from his horse and drew the gauntlet[10] from his right hand. The fingers were long and white. There was a ring, one only, but the jewel in it might have shone in the King's crown. He took the brown hand of the boy in his and looked at the face closely.

"It is the Gordon," he said, "but whence come all these bruises? There is a burn!" Turning sharply toward Abell, "You will explain this."

"The lad loaded the gun too heavily. It was old and blew up with him, sir. Thanks to the mercy of God, he wasn't hurt badly."

"God's mercy! What of your own carelessness? Allowing a mere babe to load a gun!"

"Sir, here in Maryland we don't call boys of ten, *babies*. If you think him too young to handle a gun, look at the bear on my horse yonder. That's his hunting bag for this afternoon." There was just a touch of honest pride in John Abell's voice.

"Gordon killed yonder great beast?" cried the nobleman. "Ah, well, no wonder! He is the scion[11] of the House of Ravenhurst. The earls were famous huntsmen, all of them. Edwin, remain and bring the skin. It will look well below Fire-the-Braes' antlers, eh, Godfrey? Give the fellow the reward. It is a fat purse and will repay you for your trouble, my man."

John Abell straightened his shoulders. "Keep your money, your Lordship," he said bluntly. "The boy is yours. I have no right to keep him, but I'm not selling him to you."

"Ah, if a man has a cabin in this new land, he fancies

---

[10] Long glove, usually of leather to protect the hand; may be thrown down in combat to challenge an opponent

[11] Descendant or heir of an influential family

himself already a gentleman," sneered Sir Roger Gordon. "Martin, give the peasant his brats. Walter, bring Lord Gordon his horse."

The twins struggled down from the soldier's saddle and ran to their mother. But, as Walter came forward with the horse, George drew his hand from his uncle's grasp. "I want to say good-by, please," he said.

"Walter, give the young gentleman your hand to mount. We have wasted too much time as it is."

"I'm going to stay till I say good-by," flashed the boy, "and I won't go before."

"Do as you are bid, George." It was Mary's quiet voice.

"Yes, Mother," and the boy mounted.

The horsemen trotted back across the field and down the road, but the boy's face was turned toward the wood. The little group among the trees dropped out of sight. The cabin came and went. As the last bit of smoke was hidden by the trees, the brave lips began to tremble, and the tears came, burning-hot and choking. Sir Roger gave a signal. The troop swung forward, leaving him and his nephew alone.

"Is this the gratitude you show to the uncle who has come overseas in search of you?"

"I wanted to say good-by. You wouldn't let me even kiss Mother or tell Joel—"

"Kiss? Such dirty—"

"They are not dirty—only from hard work since sunup. They are my folk. Joel, he's my twin. I mean, I always thought he was—"

"Your folk!" cried the gentleman with a laugh. "But you do not know, as yet, who or what you are. You are Charles Gordon, Lord Rock Raven, the son of James Gordon, Lord of Rock Raven, third Earl of Ravenhurst. Your mother is

Lady Margaret of Douglas, daughter of Sir Wilfrid Douglas of the line of old Sir Archibald Bell-the-Cat[12]. There are few in Scotland that can boast such blood as yours. And you are weeping for your folk! The folk of the heir of Ravenhurst!" He laughed again. "John Abell, lord of a log cabin and a pigsty, in size an ox, in brain a pipkin[13]. . . his most noble dame with a face as wrinkled and brown as the apple she baked last Candlemas. . .a dozen—nay, was it fourteen—red-headed brats. . .and these are the folk of the scion of Ravenhurst!"

A light leaped far down in those deep-blue Douglas eyes, a flame that burned up boyish tears, leaving a white-hot anger that Roger both knew and feared.

Gordon answered: "Sir, poor or not, the Abells are my folk."

---

[12] Archibald Douglas, fifth Earl of Angus (1449-1513); earned the name "Bell the Cat" in his battle with Robert Cochrane in 1482 at Lauder, Scotland

[13] A small cooking pot

4

WHEN MEN PLAY MARBLES

The good ship *Anne of Glasgow* sped, all sails drawing aloft and alow. The wind whistled jig tunes in the cordage and set the tackle blocks clapping in mimic applause. This was a good sound to the ears of Brown-head, for it sang to him of the Maryland woods. He stood by the stern rail, looking back at the ripples of the wake into the zig-zag world of wave tips, and on to the west where the gray disk of the ocean met the grim vault of the sky. He felt dumbly conscious of his own exceeding smallness in the world of waters and decidedly smaller in the strange coming world of men of which Sir Roger preached endlessly. During such sermons the boy listened as little as possible and, the moment they were over, set himself to forget. Yet one thing was bitterly clear—Brown-head was no longer George of the gay Maryland woods, but—"my Lord of Gordon." He beat his silken knee against the rail and growled.

"Ho! Your Lordship, the face you wear holds storm enough to sink the *Anne of Glasgow!*"

Gordon turned, half-pleased at the interruption, for he knew the voice. It was the man whom Sir Roger called Godfrey. Brown-head almost liked him. At least he was a pleasant fellow with whom to waste an hour.

"What has raised the present glum wind?" Godfrey ran on.

"Sir Roger," fumed Gordon. "I'd rather swallow bear's grease than hear him! He's had me in the cabin, talking high and mighty, making me walk on my toes like a top-silly girl at a husking bee, ordering me every once in half-a-crack to flop my head on my shins, and getting as mad as a slapped wasp if I fall sprawling instead of. . ."

"Making a court bow correctly. But your Lordship is learning with astonishing rapidity to—"

"Act like a jack-a-dandy for the pleasure of an uncle who does so dearly love me—baa-a!" Gordon thrust his hand into his belt wallet and drew out his only treasures: four agate pebbles, roughly rounded by many hammer-ings, a pioneer boy's marbles. Squatting on the deck, he placed three and began to shoot at them with the fourth.

"Loves me!" he growled. "So do wood ticks! Wants me for something. Crooked. Mean like—" Gordon shot a marble with a vicious snap.

"So!" whistled Godfrey, fixing his keen eyes on the boy's face. "For a ten-year lad, you are rather more than some-what shrewd, my young Laird o' Gordon. You don't like being the marble when Sir Roger is the shooter and it's his game."

The lad gathered his marbles with a sweep of his hands and jumped to his feet. "Why should I?" he demanded.

Godfrey chuckled. "Listen. Today you are the heir, the marble; tomorrow you are the Earl and Sir Roger is the marble. Wait for your turn."

It was the boy's turn to whistle. Godfrey looked out over the sea a moment, then spoke again.

"Your Lordship, you have not yet awakened to the fact that you are Earl of Ravenhurst, though as yet a trifle too young to take charge of affairs. An earl[14]—a little king in your own domain! But let me show you a picture of what it means to be chief at old Rock Raven.

"Now, there was Fire-the-Braes; he is not the first chief of your house, but the first to write his name in history. There has been a chieftain's stronghold on Rock Raven since—oh, since first God made the Scot and the devil set Scots a-fighting! A bit to the south of Ben Ender Mountain, a headland of black and jagged rock is thrust a good ten bowshots into the frith[15]. The sea beats itself to a fury roaring about its wreck-strewn base. This rock, from its shape, or from the ill-omened birds that nested there, or because of the fierce marauders[16] who made of it a stronghold, has been called since the beginning, Rock Raven. Now, Fire-the-Braes was a bold and bloody man. He carried a long two-handed claymore[17] the like of which no other man ever bore. From his wild and lonely tower on Rock Raven he sallied out for daring raids, driving home cattle, plundering, burning villages and harvest fields. It was for this he was dubbed Fire-the-Braes, a name of terror from the Isles to the English border—"

"An out-and-out villain and robber!" cried the boy.

"Softly, softly," teased Godfrey. "If any knight had named

---

[14] Title awarded by a king to a chieftain who ruled a given territory in the stead of the king; wife's title would be "Lady"

[15] A long, narrow inlet or arm of the sea where a river current meets the tide; also firth

[16] Those who roam about, raiding and plundering

[17] A large, double-edged sword

Fire-the-Braes a common robber, swords had not slept in scabbards. The chief was but a bold blade in the rough game of war. Boys throw down marbles and play 'grabs'; men play 'grabs' also."

"But—"

"Your Lordship has a keen sense of honor. Fire-the-Braes lived centuries ago when even kings were crude. In fact, your house rose from a petty chieftain's stronghold to a knight's castle by a rough jest. This Fire-the-Braes once sprang out from the bracken[18] and single-handed fought with a mighty antlered buck and slew him with his claymore under the very eyes of the King who'd sworn to hang him. But, instead, being pleased by the wild Highlander's jest, the King made Fire-the-Braes his friend, an armored knight, and warden[19] to keep other men in order.

"Yet, if your Lordship wishes to hear about a knight of honor as unsullied as the heaven-born snow, let me tell you of Lang-Sword. He was your great-great-grandfather, the man who raised Ravenhurst to an earldom.

"It was in that old time," began Godfrey, "when monarchs crimsoned their own swords and bore the scars of their own battle wounds. James Stuart[20], King of Scotland, stood on a jutting rock above the frith. The sea is no respecter of persons; the veering wind that whipped the surf sent its mist to sting the royal face. But a storm of another nature thundered in the voice of James as he eyed a seaman groveling at his feet.

"'Is this the dog that refused to obey our order?'

"'Sire,' wailed the wretch, 'I canna put my boat across

---

[18] Area overgrown with thickets of large, coarsely-leafed ferns
[19] Official in charge of a specific territory
[20] King James V (1512-1542) ruled Scotland from the age of 17 months until his death following a mental collapse

the frith. The storm-wrack's comin' fast. The sail is torn. The hull's aleak.'

"'And your coward heart would sink a galley[21]! My Lord of Arran[22], run a spear through this scoundrel who calls himself a Scottish seaman.'

"Force a jackal against a wall and he will fight a lion. Goaded by despair, the man retorted: 'If ye git the best o' an enemy, what matters it that starvin' wife and child weep o'er a dead father?'

"Indignation seized the surrounding knights. A hundred swords were drawn, but James V was a man of moods as changeable as the sea. Instead of added wrath, pity pierced the fury of his eyes.

"'So,' he said, 'and is it love of wife and child that makes a coward of a man?' He paused, and grief softened that lean, strong-passioned Stuart face. The royal home was yet in mourning for two bonny princes—sons, long-hoped, long-waited-for, that died as fast as wee lips learned to lisp their father's name. It was the man in James and not the king that spoke.

"'And have you, then, a son?'

"'Aye, sire.' Hope was born of the kind note in the monarch's voice. 'Three sons, and one runs halfway doon the hill to meet me as I come bearin' my nets at night, and one clings to the skirts of my gude wife, and one is wee bit yet and sleeps upon her breast.'

"King James turned short about and looked over the sea. A moment so he stood and then he said:

"'Go to your home, good man. Tell them their mute cry has saved you from a coward's grave and,' the royal voice sank low, 'bid the wee ones pray that God may send the

---

[21] A large, open boat propelled by oars
[22] Possibly James Hamilton (1516-1575), Third Lord of Arran

King a son.'

"Again the face of James grew stern. He gazed across the waters to the shore beyond. The frith was narrow at this point, for, from the opposite shore, the crags and cliffs of Ben Ender thrust themselves a good mile into the sea. Narrow the strait might be, but calm it seldom was. The wind puffed sharply, veering from north to east, and the scudding cloud-wrack covered half the sky. On the shore across the frith, a group of men waved torches. It was Argyll[23] signaling for orders, and there was none that dared to put the leaking boat across the strait. A clank of armor broke the suspense, and a young knight dropped on his knees before the King.

"'May it please you, sire,' said a noble at the King's right hand, 'Sir Malcolm Gordon craves audience. The youth is of the blood of bold Gordon Fire-the-Braes, as brave as he and as gallantly desirous of serving Your Majesty. He is dubbed Lang-Sword and is the Laird of yon little tower that perches there across the way like a raven upon a rock.'

"'Sire,' the face of Lang-Sword glowed with loyalty and daring, 'the word "I cannot" is not said in the House of Gordon. Let the honor of bearing the message be mine. I shall swim the frith, my Liege.'

'Swim!' cried the King, doubting his ears. 'Swim!—where a boat does not dare!'

"'Sire, I did it a year ago for pure sport.'

"'But not in the face of a coming storm!'

"'Nor did I swim then beneath a king's eye.'

"'But hark, noble Gordon, even now the surf booms along the rocks of Ben Ender!'

"'Sire, I know where the sandy shallows lie and, at worst,

---

[23] Possibly Gillespie Roy Archibald Campbell (1507-1558), the fourth Earl of Argyll

I can die but once for you, my Liege.'

"No kings ever played dice with the hearts and brains and souls of men as did the Stuart line, and now James smiled. Well was his pride pleased by this youth's devotion —almost adoration, and, when he spoke, scarcely could praise have been couched more cunningly.

"'My Lord of Gordon, your loyalty deserves our confidence. You shall know what message it is that you bear and why.' The King paused, and those who stood about His Majesty stepped off perhaps a dozen paces. 'Russell[24] has proved himself a thrice-compounded villain and traitor. His castle is a very nest for the hatching of border plots, raids, and burnings. Bid Argyll march on Russell. Raise your own clan and assist. Success attend your valor, noble Gordon. If you win the day, we pledge that you shall be belted Earl.'

"Lang-Sword kissed the royal hand and strode swiftly down to the beach. Unbuckling his heavy armor, he cast it on the sand. Then, ready for the plunge, he stepped out on a rock, paused, and dropped on his knee. And with him knelt those beside the waves and James of Scotland with his lords on the cliff.

"The Lang-Sword's prayer was brief. 'St. Mary, grant me long wind and strong blood. If I set foot on yonder shore, I vow a silver shrine to deck thy chapel in the wood.'

"King James answered, 'Amen!' Then Lang-Sword stood, hands pointed for the dive, watching for the outgoing of a wave—the tallest knight in the Highlands, lean, with knotty muscles that rose and fell like those that move under a tiger's hide. A seagull flew across the face of the racing wrack and screamed the wild defiance of the storm.

---

[24] Probably John Russell (1485-1555), the First Baron Russell and later Earl of Bedford

"'Godspeed!' called the voices from the shore.

"'St. Mary for King James!' the Lang-Sword cried, and plunged into the sea. Like a shaft of white light the body cleft air and water and was gone. A wave came trembling in, growling, shaking a fleecy mane. The head of the swimmer rose. A crest reared above him, broke, crashed over him, carrying him back a spear's length. He sank. Those on the cliff and those on the shore leaned, gasping. He rose. The long white line of foam was between the swimmer and the shore.

"'Ho, Scot! Well swum!' called James. 'By Mary's virgin soul, I swear to deck that shrine with blood-red rubies!'

"Thunder muttered along Ben Ender. Flashes of lightning played on the cloud like lancers tilting before a battle. The swimmer had gained three bowshots' space against the sea. His head was a dodging speck and the King dared not rest his eyes lest he lose sight of it. The storm broke, rain swirling to the mad onslaught of the wind. The frith rose and sank in white, roaring heights and bellowing caverns. The lightning shot its jagged bolts from sky to ocean —and the swimmer?—the tempest had swallowed him.

"James Stuart strode the cliff. Sometimes he prayed aloud and sometimes cursed himself or any that dared venture within earshot of the royal wrath. An hour passed. The storm drew back among the hills, ravage-glutted, exhausted, muttering.

"'This day was lost the noblest knight that ever risked life for Scotland's king.' So said James Stuart, his face gloomy as the sullen frith below. But Arran, peering through the mist, gave a sudden pluck at the royal sleeve. 'Ho, my Liege, a light on Ben Ender! The Argyll signals! Two to right, three to left. They have the message! Holy God! Lang-Sword has crossed the frith!'"

Godfrey paused, for Gordon stood with his right hand clenched as if it held a sword. He drew his breath through parted lips and his eyes were like a war eagle's.

"Aye," cried Godfrey, "your young Lordship is a fine keen splinter of old Lang-Sword's steel!"

But the boy was not pleased with the compliment or with anything that delayed the tale, for he broke in, "And Lang-Sword raised the clan, joined Argyll, and then—?"

"Like a good knight and true, he set out after Russell, chased him well up into the morasses[25] beyond Ben Ender. The Lowlander fled north toward the Laird o' the Isles. Lang-Sword harried the Russell lands and followed. With Argyll, he crept upon Russell in the wilds beyond Straithbogie and caught him in act of treason. He was pledging to lure King James to his castle and let the Isle-man capture the royal person. All this, Bluff Hal of England[26] was paying for. As your Lordship knows, English kings have ever tried to put Scotland in their hunting bag.

"Russell was hanged, drawn, and quartered as a traitor should be, and Lang-Sword was given all Russell's forfeited lands, made an earl, and became a trusted counselor of good King James. In truth, the plunge of Lang-Sword into the frith was a leap into the high seas of royal favor."

"Good!" cried Gordon.

---

[25] Areas of low-lying, soggy ground; marshes or swamps
[26] Common nickname for King Henry VIII, who reigned England from 1509 to 1547

5

CASTLE RAVENHURST

It was harvest time before the long journey on sea and land ended. They had changed horses at the last inn, and the carriage rattled merrily along the Highland road. The tired boy had watched the haymakers, field after field, until he had fallen asleep. Sir Roger sat scowling, tapping his boot with his scabbard[27]. Godfrey, who seemed to be something more than a servant, sat watching him.

"Three long years of labor, and now failure," growled the nobleman.

"Failure! Is it a lord of the House of Gordon who cries 'failure' when the first knot comes? We have the heir, and old Ravenhurst will yet be the greatest earldom in Scotland."

"The heir, we have him, indeed. But what an heir! We would do better without him. Bred on the farm, he has the

---

[27] A sheath or covering for a sword or dagger

31

manners of a clown. Still, he is learning. At least he can bow without falling down. Time and training will remedy his lack of culture. It is the Catholic Faith in him that ruins all."

"The faith of a ten-year-old boy ruins all! Oh, Sir Roger, is this the spirit of the noble House of Gordon?"

"You see for yourself his stubbornness."

"Stubbornness! That is the best point in the lad. Do you think a weakling could ever win back the lands of Ravenhurst? Our work is to turn his strong will from his Faith to what we wish."

"Very easily said, my good Godfrey, but it cannot be done. What else have I striven to do since the day I found him? Right at this moment that red-bearded Abell has more influence with him than I."

"Sir Roger, it is a hard matter to skin a deer with the handle of a knife; the blade does such work much better."

"What do you mean by that?"

"I mean what I have said from the first: don't try to drive the boy, lead him."

"Lead him! A ship's cable would not draw that boy one step."

"My Lord, I said *lead*; I did not say *draw*."

"No more of your riddles, my good Godfrey, speak plainly."

"Sir Roger, fire and sword could not turn that boy from his Faith now, while he loves it; but let him alone, and he will forget both Abell and his teaching. Tell him of Fire-the-Braes and Lang-Sword till he longs to be as great an earl as they—nay, even the greatest of them all. Then, in later years, when it is a choice between lands, castles, and the king's favor, or the Catholic Faith and poverty, there may be a struggle; but the Faith will go to the wall."

"Perhaps, and perhaps he will die for leading some fool's-chase of a rebellion. That has happened before."

"True, but he is only a child. A child's faith dies easily if it is not nourished. The one I fear is his mother. If you will follow my advice, he will never see her, never even know that she lives."

"I need the mother's evidence that he is the heir. Lady Margaret will not dare to cross my will; she knows the penalty." Sir Roger's face grew very ugly.

"The Lady Margaret will not dare? Remember, that frail and gentle woman is a Douglas. Who has ever yet bent the will of a Douglas? Let her once speak to him, let her but once tell him of the old Earl, or of that fool—Gordon's father. . . . Oh, have a care! It will be an easy task to lead the boy, but the boy with his mother at his back—aye, that's another tale. She will have more influence with him than a dozen Abells."

"Douglas or no, my Lady will fare ill if she cross wills with me. There is such a thing as the will of a Gordon as well as that of a Douglas. I am no weakling to bend to a woman. Let her once dare open her lips. Let her once dare! I will execute the law to the fullest extent!"

The sleeping boy stirred. Sir Roger's voice grew suddenly pleasant. "Ah, little nephew, you are sleeping at a strange time. We shall see the castle in a few moments."

"Yonder is the spot where Gordon Fire-the-Braes killed the great deer." Godfrey pointed to a glen leading into the heart of the mountain.

"Did you not tell me that the antlers are still in the castle?" The boy was wide-awake now.

"They are in the old Earl's room above the fireplace. You may see them tonight if you wish. Old Fire-the-Braes was a great man in his day."

Sir Roger looked at the eagle light in the boy's eyes and smiled at Godfrey. "Do you see that point of rocks jutting out from out from Ben Ender into the frith? In the lee[28] of that is the spot where Gordon-o'-the-Lang-Sword landed when he swam the frith from shore to shore and carried the message for the King."

The Gordon leaned forward eagerly. "Was there ever a greater earl than the Gordon-o'-the-Lang-Sword? Godfrey has told me so many wonderful deeds that he did."

"Indeed, he was the proudest of them all. The earldom reached its greatest extent in his days, but he died at Solway Moss[29], fighting for King James. The days have been evil for the House of Gordon since then."

Sir Roger paused a moment to look at Godfrey, for the boy's face was all aglow.

"Land after land was taken from us till, when I became regent[30], we had little more than the bare rock on which the castle stands. I have gained a good portion for you, and you must do the rest. I will do all that can be done until you are a man, but you must be the Earl who raises Ravenhurst even higher than she was before she fell."

"I will try, my Lord." The Gordon spoke very slowly. His square little jaw grew a bit sharper. His eyes shone with a wild Douglas fire. Godfrey looked at Sir Roger and smiled.

The road made a short turn round a cliff. In the depths below, the water foamed among the rocks. Far off down the frith, five great gray towers stood out in the sunset.

---

[28] That side opposite or away from the wind

[29] Battle fought in November 1542 between King James V and King Henry VIII near the River Esk

[30] A person who governs instead of the rightful sovereign in times of minority, absence, or disability

The slant rays sifting down among them touched here and there a battlement with gold and deepened the purple shadows. From the seaward tower came a puff of white smoke and then a roar. Sir Roger rose in the carriage, lifting his plumed hat. Over the water the sound of a great bell rolled. The rocks caught the echo, and many an elfin[31] note made answer from crag and cliff and forest far up, even to the summit of old Ben Ender.

"What is all this noise about?" whispered the lad. "Tell me, Godfrey, or I shall make a blunder."

"Will you never learn that you are the scion of the House of Gordon? The cannon and the bells of old Ravenhurst are welcoming you, my Lord."

The road turned in among the hills again. The castle was out of sight.

"Lowlanders[32] have taken our lands and made my people slaves. You told me so long ago." The Gordon spoke very slowly.

"But an earl as great as Lang-Sword could win it all back again. You must be that Earl."

"I will do my best, Uncle."

"There is just one thing standing in the way." Godfrey shook his head and frowned sharply. His lips said, "Not now! Not yet!" But they made no sound.

Sir Roger continued in spite of the warning; he was as certain of victory now as he had been of failure. "One thing stands in the way. This one thing will ruin all if you have not the sense to give it up. You cannot be a Catholic and

---

[31] Having a magical charm or quality; otherworldly

[32] Those who reside in the Scottish Lowlands; Scotland is divided into roughly three geographical regions: the Highlands, the Central Plain and the Southern Lowlands; the Lowlands contains the latter two regions or roughly half the country

win back to Ravenhurst her rightful place in Scotland. The King is for the new faith[33] and will put down with fire and sword any noble who stands for the old."

"My Lord," said the boy, looking straight into his uncle's eyes, "the earldom costs too much. 'There is nothing worth the buying if the price be the fire of hell forevermore!' Daddy Abell said so."

A chorus of shouts drowned Sir Roger's answer. "The Gordon! The Gordon! Hail to the young chief! Aye! Sir James' son and no mistake!" It was a group of herdsmen watching from a cliff.

Another turn among the crags and he could see the road winding up to the castle and the crowds of peasants, throng after throng, along the wayside.

"The Gordon! The Gordon! Aye, in very truth the Earl's own son. God's blessing on his young head! The Gordon! The Gordon!" Right and left the lad threw silver bawbees[34] out among them as he passed on the long way up to the castle.

The great gray drawbridge came clanging down across the moat[35]. A double file of soldiers marched out, cheering as only soldiers can. "The Gordon! The Gordon! Welcome to the chief!" They crossed their blades, and the lad walked on beneath a shining arch of steel. Straight across the courtyard, between the files stepped the sturdy little figure. The castle doors swung open. Long lines of servants in the great hall bowed and cheered as he passed along

---

[33] Faith of the National Scottish Church (The Kirk) established after the Scottish Reformation of 1560 when it broke from the Roman Catholic Church

[34] Scottish coins of small value, such as a halfpenny

[35] A deep, wide trench surrounding a fortified place and filled with water

the polished floor.

The massive carven doors of the drawing room slid back noiselessly. Someone in green and gold called, "Sir Charles Gordon, Lord Rock Raven—Sir Roger of Gordon." The boy looked about him in wide-eyed wonder. Never had he dreamed of such a place. Candles—it seemed to the boy there were a thousand—made the room as light as day. Pictures, great ones from floor to ceiling; statues, massive furniture, and rich tapestry[36]; ladies in crimson and ladies in gold, ladies in purple and ladies in blue; gentlemen dressed like peacocks, with gold lace and jeweled shoe-buckles; here a plaided chief and there an English noble. From a hundred throats burst the old, old cheer that had greeted the earls of Ravenhurst these hundreds of years: "The Gordon! The Gordon! Welcome, my Lord, thrice welcome!"

Among them all, the puzzled lad saw one kind face. It was a little woman with snow-white hair, a face worn and thin as if from much suffering, two dark-blue eyes that looked straight into his own. He turned to her as to a friend.

"Aren't you somebody that belongs to me?" he whispered.

The woman took his face in her frail hands. She looked at him long and lovingly. "I am your mother, Gordon, and you are welcome home."

"Ah! Lady Margaret, you must not keep his young Lordship all for yourself. Let us kiss him, too," cried gay voices.

Sir Roger frowned. He had always feared that the boy would show his farm rearing by his clumsiness, and now, at this all-important first appearance, there he stood— timid, stammering, clinging to his mother's hands. Not

---

[36] A heavy, woven cloth with picture designs used for hanging or upholstery

one of those graceful bows, not one of those neatly turned speeches! Oh, how carefully he had trained him just what to do and say! The red flush brought out the tan and freckles and made him look so common.

Sir Roger remarked nervously, "His Lordship is browned by the voyage."

"Since when has a weathered face been a disgrace at Ravenhurst?" queried Lady Margaret gently. "In truth, there never was a carpet-knight[37] among the lairds[38], from old Gordon Fire-the-Braes to your most noble brother."

The lad saw that his mother's words had angered his uncle. He put one arm about her, as if to guard her, and looked straight at them all. The bashfulness was gone, and there was in the boy's figure a certain dignity.

"How much he resembles his father," said one.

"Aye, too much like the Earl, I fear. God grant him a better end."

"But then," remarked a noble who seemed of some importance, at least in his own eyes, "—but then he has you, Sir Roger. You will do your duty. We need have no fear of the mother's proving unwise while the uncle is at hand."

"I will indeed do my duty, my Lord, both by the heir and by Ravenhurst," Sir Roger answered somewhat stiffly. "Lady Gordon will wisely remember that there are laws concerning the imparting of knowledge on certain dangerous subjects to youth of our land."

The dark eyes of Lady Margaret looked straight into Sir Roger's. "I thank your Lordship for your kindness.

"I am well aware of the laws of which you speak and

---

[37] One not knighted on the field of battle but dubbed by Court as a favor; a knight who spends his time in luxury and idleness
[38] Scottish lords or owners of landed estates

know how to conform myself to them." Her voice was sweet and low, but there was a ringing firmness in her tone, a light in the depths of her eyes. She seemed to be a mother eagle guarding her young.

6

BY THE OLD FIREPLACE

T his is the old Earl's room. It will be yours now," said nurse Benson, swinging open a great carved door. "May you have a good night's rest, my Lord." The aged servant bowed and closed the door, leaving Gordon alone in a large room.

"Now, this makes two people here that I like. There's my mother and there's Benson. Nurse said she cared for my father when he was a 'wee bit bairnie[39].' That's why she gave me pigeon pie. He always wanted pigeon pie.

"Oh, what a beautiful fireplace!"

Indeed, it was a fine piece of Flemish carving. Two yeomen[40] standing on the hearth held the mantel on their spears. The shelf was bare, covered only with white linen. At the ends of it, two knights stood crossing swords above a picture. Above it hung a great pair of antlers. "Those deer horns must be old Fire-the-Braes'. Uncle said they

---

[39] In Scottish, a bairn is a child or a baby.
[40] Officer or manservants in a noble or royal household

were in here. I wonder—is that his picture, too?" The boy held up the candle to examine it. The painting represented an old warrior, white-haired but large and strong of limb, a kind face that smiled at one, and the jaws square to ugliness. "It can not be Fire-the-Braes. He lived so long ago. Perhaps it is the Gordon-o'-the-Lang-Sword . . . but where in the world did they get that picture of me?" For a lad stood by the warrior's knee, who smiled from the canvas with a face Gordon had seen too often in the fishing pool not to recognize.

Then other memories came. He saw another fireplace, not so beautiful as this, but wide and low and very comfortable: Mary Abell at one end of the hearth, spinning with swift, sure fingers; Daddy at the other end, his pipe in the corner of his mouth, the zip-zip-zurr of his whetstone[41] on the ax; Joel and the twins rolling over one another on the cabin floor. The boy leaned against the fireplace and cried for the first time since he had seen the last bit of smoke from the Abell cabin slipping behind the trees.

There was a gentle touch on his arm. "We never place anything on this mantel, my son," and a white hand raised the candlestick. "Are you lonesome in this grand old house?"

"I was thinking of Joel and the folks at home. I couldn't even say good-by."

Lady Margaret sat down in a wide armchair and drew the boy down beside her. "Who is this Joel, my son?"

"Joel, he's my twin. I mean, we always thought we were twins. I didn't bid him good-by." Then, with a little wonder in his voice, "But you are not angry! Uncle Roger was angry with me because I cried for my folks. He thinks being poor is a disgrace."

---

[41] A hard, smooth stone used to sharpen knives and tools

"Gordon," said his mother earnestly, "I should indeed be grieved if you had no love in your heart for that woman who, in spite of her poverty, took a homeless babe to her heart and was so true a mother that you never dreamed you were not her son. Some day, if God gives you your rights, you must do great things for them, but all that we can do now is to write and let them know of your safe arrival."

"Oh, that would please them. Daddy couldn't read it, but they'll wait till Father Cornwall comes."

"Father Cornwall!" Lady Margaret's face lost all its gentleness. Her eyes were as stern as the old Douglas steel.

Oh, why did everyone hate the Faith he had been taught to love? His hand gripped the arm of the chair till the knuckles stood out hard and white; yet, he looked straight into those stern eyes and answered:

"The Abells are Catholics, and I am a Catholic, too."

His mother was not looking at him now. Her eyes were fixed on the old fireplace with a look of deepest joy. "Holy Mother of God," she was saying, "I thank thee that thou hast kept thy trust."

"Mother, if you are a Catholic, what made you look at me like that?"

"I wished to learn of what metal[42] you are formed, my son. There is one weakling in the House of Gordon. Had you shown a spirit like Sir Roger's, had your will bent because you feared me, I would have disowned you, my son, though it broke my heart.

"The Earl of Ravenhurst must always stand for God and our blessed Lady, let the cost be what it may."

---

[42] Basic character; spirit; courage

A gleam came into Lady Margaret's eyes. "Now, most noble Sir Paul Pry, now will the Countess of Ravenhurst conform herself to those laws of Scotland, aye, fit herself most snugly into this first opportunity. The good uncle is very busy talking about himself and all he has done, or maybe not done, in the colonies. The cunning Godfrey also is busy. He must needs open the chest and show the wampum[43], the tomahawks, and even a bearskin, though I doubt somewhat the truth of Sir Roger's tale of his great bravery in killing the monster."

"Killing the bear! He is not claiming my pelt, is he? He didn't have a thing to do with it. I killed that bear myself."

"You killed that beast? Did you more than help some hunter just a little?"

"The old bear had us treed. She rammed her snout right up on the gun. I couldn't have missed her if I had tried."

"My son, I came here tonight to speak of things more important than a bear's pelt."

There was that in her voice which made the boy look up with swift constraint of every muscle. Lady Margaret smiled, for she saw the war spirit that pulsed in his frame, and she knew him to be worthy of her confidence, though but a boy in hand and heart and brain.

"I have much to tell you this night, my son," she said, and her deep eyes seemed to read his soul. "Things of import—matters that could not be trusted to a coward. It was for this reason that I tried your metal, boy, and your mother's heart was glad to hear it ring back true Gordon steel. Of the things I tell you this night, speak nothing. You are yet a boy and do not know friend from foe. What-

---

[43] Beads made of small shells and strung on thread; used as money by Native Americans

44

ever be your need, put no trust in Godfrey Bertrandson."

The lad's brow drew up in a puzzle. "I thought you were going to say not to trust Uncle Roger," he blurted.

Lady Margaret laughed, "Why should I warn where there is no danger? You have already taken the measure of Sir Roger, but I warn you, trust nothing to Godfrey Bertrandson."

Then suddenly after a pause, like an arrow shot from under a shield, the mother sent a question:

"What do you know about your father?"

The boy frowned a moment as if searching his memory. "Not much, Mother, I guess his name is all they told me."

She seemed relieved. "So, you shall learn of him from me, and that is well," she said. There was in her eyes a look, deep, unfathomable, as if a mingling of joy and pain. "I was an orphan in this house," she continued, "a child of Douglas blood, but penniless. James was Earl of Ravenhurst —not as it is today, but as it was in a time of which you will learn, a bleak wintertime of poverty and pain. Yet there are gifts that gold and fame can never buy, for God alone has the giving of them. God gave to James and me a love that was blessed before His throne in heaven. Here, standing before this fireplace, we were married. You smile, my son. Some day you will know that this great room in the seaward tower is the room of memories to all of Gordon blood, and this fireplace is a sacred thing to all who know its history. James and I had waited long for our wedding day because no priest had come this way in many years. He was no longer young, nor yet was I, but we would have gone single to our graves rather than be wedded by any other than a priest of God's Holy Church. God sent His minister to us, and the castle rang with mirth and song. Never was there a gayer wedding, nor was there one laugh less light because both bridal pair and merrymaking clan had nothing but oatcake and ale to feast upon.

"Three years God gave joy to James and me, and then He sent the cross, my son. For it was ten years ago on this very night that the King's dragoons[44] came for your father. James was standing by my side as I lay on the couch yonder. He thought me to be dying. We could hear the heavy boots of the soldiers tramping in the hall below. 'Courage, little comrade-at-arms!' he whispered. 'The battle lowers. The bugle of Christ calls "Forward!" Shall we falter in the charge? We follow a Leader Crucified!'

"Then came the clanking of their armor as they climbed the stairs. James took you from my arms, wee bit of a newborn babe that you were, and carried you over to the fireplace. A little image of our Lady used to stand there. He laid you down before it and prayed, 'Holy Mother of God, Margaret is dying. I am going God knows where. See, there is no one to guard the Faith of our child. Holy Mother, we leave him in your care.' James brought you back to me. 'Fear nothing, Margaret,' he whispered. 'The Blessed Mother never yet has failed those who trust in her.' Then he kissed us both and went out, and the dragoons took him. But, my son, I would that you could know the joy in my heart this night when I see how faithfully our Lady has kept her trust. O Son, we shall cling to each other and trust the sweet Mother of God!"

"Where is my father now?" asked the boy, his bright eyes wide with wondering love.

"God alone knows," she answered. "I never learned what befell him. So many years have passed that I hope he is dead!"

---

[44] Soldiers trained to fight on foot but who often traveled by horseback; can be classified as "light" or "heavy" dragoons

"Hope that he is dead!"

"Yes, Gordon, I hope that my brave and noble James is dead. For if he is dead, he is with other martyred Gordons who stand before the great white throne; but if he is living, he is in some foul dungeon, suffering hunger, thirst, the rack—I know not what."

Margaret was not weeping; she had borne her pain too long for that. But the lad knew now why his mother's hair was white, and in his childish way he strove to comfort her.

"Mother," the boy ventured, "perhaps—you see, Father Cornwall was so wise, I guess all priests must be—the next time we go to Mass, the priest could help us find out about Father."

Lady Margaret smiled. He was so eager to comfort her, so powerless.

"My son, you have forgotten that we do not live in Mary's Land beyond the sea. I have been present at Holy Mass five times in my life. Even should the Holy Sacrifice be offered near us, there would be small chance of our being there. Sir Roger watches like a hawk. I shall tell you what I do. When on a Sunday I am longing to live in lands where Mass bells ring, I come in here and kneel beside the old fireplace. This is the sacred relic of the House of Gordon. Many times in by-gone years, the priests of God made of this mantel an altar. Many times within these walls, the angels covered their faces with their wings, saying, 'Holy! Holy! Holy! Lord God of Hosts!' Once did wicked men spill here the Blood of God. That silver spot upon the hearth marks the place where the drops of Precious Blood fell years and years ago. Therefore, to this holy room I come and kneel by the fireplace and pray awhile and kiss that little silver spot and beg the good Lord Christ to come to me in spirit since I cannot receive

Him in the Holy Sacrament. You can do this, too, but we must not come together and we must not stay more than two or three minutes. If Sir Roger were to learn of it, even this small comfort would be denied us."

"Uncle Roger is mean to you!" cried the boy with sudden anger. "But now that I am here, if he dares say a thing to you, I'll—"

"You will keep your temper and say nothing. That is
what you will do when things go wrong. If you fly into a
passion, you will do great harm and no good. Keep this little thought to be your comfort at such times. Nothing Roger
says can wound me. Only those we love can cause us grief.
Let me see you growing up, day by day, such a son as the
child of such a father should be; then your mother will be
a happy woman, come what may."

Gordon felt the strength of her will across his own, and
the love in his heart for her deepened into reverence. They
were silent for a time, and when his mother spoke again,
it was of other things.

"You have not yet told me of those kind folks who gave
you shelter in your childhood," she said. "How was it that
they found you?" There was something in her tone that
made him wonder at her question.

"I don't know much about it," he answered, and again
he noted a look of relief in the depth of her eyes. "Daddy
said that Father Cornwall found me and brought me to
them. They named me George because I called myself
'Dordie.'"

"Did you say anything else?"

"Only to ask for 'Dunkie Teewee.'"

"Did they tell Roger that?" Lady Margaret's voice was
swift and sharp.

"No!" cried Gordon, startled at her tone.

"Thank God," she said, and smiled at his troubled face.
"It was for your Uncle Stephen that you called. Well indeed would Roger know the meaning of your wail for 'Dunkie Teewee,' and one more nail would be driven into my
poor brother's coffin."

The puzzled boy stared at her.

"You were lost a long time from Uncle Roger, but you were not lost at all from your mother, my son. After the dragoons took your father, I was ill for many months. A year later, they again thought me to be dying. Even faithful Benson thought my last hour had come, and she sent a messenger for my brother. Your Uncle Stephen is one of our brave hunted priests that neither prison nor the fear of death can drive from Scotland. He came at the risk of his life to give me the last rites[45] of Holy Church and took you with him, promising to find a home for you where your Faith would be guarded. He passed out with you hidden under his long gray cloak. A trusty clansman rowed him to a seagoing frigate[46]. I had supposed that my brother meant to take you to France and place you with our kinsman, Cardinal Beaton; but Stephen is a saint, and saints do not reason as worldly people do. He considered your soul alone and placed you where he thought that pearl most safe. I was not pleased with his choice, but he said, 'Where was the only Son of the King of kings placed—in a castle or a cot?' I said no more, for Stephen is a saint."

"Why didn't Uncle tell Daddy Abell instead of just setting me down by the roadside? That was a queer thing to do."

"Rather, it was a wise thing to do. Had this kind farmer known whose child he took into his house, Sir Roger would have put him in prison for helping to kidnap you. Neither did Stephen go to a strange land and set you down by a roadside and leave you to the hand of chance. He knew well the wisdom and charity of the good priest to whom he entrusted you, and he remained in hiding a few

---

[45] The sacraments of Penance and Reconciliation, Anointing of the Sick (formerly called Extreme Unction), and Viaticum (Holy Eucharist) given to a person before death
[46] A fast, medium-sized warship

weeks till he had learned what manner of man was the John Abell in whose care you were. Then, my son, when Stephen and our trusty clansmen thought the time was ripe for your return, we paid a seaman to give Sir Roger a clue that he might search for you and bring you back to us."

"But it is all so queer, Mother. Now there is this picture of me you have over the fireplace. How did you get it?"

Lady Margaret laughed. "This is not your portrait. It is your father's. Now do you know why it takes but a glance to let any clansman know whose son you are?"

"And the old warrior, is he Gordon-o'-the-Lang-Sword?"

"Oh, no, that is your great-grandfather, Angus Gordon, commonly called the 'old Earl.'"

The boy was a bit disappointed. "I never heard of an Angus Gordon. I thought he looked brave enough to be Lang-Sword. Godfrey said he was the greatest earl of them all."

"No doubt Godfrey thinks so. But I shall tell you of both these heroes, and you shall say which was the braver knight. It is not titles, lands and gold that make a man great. You shall learn who are the great men of your house, who have done heroes' deeds, and why this old fireplace is sacred to all of Gordon blood."

Lady Margaret smiled, and there was triumph in her glance. Then her look grew suddenly grave. "My son, I shall tell you many tales in time. Yet, lest unknown need should catch you unprepared, I must give you one more word of warning. If you have need of help in any hour of trouble, call on Benson; failing her, old Edwin, the gate warden, is true. But be watchful—sometimes walls have ears—and do not speak unless your need is very great. Trust no one else. Should you be forced even to fly from the castle, you have loyal clansmen living in the fastnesses[47] of Ben Ender's glens[48]. Their chief and the best of them all is Muckle John-o'-the-Cleuth. A secret passage opens from this old fireplace, the same way by which you fled when Friar Stephen carried you in his arms. It is not known to Sir Roger. There is a spring in the hand of the wooden soldier on the right side of the mantel. Turn the sword twice to the right and press down; a panel on the left of the fireplace will slide back into the wall. This is the beginning of the passage. The end is in the woodland near Ben Ender. When once in the open, make your way to the frith and follow the shore to the glen—"

"But, Mother," interrupted the boy, a look of apprehension darkening his eyes, "if we had to go away, you would be with me and you would know where the paths are."

Lady Margaret did not answer. The white fingers clenched on the arm of the chair, but only for a moment. "It is not wise to face trouble till it comes," she said, with strange quietness. "Be brave and silent, my son. We shall trust to God and our Lady, hoping that all may go well."

She had given these instructions in a tense, clear, exceedingly low tone, her lips scarcely moving. But with the last word her voice rose to a merry note, and she began to sing a sweet old ballad about a Douglas lost in battle for the love of the Heart o' the Bruce[49].

Something in her eye told the boy to ask no question. Half instinctively Gordon realized that there had been a sound in the outer hall a moment or so before, and he heard it again—a faint creaking as if a weight were against the door.

---

[47] Remote, secret places; strongholds
[48] Narrow, secluded valleys
[49] Robert the Bruce, King of Scotland from 1306-1329

7

MY FRIEND GODFREY

There was a ray of light teasing Gordon's eyes. He turned sleepily toward the wall. How did he happen to be in bed? Who put him there? He could not remember undressing at all. Was it his mother? She had been talking to him . . . about his father. What? Oh, yes, he was in prison somewhere or, perhaps, dead. She had been telling him things . . . about a hero greater than Lang-Sword . . . about a sacred stone and a fireplace. No, she did not tell him . . . only started to do that . . . and then broke off suddenly as things will stop in a dream.

Gordon opened his eyes. "My, how late!" he thought with a start. "It's broad daylight!"

Gordon turned the coverlet back, rolled over, stared a moment, began to rub his eyes.

"I am not in the same room. Yes, I am," he puzzled. "The bed is the same, the windows, and the pictures, but the fireplace! That is not the fireplace I saw last night! It can't be the same room. Yes, it is! There is the chair where we sat. There are the antlers belonging to Fire-the-Braes. Last night they were right up there on top, but not on top of that fireplace. I am all turned round."

He sat still upon the edge of the bed. There was indeed a great carved mantel, a beautiful work of old-style art. There were four pillars, two above and two below the mantel. But the two which rested on the hearth were not yeomen of the guard, and the two above were not knights, but oaken trunks round which a grapevine twined. Here and there clusters peeped temptingly from among the carved leaves. A beautiful work of brush and chisel, but not the fireplace beside which he had been seated while his mother spoke of long ago. There was a painting above the mantel just beneath an arch of vines, but not the one he had seen last night beneath the crossed swords. The same place, the same size and shape, but not the same picture. It was not an aged warrior and a lad, but a kilted chieftain of long, long ago, standing with one foot upon a fallen deer. Below, the gilded title shone in the sunlight: *Sir David Gordon, Lord Rock Raven, First Laird of Ravenburst, commonly called "Old Fire-the-Braes."* Lady Margaret had said the mantel was held sacred, but many odd trifles lay upon it—French knickknacks and shells from beyond the sea. The blackened hearthstone showed no trace of that silver spot. Nothing seemed the same.

The door opened, framing Godfrey's smiling face. "Well, my Lord, are you awake at last? If you had slept a little longer, you might have slept the clock around once more."

"Very late, isn't it?" But Gordon's mind was elsewhere.

"No, my Lord, it is still quite early, two o'clock by the

sundial, sir."

"Two in the afternoon!"

"Two by the dial, my Lord."

"Why didn't Benson call me?"

"Benson? Pray, who is Benson?"

"Don't you know Benson? She is the kind old woman who gave me my supper."

"Oh! You mean Betsy."

"No, I mean Benson!"

"Your Lordship might call her Ben's daughter, though, if my memory plays me no trick, her father's name was Tarn. I think she will not take kindly to the name of Ben's son, but, call her what you may, don't say she is a good old soul. Betsy is a blooming lass, turned sixteen last Candlemas[50]."

"She is old, and her name is Benson! I know because she gave me my supper."

"Have your own will, my Lord. But I would not take your word, nor even your oath, for anything which happened last night. Aye, but you were one right royal sleepyhead! The guests were scarcely seated when down went your head on your mother's silken knee, and there was no waking our young Lord at all, though the great folk from miles around had come to see you. So Betsy was called, and she led you away. 'My sakes, Master Godfrey,' she said to me later, 'I brought him a fine pigeon pie, but down goes his head on the table and off to sleep again, poor tired lamb. I led him to his room just now. Will you run upstairs and put him to bed?' So up I came. Here you were, standing

---

[50] The ceremony of the blessing and distribution of candles to celebrate Simeon's prophecy of Christ as a light to the Gentiles (Luke 2:32); celebrated February 2nd; now known as the Feast of the Purification

with your head against the fireplace, sound asleep on your two feet, and asleep you've been ever since."

The puzzled boy rubbed his eyes again, and his mind struggled to clear itself.

He did have his head against a mantel, but not that mantel. It was his mother, not Godfrey, who found him, and they sat a long time in that great leather chair by the fireplace, but not that fireplace. He would ask his mother about it sometime when they would be alone. It wouldn't do to ask Godfrey.

Then he spoke aloud, "What did my mother say when I was not there for breakfast?"

"Oh, she had no time to trouble herself about so small a matter. All the great folk rode over to Lindsey Hall quite early. The young Lord of Bethune is to be married this day fortnight[51], and the gentle Lady Anne of Lindsey is to be his bride."

"Why did she go so soon? The wedding is not to be for two weeks. My mother will not be away all that time, will she? What would she be doing?"

"Doing? What would any lady be doing? Dancing and riding out with the hunt, to be sure, having a gay and merry fortnight."

"I cannot see why an old lady like my mother would want to dance so much. And she won't come back at all till after the wedding?"

"Perhaps not then. You must have a bee in your bonnet for calling people old. It is well for you that Lady Margaret did not hear you say she is one who is no longer young."

"Well, she is old!" Gordon cried almost angrily. "Her hair is snow-white."

---

[51] A fortnight is a period of fourteen consecutive days. "This day fortnight" would be two weeks from today.

"Snow-white! The Countess of Ravenhurst is so old that she is snow-white! That would be a joke for her rivals! What a sleepy-eyed child you were last night! Your sweet mother is fair, very fair, my Lord. As to her age, what sort of gray head have you that your mother needs be aged?" Godfrey laughed merrily. "My Lord, 'twas just eleven years last Christmas that the old bell rang out her welcome to Raven-hurst. Many a fine ballad was written and sung in honor of the gallant young Gordon and his bride, the White Rose of Douglas. Here you are trying to tell me she is old, aye, even white-haired. Come, come! There are many who say the Countess of Ravenhurst is the most beautiful woman in Scotland. Her age, would you know it, is six and twenty, but none would guess it."

"You have never spoken of my father before," cried the lad. It hurt him to hear Godfrey speak so lightly of his moth-er. They could not be the same—that frail, sorrow-worn mother of last night and this gay lady of the world . . . but had his mother ever spoken to him? Godfrey had found him asleep with his head against this fireplace, not that other one. Could all the long, strange talk of last evening be but a dream? "You never spoke of my father before," he repeat-ed. "Please tell me of him. Where is he?"

"You never asked before. I do not like to speak of sad things. He is dead, my Lord. The old castle rang with hunt and song for two short years, and then Lady Margaret was a widow. Your father died quite suddenly. A bit of a cold caught while hunting was all it seemed at first, but he was gone in a fortnight."

The boy sat looking up at the fireplace with a troubled countenance[52]. Was the brave father of last night only a

---

[52] Appearance, especially the expression of the face

dream? But it would not be wise to ask questions. He was sure of that.

"Come, come! Let us talk of more pleasant things, my Lord. Now, if you wish Lady Margaret to be pleased with you when she returns, see how much you can learn in a fortnight."

* * * * *

How the lad did study, but then what else was there to do? He had no playmates of his own rank; others were too far beneath his dignity as heir of all Ravenhurst. How he longed for the old free days when he had no dignity. So he put his whole heart into his studies, and every scrap of work he did was saved to show his mother. That little mother he had known but a few hours, yet he loved her more than Daddy Abell, yes, more than Mammy, too. His heart filled up when thinking of them, yet he knew he loved her more. "She is really and truly my own mother. That must be why. When she comes home, she will straighten out all the puzzles about the first night." So he thought as he stored away those treasures, sheet after sheet.

Gordon had been hard at work for three weeks. There was pride in his eye as he placed his last page upon the others. Godfrey smiled. "Well, my Lord, that pile in the drawer must be thick now. What are you planning to do with them? Build a monument or use them for the breast-works of a fort?"

"Oh, you are laughing at me, Godfrey. You see, Mother will come home in a day or two, and I want to show them to her."

"Show her the last two or three then. She would hold up her dainty hands in horror if she should see your first attempts."

"Uncle Roger would laugh at them, but she will not. She will know I did my best. Anyway, the last are better. You used to say, 'How much paper between those blots?' and now it's, 'How many blots on that paper?' There is only one blot on this, just the place where that 'h' got its hump on the wrong side and I tried to turn it over."

"It looks as if you turned the inkhorn[53] over and a spider took a stroll across the page. But never mind, you will be a scribe[54] some fine day."

"O Godfrey! See where the road turns the point of the cliff! It's the carriage! O Godfrey, it's the carriage! There goes the big bell!" and the boy was gone. Racing down halls, sliding down banisters, banging doors, he arrived in three short minutes at the castle gate. Then he waited, and then he thought. He had been good, that is, he had been quiet, for three long weeks. Now, just when it was almost over, he had been a wild man of the forest once more. Sir Roger would hear—oh, well, he was used to his uncle's sarcasm[55] —but his mother? Would she be angry? The soldier just beside him—there was a twinkle under those bushy eyebrows—was he laughing? He had saluted most gravely, but if he were laughing, then the heir of all Ravenhurst had disgraced himself before the soldiery[56]. "You see," the lad gasped, "you see, my mother is coming! You see, I forgot my dignity. Please, I could not help forgetting about it. I want her so!"

---

[53] A small, round container made of horn or a similar material that holds ink for writing
[54] A writer or journalist; a learned person
[55] A mocking, often ironic, remark intended to hurt
[56] Military personnel; the profession of soldiering; soldiers as a group

The twinkle had grown till the grim old mouth was smiling also.

"Lady Margaret's a-comin', be she? No wonder ye swooped doon on the wing. As ye flew a-boundin' o'er the hedge yon, I could but just make my ald eyes tell me 'twas the young Laird himsel' an' no the gay Laird Jamie o' the long ago."

"Jamie? You mean my father? Wasn't he always quiet? Did he ever forget his dignity?"

There was a chuckle, low and rumbling, in the grizzled soldier's throat. "I do na mind the day when Laird Jamie had a dignity to forget. If I was na haulin' him doon fra a battlement[57] edge, I would be a-fishin' him oot o' the moat. 'Twas his young Worship, Laird Roger, what had a' the dignity to be found fra the Orkneys to Lands End[58]; but Laird Jamie, my ain bonny[59] Jamie, he was ever bold and free as the winds o' Ben Ender. Yer father was a straight-doin', upstandin' Scot as were all o' the Gordon chiefs before him. And there will be na body who can ever turn ye into a prancin' prig[60]. Ye'll be as the earls who are no more, for ye are a true splinter fra the ald Gordon steel."

"But I ran in the halls, and I slid down the ban—"

"Worry na more! None but servants saw ye. Ner lad ner lass o' them would tattle on ye for a bag o' bawbees. But, sh! Godfrey be comin', an' he may howl to Sir Roger that ye broke a' the plumes[61] o' yer dignity if he find ye talkin' wi' a common soldier. Yet, one word more, my

---

[57] A narrow wall built along the edge or top of a castle wall for protection; has open spaces for shooting
[58] Lands End and the Orkney Islands are situated in the far south and far north ends of the island of Britain, respectively
[59] Pleasing to the eye; attractive; fine
[60] A snob; someone who is annoying and arrogant
[61] Large, showy feathers

Lairdie—if ever ye ha' need, ald Edwin's at yer service."

A thought flashed through Gordon's mind, keen and clear as the call of the curlew[62], an echo from that first night: "Old Edwin, the gate warden, is true."

When the tutor came sedately down the great stone steps, he beheld the heir of all Ravenhurst standing on the velvet sward[63] gathering rosebuds. The old soldier? Never a stone in the ancient gateway was more rigid than he.

The chains rattled and groaned as the drawbridge came creaking down across the moat. There was a hollow sound of horses' hoofs, and the carriage rolled in. Sir Roger stepped out, alone.

"My mother?" The boy's voice had a choking sound. "My mother? Is she ill?"

"Oh, no, Gordon, there was no need for her to leave the merrymaking. Matters of state brought me, but she may as well remain till the end."

"When will she come, Uncle?"

"In a week or so, perhaps. Have you studied well?"

* * * * *

The days slipped away one by one. It was fully six weeks since Sir Roger's return. Still the pile in the drawer grew. Gordon was placing his last task upon the others. Godfrey laid aside the grammar.

"Well, my Lord, how soon will you need a new drawer for that collection?"

"Mother will come in a day or two, surely. The drawer will not overflow before then. She will be so disappointed if she cannot see them all."

---

[62] A long-legged, brown shorebird
[63] Grass-covered soil; lawn

"Are you sure of it? I fear it is you who will be disappointed for your pains. When you carry that cartload to her, she will say, 'Run along, child, and do not trouble me with that rubbish. The maid must arrange my headdress.'"

"Don't, Godfrey, don't! My mother is not such a woman! I would hate her if she were like Sir Roger."

"Your mother is a most excellent lady. But have a little common sense: do not trouble her with trifles. You have one grave fault, my Lord. You are a dreamer. You have built an angel in your mind and named her Mother. Then, forsooth[64], if the real lady fail to have golden wings, you will hate her. Have a care, your dreams may cause the loss of your head one fine day. You worship a dream-church even as you worship that dream-mother."

"No, Godfrey, it is you who are the dreamer. I think my mother is a true mother, just as Mammy Abell was, but I *know* that the Church is true."

"My little Lord, do you see the oaks over on Ben Ender? Last spring their leaves were tender green. They grew more beautiful with lengthening summer days. Now the glory of autumn is all but faded. A few more northern winds, and the oaks will be bare and ugly. They are a picture of your dream-church. Fresh and fair in her beginning, but days of strength, days of glory came and went, and now she is all but dead."

"Oh, no, Godfrey! Are the oaks dead because the leaves have fallen? Neither is the Church of God dead!"

"Now, bravo! There is eloquence as well as wit in that. Your brain will be as keen in argument as was Lang-Sword's steel in battle. Let your training be what it should, and, mark my words, the day will come when the House of

---

[64] In truth; no doubt

Lords[65], aye, even the king himself, will hang breathless upon your words."

"Oh, it is not that I know how to argue, but you have the wrong side, Godfrey. The side that is not true always has a hole in it."

"Well, is this a lesson or a tale in which you are so interested?" Sir Roger was standing beside them, a letter in his hand. "Pardon the interruption, but Lady Margaret has sent good news. It will be of great benefit to you in time."

"Oh! Is she coming home tomorrow? What is it?"

"Coming home! Oh, no! I doubt that you will see her again before reaching manhood. She has been chosen maid of honor[66] by the Queen and must go to London at once."

Sir Roger withdrew; he seemed in fine spirits. Gordon walked over to the window and stood there kicking his foot against the wainscoting[67], whistling—anything to conquer the tears. Then he walked slowly to the drawer, took out that treasured pile, and threw it on the coals. He leaned against the mantel and watched them burn.

"No!" he muttered. "No, she was only a dream."

---

[65] The upper house of Parliament or the legislature in Great Britain (The lower house is called the "House of Commons."); similar to the United States House of Congress

[66] A female attendant to the Queen; sometimes a paid position, sometimes unpaid

[67] Wooden paneling used to line the walls of a room

8

THE RUIN IN THE WOOD

March came. The lad stood by his window, watching the sunrise. "Oh, how warm! It is really spring at last. I am going for a ride before breakfast."

He ran out into the hall. Godfrey was there.

"Good news, my Lord! Sir Roger decided last night that he would send you to Glasgow to prepare for the university. You will go in the fall."

"Oh, Godfrey! Are you going, too? And there will be all those football games!"

"Football, is it! You must do more than play football. You must become a learned man so that you can bring your earldom to its proper place."

"Oh, I know. I mean to study, but I have not played with a boy for almost a year."

"Yes, yes, I understand. I know how you feel—quite natural for a lad. But here comes your uncle."

"Well, my little Gordon." Sir Roger was smiling. "A messenger brought this letter a few minutes ago. It is as much for you as for me."

The lad took the note, a dainty bit of parchment[68] with an odor of roses about it. His mother was now in great favor with the Queen. She had made a conquest[69] and was soon to marry the earl of something or other. He could not make out the name nor the long title. There was not a word about himself, not so much as "my love to the boy." She had forgotten him. The bitter spot, which had been burning all winter, was almost past bearing. He did not ask if she were coming home. He wished never to see her again. Why should he? She had no love for him.

"Gordon," said Sir Roger, as he took the note from the boy's hand, "I am much pleased with your progress in study. You have a brain and use it. Now, I am going to give you the best education to be obtained in Scotland."

"Oh, thank you, Uncle! When am I going?" The lad was thinking of football. "I do want to go so much, and I'll study, oh, I will study, Uncle!"

"Godfrey will take you to Glasgow next fall. But remember, you do not stir one step till I have your word that there will be no Catholic nonsense while you are gone."

Gordon did not answer with the indignant "No" that had always come before. His heart was full of bitter, stinging anger. He was longing for boyish games, as only a lonely boy can long. He turned on his heel and walked down the hall toward the stables with a quick, short step. Sir Roger would have followed, but Godfrey touched his arm. "Let well enough alone, my Lord. Let that dose sink in."

The horse had been in the stable for days. He would not stand still even while Gordon mounted. They were under

_____

[68] A superior quality paper that resembles sheepskin
[69] Someone whose affections have been won

the old arch in a flash and onto the drawbridge before it was fully down. The steed gave a little snort and tossed his mane. Away he flew toward the wood. Gordon leaned forward. Away, away through the clear sunshine, over the hedges, over the ditches with a catch in his breath, dodging under branches just bursting into leaf. Oh, what a glorious ride!

The horse stopped, panting, at the edge of the wood. God's sweet sunshine had put a better spirit into the boy. "Good ride, old fellow, good ride!" he cried, slapping the horse's shoulder. "Take it easier if you want to, you are getting hot."

A bird in the great larch above him set up a bit of spring tune, and Gordon whistled in answer. His hand was deep in his pocket, as boys' hands are sure to be. Something hard touched his fingers. He drew it out—only a brown rosary.

Gordon held it up and looked at the simple thing, wondering how it came to be in his pocket. He had forgotten all about that rosary he meant to say every day for the folks back home in Maryland. They had promised to say one for him. Would they have forgotten? No, not Daddy Abell. When he said he would do something, he did it.

Gordon slipped the beads through his fingers. They brought memories: the old cabin, Mother kneeling by the cradle rocking it with her foot, Father leading the prayers, and all the little Abells answering, "Holy Mary Mother of God, pray for us sinners." He saw Daddy reaching one hairy hand to give little Which a cuff for tickling Tother's feet, but never pausing in the prayer. Then he remembered the old log church. Father Cornwall's solemn voice, but still the same sweet prayer that the angel said: "Hail Mary, full of grace." And the great day—it was only a year ago—when they made their First Communion, he and Joel. He thought of the joy of that moment when, kneeling at the altar rail[70], he saw the priest raise the Host above the chalice and the long-awaited moment had come. He thought of the promises, boyish promises, earnest, loving, whispered to the Lord Jesus.

He remembered with a start that he had given no answer to Uncle Roger in the hall. Daddy Abell seemed to be standing at the edge of the woodland and saying, "No man can lead you into sin if you don't follow him. Stand on your own two feet and be a man."

Suddenly, the horse stood still. There was a wall of trees in the way. They were so close to each other that none had a chance to grow. Some seemed dying; others were dead. The row stretched out to right and left as far as he could see.

"It looks like a hedge that has not been cut since the owl knows when," he thought as he turned to the right and rode along. He found an opening farther down and looked through. On the other side was a field with a strange row of trees running around it.

"Looks as if it used to be an oat field," Gordon mused, "with all those bunches of old straw among the weeds. But that must have been long, long ago. Look at all those young trees growing in the field."

A bush moved, and a deer sprang from behind it, head raised, ears alert, and foot uplifted. A frightened sniff, a

---

[70] A horizontal bar that separates the sanctuary from the body of the church; when Holy Communion is received by the faithful on their knees, may be called the communion rail as the faithful line up kneeling in front of this rail and take turns receiving our Lord's Body and Blood

scamper of hoofs, it was gone. The horse, a hunter bred, dashed through the opening between the trees. Gordon, quickly dropping his head against the beast's neck, barely escaped the fate of Absolom. They bounded away across the field, over the bushes, and under the trees. Then the deer swerved suddenly and sprang through an opening in the dense hedge.

"I am not going through that place, old fellow," cried the lad, tugging at the reins. "Maybe you can get through there, but I want my head for a day or two more." Gordon had a good wrist for his age, but the horse had a good neck for his age. The animal was full grown, the boy was not. "Can't stop him," he gasped. "It's jump off or be raked off."

Loosening his feet in the stirrups, he dropped the reins and jumped. Gordon struck, rolled over a few times, and lay still until the dizziness from the fall had passed. Then he sat up, rubbed himself, and took stock of his injuries. "Kind of shaken up inside. . . head aches some . . . knee stings . . . nothing but a bruise and a skinned place—guess I'm all right."

Jumping up, he ran to the opening and slipped through. The horse was gone, so was the deer. Gordon was standing at the edge of an old flower garden. The weedy bed beneath his feet had once been a star of roses over which a crested boar's head grinned from its place on the great sundial. A Cross of Malta[71] lay beyond with a marble fountain at the center. But the rosebushes were choked with dead thistles; the gravel was covered with moss, and the frog in the broken fountain croaked to the lizard that sprawled on the sundial.

The building had once been majestic, but fire and time

---

[71] An eight-pointed star symbolic of the military order of the Knights of Malta

had made it a vast ruin. The cloister[72] lay in blackened heaps, half covered with moss and vines. Here and there an arch yet stood, held more by the ivy than by its own strength. The Gothic windows of the minster[73] were broken and blackened, but the morning sun glinting through them sent long prisms of light across the weed-grown lawn. The lad crawled over a broken windowsill. From the jagged pane above him smiled our Lady, Queen of Heaven.

"My mother," Gordon whispered, "my mother, she is like Sir Roger, but you loved your Son. If I have you, I have a mother still—and I all but turned against the Faith this morning!"

Gordon dropped down into the ruined minster. The carved stalls[74] were about him. Many had fallen and some were half buried beneath parts of the roof that had come down years before. There were heaps of dead leaves on the moldering[75] beams, plants growing upon them, and many vines. A sapling oak leaned over the altar, slender, graceful. Beneath it, the tabernacle door hung open on one hinge. A robin, perched there, looked at the boy with frightened eyes. Her nest was in the holy place. Gordon paused on the altar step, and the bird flew to the tree.

He put out his hand to take the nest, but stopped. "I wonder which is worse, to leave the nest there or to put my hand into the tabernacle?"

"Let the poor bird in peace, Gordon," came a low powerful voice.

---

[72] A covered walk that runs along the walls of monastery or convent buildings
[73] Church of a monastery or convent
[74] The fixed seats of the choir, wholly or partially enclosed on the back and sides, where the Divine Office is chanted
[75] Disintegrating; becoming rotten

The boy turned with a startled cry. Halfway down among the ruined pews stood a tall figure in a long gray cloak[76]. His face seemed but a yellow skin stretched across the skull, but the deep-blue eyes were full of life. They were kind eyes, and Gordon lost his fear as he looked into them.

"See, you have frightened the little bird. She is doing no harm where she is. That place has not been God's altar for eighty years and more. How is your mother?"

"My mother!"

All the anger of the morning burned in the lad's voice. He spoke out wildly, spoke as he had never done before, even with Godfrey, told it all—all that had been burning in his heart these long bitter months.

"And you believed this . . . all this. . . ."

"Believed it! Isn't it true?"

"Not one word of it!"

"Where is my mother, then?"

A great hope was springing up in his heart. Perhaps he had not been dreaming. Perhaps his real mother had sat with him beside the fireplace on that first night.

"I do not know where she may be."

"Then how can you say the story is not true?"

"Why do I know this wild tale is untrue? Gordon, I know Margaret of Douglas. Poor Margaret, how much she has suffered! And you, boy, how could you believe such things of your own mother?"

"But Godfrey said so! Uncle Roger must have lied to him.

"Godfrey is your friend, the best friend you have, is he not?"

"He has always been kind to me."

---

[76] The habit of a member of the First Order of the Franciscans or the Gray Friars; established by St. Francis of Assisi in 1209

"Oh, yes! Very kind! He tells you what a bright boy you are and that you will be the greatest lord old Ravenhurst ever had."

"How did you know that?" The boy flushed painfully.

"Godfrey is Bertrand's son. Do you know who Bertrand was? Not yet? In time, you shall. A devil with the oil of flattery upon his lips is a double devil, boy." The stranger paused as if in thought. "So Margaret has been gone for seven months. Did she speak to you about your Faith or your father before she disappeared?"

Gordon was troubled. Had his mother really spoken to him on that first night? If that gentle, sorrow-worn mother were not a dream, she had forbidden him to mention the subject of which they had talked.

"You need not fear to tell me," said the stranger, seeming to read the lad's thought. "You know to whom you are speaking, do you not?"

"No, sir. Who are you that knows so much about my mother and me?"

"Stephen Douglas."

"Uncle Stephen? Dunkie Teewee?"

"You have changed much since you used to call me by that name. Did your mother speak of Sir James or of your religion?"

"Yes, Uncle Stephen. That is, I don't know if she did or if I dreamed she did. I think she talked to me a long time on the night I came from Maryland. Maybe she didn't, but I think she told me about my father and was going to tell me more, but she stopped strangely all of a sudden."

"Do you know what penalty she was to pay for such talk?"

"No, Uncle."

"Sir Roger told her that if she ever dared to speak to

you of Sir James or of your Faith, he would execute the law to the fullest extent. Do you know what that means?"

"No, Uncle."

"If a widowed mother persists in teaching the ancient Faith to her children, any relative of the new faith may take her children from her. Roger said that if she went against his will, she would never see your face again."

"If she had told me. . ."

"Margaret would not have told you her own danger. No doubt, Godfrey had an ear at the door. Your mother knew the risk and took it. Fearing you might get into trouble by some foolish attempt to rescue her, she did not tell you of Sir Roger's threat. That would be Margaret's way. God grant the traitor had enough mercy to put her in a cell above ground."

"Where do you think she is?"

"Some place in the old castle in or under the north tower. The dungeons[77] are there."

Gordon scraped his heel back and forth among the dry leaves.

"She has been suffering all winter long, and instead of helping her, I have been thinking mean things."

"Let it be a lesson to you. Never allow anyone to come between you and your mother, or between you and your God. Those two friends are true."

Gordon stood with eyes of dumb agony. The gray-cloaked friar[78] waited, watching. He knew the metal of that boy and let the pain give the caustic cure, burning out whatever mite[79] of dross[80] could be within that strong young

---

[77] Dark, underground cells of a castle; used as a prison

[78] A monk or brother who works outside a monastery

[79] A small amount

[80] Worthless material; scum

soul. At last, Gordon drew a long breath as if shouldering a load. He looked up at his uncle. On his boyish face was the light of awakening manhood, a deep strength scarcely expected there. But because it was impossible for him to open his full heart as yet, when he did speak it was a mere commonplace which he asked.

"Uncle, what does my mother look like? Is she a little, white-haired, frail old lady? Godfrey said I had been dreaming. He said my mother is young and very beautiful."

"Your mother is not old in years. She seems old because she has suffered so much since that night when the dragoons came for your father. Sir James let me make his castle my headquarters. You know I am an outlaw, child. To give me food or shelter is a crime punishable by death. I fear your father gave his life for mine. Could you but remember that night which followed the arrest of your father, you would know if your mother loved you or not. Toward morning, her heart was so faint that Benson whispered to the other watcher, 'Begin the beads again, Jeanie, her soul is passing.' But Margaret's eyes opened wide. 'Pray!' she gasped. 'Pray that I may live. I cannot die. God helping me, I will not die. I must live for my son's sake.' And you, boy, you could let that smooth-tongued Godfrey make you hate her! No, no, those words were too sharp! Forgive me, child! You are only a lad. How could you know the depths of your mother's love?"

But Gordon suddenly spoke out the thought that had been on his lips a moment before when he could not control himself to speak it.

"Uncle Stephen, Mother said you are a priest."

"Well, I am, child."

"Then couldn't I . . . couldn't I . . . go to confession to you here? And I am fasting. Perhaps . . . that is . . . is there any

74

way for me to receive Holy Communion? Maybe then I wouldn't be so. . . ."

Friar Stephen took the tear-stained face in his hands.

"I have frightened you overmuch, my son. You have been sorely tempted, but I do not think that you have sinned grievously. If Sir Roger were to hear that you had received the sacraments, he would be very angry."

"He often gets angry. I shall not mind that."

"This will be a very different sort of anger. He is cruel, as all cowards are. There will be no one who will dare to defend you." Stephen spoke slowly, as if weighing his words; yet he knew what the answer would be.

"My father suffered, and Mother is suffering now."

There was joy in the soul of Stephen Douglas. Many were the prayers he had said, many the penances offered that this day might come.

"So you are ready, Gordon, ready to take your first step on the path of those who suffer for God." Then, taking a kerchief from his cloak pocket, the friar began to bind it over the boy's eyes.

"Why are you covering my eyes?" cried the startled lad.

"It is not wise for you to know where the good Lord is hiding."

"Do you think I would tell?" cried Gordon, cut to the heart.

"No, no, child! You would not tell. I did not mean that, but Godfrey will ask sharp questions and judge by your face when he finds the truth. Bertrand's son is cunning, but he cannot learn from you what you do not know. So, you will go with the bandages over your eyes. There is a long walk before you. Say your prayers as you go."

A long walk it was indeed, with many turns and twists. At last Friar Stephen spoke.

"Be careful now! We are to go down steps."

Down, down, down they went, and then on again. It was damp and cold. Gordon knew it was a cellar but never thought the prudent friar had led him about in the wood only to take him into the same ruin from which he had brought him. At last, Stephen turned a key in a lock, opened a door, and removed the bandages. They were in a place that Gordon could scarcely see. No little trembling light burned through the darkness. The enemies were too many. Only the holy stillness spoke of the Guest Divine, and Gordon knelt to adore.

9

THE MERCY OF A COWARD

Roger and Godfrey were in high spirits now that the heir was won—almost. They chatted a good half-hour, laying new plans. Sir Roger remarked, "Gordon should be coming back from his skylark[81] ride or he'll be late for breakfast." Turning toward the old Earl's room, he added eagerly, "No doubt I can see him from this window."

Like a spurred colt, Godfrey sprang alert; yet his voice was but mildly persuasive as he suggested, "The view from the hall window is far better, my Lord."

"But the Earl's is nearer," laughed Sir Roger as he strolled to the door.

Godfrey whirled, ran noiselessly to the stairs, down, and out of sight.

Humming a snatch from an ancient ballad, Sir Roger swung open the door of that room of memories to all of

---

[81] Playful; frolicking; boisterous

Gordon blood, that room which the weakling of the House of Gordon usually avoided.

One glance and the smile died. With a hiss of fury, he turned on Betsy and roared: "How comes this! The fireplace! Remains of a fire on the sacred stone! Carvings! Painting! Who dared?"

"Please, my Lord? The young gentleman just rose! I had no time to clean! I'll have—"

"Clean it? You know well, every servant knows well, that there must never be a fire on this hearth!"

"Please, my Lord, we thought you had changed your mind, my Lord. Your orders, my Lord!"

"My orders! Who said it was my orders?"

"Master Godfrey, my Lord!"

"Bid Godfrey come at once!"

"Yes, my Lord," and Betsy hurried away.

Sir Roger walked up and down with a stiff and snapping stride. "It is not that I have any Romanism in me," he argued as if addressing someone in the back of his own mind. "I am not a Roman Catholic. I was never one, at least not since my reason has been that of a man, a brilliant and thoroughly educated man. But, it was my mother's request, her deathbed request, that nothing should harm the sacred stone. Sacred? No, no! Not sacred! A little wine fell on it years and years ago. Only a little wine! A man must respect his mother's last request, her deathbed wish. Every gentleman does that. Yet, if someone . . . if Godfrey had seen my anger, he would have said—but he did not see me. Good!"

"Please, my Lord, Godfrey cannot be found, my Lord," came Betsy's quivering voice from the doorway. "But Ben's with me to help. We'll fix everything just as it used to be. The tree trunks were only slipped over the soldiers. The stone you wished kept so clean? It has not been harmed, my Lord. We placed another one on top of it."

"Less talk, girl. Set to work. As to the tree trunks, they are mere casings made in the days of Sir Angus to disguise the fireplace when . . . um . . . when state papers concerning Mary Queen of Scots[82] were hidden there. But take them off. They are clumsy, unsightly, and disfigure the apartment. As to the stone, it must always be kept clean because . . . um . . . because the fireplace is an heirloom, valuable only as such, but not to be marred by common use."

Sir Roger stalked out of the room of memories, still battling within his own mind to convince that someone in the back of it. "Cleverly turned! Yes, rather. Let Betsy repeat my words. Who would say there was anything . . . um . . . unusual?"

Seated in the library, Sir Roger read for five minutes, sent for the butler and fumed at him, called for his horse and raged at the groom because he saw a tangle in the mane, went down to breakfast that had been awaiting his pleasure almost two hours, sniffed at everything set before him, nibbled a bit of this, took a taste of that, and bolted a goblet of strong red wine as he shot one last word to silence that adversary[83] within him: "Wine, nothing but wine, a few drops of blood-red wine fell on the old hearthstone years and years ago."

Suddenly, there was a noise in the hall as of a heated argument. Sir Roger jumped from the table and ran out, slamming the door. The voices died to whispers: "Riding all alone in the forest without a groom."

---

[82] Daughter of King James V; crowned Queen before she was a week old in 1542; reigned (despite imprisonment) as Queen of Scotland until her execution for alleged conspiracy to kill Queen Elizabeth of England in 1587

[83] An opponent; an enemy

"Scarce more than a bairnie!"

"There comes Sir Roger!"

"You tell him! It's your fault!"

"And be clapped in the tower! Not I!"

Old Edwin broke through the group of cringing servants and said to Sir Roger quietly, "My Laird, we ha' all fear that harm ha' befallen the Gordon. His steed ha' trailed in wi' empty saddle. Godfrey be waitin' by the gate wi' yer steed, my Laird."

Sir Roger hurried away. A few moments later, the horsemen clattered out through the great gate. The dogs picked up the scent and started toward the woods.

Halfway across the meadows, Godfrey pointed to a tree near the edge of the forest and shouted, "There he is!"

"Gordon is not limping."

"No, my Lord, but I don't like his step."

"Why? Nothing seems wrong with him."

"He is not injured, but. . . ."

"But what?"

"Look at him, my Lord: head up, chest out, tramping along. He has his mind made up. That's certain. What do you make of it?"

"Good! Gordon has decided to go our way."

"Let's hope so, but I doubt it. Look at the jaw of him: all the will of the House of Gordon up and bristling for a fight."

"Fight? But why?"

"That's exactly what I wish I knew, my Lord. Perhaps Gordon was not thrown. If he got off his horse to talk to someone, Bolo could have broken away."

"It would mean foul luck for us if Muckle John saw the boy ride to the woods alone and contrived. . . ."

"But this is a fair day. Muckle John should be far out at sea before sunrise, a-fishing."

"Stephen Douglas? Is it near enough to Easter for him to be skulking[84] around the old ruin?"

"May the fiends defend us from him! That cutthroat[85] of a priest has spoiled more plans of mine than any other man living. If Gordon has been with him, there will be no doing anything with that boy for a year. Hold! No, my Lord, no!" Godfrey cried out, for Sir Roger's horse was plunging ahead under spur. "Wait! Go slowly! We must find out first!"

"Find out? Exactly what I shall do! Not be able to do anything with Gordon for a year, eh? If that brat has been with Stephen Douglas, he'll learn before he is an hour older with whom he is dealing." Roger's sallow[86] face grew still more ugly.

"Oh, have a care, my Lord, have a care!" Godfrey pleaded as their horses thundered toward the woods. "Don't try force! It's the worst—"

"Don't try force! Don't try force! That's always your tune. Much good in smooth ways!"

"You saw this morning the effect of my smooth ways. Think. If the boy has been with Stephen Douglas, he may be heart and soul set to be a martyr of the Gordon line. I'll see that priest on the scaffold[87] yet, but don't try force on the boy now. You'll only rouse all the stubbornness in him. Then, too, if he has been with the priest, he may have received the sacraments, and—"

"You believe in sacrament-magic?" sneered Roger.

"No. But sacraments have a strong effect on those who

---

[84] Moving about secretly; lurking; hiding or practicing evasion

[85] An unprincipled, dangerous person; a murderer

[86] An unnatural or sickly pale complexion

[87] A platform used for the execution of prisoners by hanging or beheading

have as strong a faith in them as Gordon has. Go gently with the lad until we have the facts. Get him up to the castle quietly. Then call out every man you can trust to beat the woods for Douglas."

"I'll put the bloodhounds[88] on that outlaw. Trust me for that! But, go gently with the boy? If he has received the sacraments, I'll teach him the magic of pain. I'll—"

"Oh, have a care, my Lord! Remember your brother James. Remember the will of the House of Gordon. Neither you nor any other man can break his will. Oh, think, sir! Have a care!"

"And of what house do I come? Am I not a scion of the House of Gordon? Can you break my will?"

"Weakling of the House of Gordon!" snarled Godfrey, but his voice was lost in the thud of hoofs.

The little Earl of Gordon had seen the racing horsemen, and he was coming straight toward them, a slim, boyish figure in the shadow of those ancient trees. His square jaw was set, the iron jaw of Fire-the-Braes and Lang-Sword, the firm jaw of the old Earl and Sir James, the jaw which for centuries had marked the chiefs of Clan Gordon; but his eyes were Lady Margaret's, deep-blue, almost black, with the Douglas fire burning in the depths of them. Bell-the-Cat would have been proud of this boy had he seen him. But, to the lad, it was Daddy Abell's face that rose in his mind; and in his heart he spoke as if to the frontiersman, "Uncle is coming, blazing mad. Maybe I must fight it out with him now."

Sir Roger drew up his horse with a jerk that turned the foam red from the points of the bit. "Explain your conduct!" he roared.

---

[88] Dogs trained to track by scent; any type of relentless pursuers

"Conduct?" sparred Gordon warily.

"What were you doing that your horse should come in with an empty saddle?"

"Oh, is that it? I'm sorry if I caused trouble, sir. Bolo took after a deer. I couldn't hold him. I had to jump off or be raked off, sir."

"Very slyly put! Nothing else detained you these three hours? Did you talk to any person in the wood? Speak up! Don't try to deceive me!"

Gordon's tongue was never made for cunning speeches. It was always "Yes" or "No" with him. Tell a lie? Never. Tell the truth? Betray a priest? Not while the breath of life was in him.

"No words are needed. Your face speaks for you. You were talking to someone. Was it Stephen Douglas? Deny that if you dare."

Godfrey cut in sharply, "Gordon, you did not mean any harm, I know, but you went to confession to him in the old ruin. Didn't you?"

The lad's face brightened. "Guessing wrong this time." The flashing thought had scarcely crossed his mind.

"Not at the ruin, eh! Where then? At the cave among the cliffs? The cavern by the frith side? The hollow back of Ben Ender?"

There was joy in the lad's heart. What he did not know could not be learned from him.

"Answer, will you?" snarled Sir Roger, springing from the horse.

"The Gordon does not know, my Lord. Can you not tell it from his face?" cried Godfrey. "Friar Douglas often binds the eyes of children whom he thinks too young to trust."

"You can answer like a gentleman, whether you know or not. Answer! Answer, will you?" Sir Roger struck the boy with his whip.

There are few things that hurt like the sting of a fine supple lash. Gordon sprang back with a sharp cry. A narrow red line rose up across his face. "Answer, will you? You dare to be stubborn with me?" The whip rose again.

"Don't, my Lord, don't!" Godfrey cried. "The child does not know, I tell you!"

"Keep your place, Godfrey Bertrandson! You have done enough harm and to spare! Gordon would have had this lesson long ago but for you. Stand aside! You dare to step

in my way! This boy shall learn with whom he is dealing. Open-faced rebellion! Receiving treasonable sacraments! Talking to outlawed priests! Refusing even to answer when spoken to! Much good your religion does you, young gentleman! Did you ever hear of the Fourth Commandment?"

"Fourth Commandment says, 'Honor thy father and mother.' Doesn't say one word about uncles."

"You can find your tongue soon enough when you wish to give impudence[89] with it. You will know whether or not you must obey uncles when I finish with you! Stephen Douglas is not your uncle, I suppose? But you do his bidding! Young upstart!"

Sir Roger struck quick, sharp blows while he spoke. The lash hissed through the air and writhed around the slim body again and again. The child staggered this way and that from the force of the blows. Once or twice, when the burning whip struck the rising welts, there came a sharp cry. That was all. He did not say one word.

Sir Roger's arm was growing tired, but the square jaw was still set, and the blue eyes looked straight into his. He began to realize that the boy's will was stronger than his own. "Weakling of the House of Gordon!" That taunt had been thrown at him since childhood, and now, here was a boy with a will stronger than his own. Pride stung him. The whip fell again and again, but Gordon saw that the coward was weakening. The light of victory shone in the blazing Douglas eyes. There was new courage in every line of that little body still staggering under the weight of the blows.

The look in Gordon's eyes stung Sir Roger's pride anew. Yield? Godfrey had seen everything. Yield? Even the groom would sneer. He tried to strike with the same force as before,

---

[89] The quality of being offensively bold and rude

87

but his arm was weary, aching. The whip dropped. He had not the power to give what the lad had the courage to take.

"You may be thankful that I am too merciful to give you more." Then a thought occurred to him. "But you deserve no mercy. Go at once to the castle and, without pausing, go straight to your room. You will stay there without food or water till you tell me all that happened this morning —yes, and until you promise to quit the Catholic Church once and for all."

Sir Roger was in great glee. Here was a punishment that could be carried out to the bitter end. It would cost himself no pain.

10

SECRET OF THE FIREPLACE

Betsy was wiping the last suds off the hearthstone when Gordon walked swiftly into his room. He stopped in amazement. The fireplace was before him, not the fireplace of the last few months, but the one beside which he had sat with his mother on that strange first night.

"Betsy, why Betsy, what has happened?"

"Land's sakes! I do hope your Lordship won't be put out about it! Sir Roger, he would have it changed back again like it used to be."

"Put out? No, indeed, but how did it happen?"

"God bless you, my Lord. You never fuss about things at all. But his Lordship Sir Roger! What a temper he flew in when he found it was changed. Master Godfrey gave us the orders, and we did it whilst you slept. 'Twas the first night. He bade me play off that I was Benson. 'Land's sakes!' says I to him, 'Benson and I don't look alike. She's old enough to be my granny,' but he would have it."

Betsy twisted the rag with a snap. "But—for the mercy of our Lady, lad, what's happened to your face? Sir Roger—no one else would dare! I'll run for some salve."

"It's nothing, Betsy, never mind."

"Don't you suppose I know how that stings? I'll go right now, my Lord."

"No, Betsy, no! I'd rather ask you something. You know some—I mean, do you know where my mother is?"

The girl dropped her rags and brush to stare.

"My Lord!" she gasped. Then, after a pause, "There is nothing I would not do. You . . . you . . . but the risk isn't just to me. My old mother, she's a widow, my Lord. The few pence I make is all she has. . . I . . . I can't lose my place."

"You do know something. Tell me, Betsy. No one shall ever find out from whom I learned. I want to find my mother," pleaded the boy.

"Well, 'tis little enough, my Lord. Only none of us servants ever believed that Lady Margaret went gallivanting[90] off to London—not but what she would be an honor even to the King's court—but the tale did not fit. Some things do not fit with some people. The Countess is gentle, my Lord, kind, very kind and cheery always, but not gay[91]. She was always planning things for the poor and sending little comforts to this old granny or that down in the village. The tale that she was running from one frolic[92] to another did not fit, and not one of us believed it. We were ordered on our lives not to let the village folk know she was no longer at the castle, and from that time Godfrey began to get two extra portions from the cook. He always

---

[90] Traveling or roaming about in search of pleasure
[91] Given to social pleasures
[92] Scene of fun and merriment

feeds the prisoners, and that made us think. . . ."

"Prisoners! Where are they kept? I never saw one."

"Oh, there are always prisoners in great castles like this. They are kept down in the dungeon under the north tower. My Lord, you had better mind your eye today. Don't cross Sir Roger when he's in a temper. He would as soon put you into one of those black holes as eat his supper. I am fearing you are in trouble with him now. No one else would dare to strike your Lordship. I'll run and get something to take out the pain."

"But don't you know anything else?"

"No, my Lord, nothing more," and picking up her pail and brush and scrubbing rags, she hurried out.

A heavy step came down the hall. The key turned sharply in the lock, and the steps went away again. A few moments later, Betsy tried the door, whispered her comfort through the keyhole, and went back to her work.

The long hours began to drag. It was one thing to bear the blows as they fell, when his nature had risen for the battle, but quite another to endure the never-ending smart of the wounds which the lash had made. He walked up and down with quick, impatient steps, then flung himself on his bed, only to spring up again in restless misery. The old wag-at-the-wall, steadily ticking all day long, told minutes that seemed to be hours. Still no one opened the locked door.

Thirst had come with the fever.

There was a sudden clank of keys. Gordon whirled to face the door. In came Sir Roger. He smiled coolly. The new punishment worked well. Between pain of body and of mind, the boy was very near to madness.

"Have you had enough of disobeying uncles?" he sneered. But the child turned in a frenzy.

"You take my mother out of that dungeon!" he yelled. "Underage or not, I'm Earl. You shall pay for this and for your lies and for—" Sir Roger's grating laugh interrupted him.

"Hunger will tame you, my angelic nephew!"

With a sudden, high, piercing cry, the maddened boy sprang at him. Sir Roger jumped back, opened the door, and was out with more speed than grace.

Shaken and weary, the lad stumbled to the armchair and flung himself into it, but the chair awakened memories of his mother. Sorrow welled up in him, and the pain of his wounds rose with the lull in excitement. A moan burst from his lips, but it was choked on the instant.

"No!" he muttered, "Uncle Roger shall never hear a whine from me. He shall never see the mark of a tear. He can do without that much fun!" Then slowly the thought dawned on his mind, "And . . . and . . . in a way . . . I did deserve what I got. No boy was ever so mean to his own mother."

Gordon slid down on his knees and knelt a long time with his head bowed on the old chair.

Minutes snailed on. The burning of thirst outdid the stinging of welts in causing sheer misery. Gordon could endure inaction no longer. He sprang up and began pacing the room, jaw set, eyes blazing.

There was no sound save the growl of the old wag-at-the-wall doling out the moments, "Tick-tock, tick-tock." At long last, it groaned, "Nong, nong, nong," and a bugle blared in the courtyard below.

Gordon sprang to the window, thinking with a swift surge of hope, "That's change of guards. Old Edwin will be at the gate. Maybe he can help."

Down on the walls and in the court below, soldiers snapped out of and into their positions. Edwin, stiff in the joints but straight as a spear, clanked to his post by the gate.

Gordon stood waiting.

The wag-at-the-wall whined on, "Tick-tock, tick-tock. Ed-win, Ed-win, he would, he would, if he could." The monotonous sound beat on the boy's eardrums until the irritation all but surpassed the pain. He beat his fists on the stone window ledge, but he did not stir from his place.

The agony wore on.

Again the old "wag" moaned, "Nong, nong, nong, nong." But Edwin had not yet so much as glanced up at the window where Gordon stood.

"Tick-tock, tick-tock, Ed-win, can-not, can-not, for he would, if he could, can-not, can-not."

A light flashed into Gordon's eyes, blinding him. He sprang backward, returned, and was driven back again rubbing his eyes. Cautiously, he slipped to the side of the window and looked down.

A disk of light began to play on the ceiling. It was coming from the hilt[93] of old Edwin's claymore. His gnarled hand was just below the spot.

The disk of light moved in a peculiar way along the ceiling as if drawing something, first in the horizontal, then in the vertical, horizontal and vertical, horizontal and vertical. Then the light died. Edwin's hand had slipped up and was shading the point on the hilt from which the flash had come.

Gordon waited. Nothing more was done.

He studied the ceiling, trying to find out the meaning of the signal.

"What did Edwin draw?" Suddenly Gordon's face brightened. "Deer horns! He drew deer horns, first lying straight

---

[93] The handle of a weapon or tool

across, then standing up and down. Deer horns? Fire-the-Braes' antlers! Did Edwin signal, 'Turn the antlers around'?"

Off went his shoes and socks, for a pioneer boy can climb better barefoot. Up he went from the yeoman on the hearth to the mantel shelf. Gripping the bronze shield of the House of Gordon with his left hand, he took a firm hold on the antlers with his right.

But what then? The boars' heads on the old shield grinned at the boy. The antlers would not budge for him no matter how desperately he tugged. The deer's head had never known a deer's body. It was a finely done bit of wood-carving.

The antlers could not be turned sidewise, but maybe they could be pulled forward. Gordon tugged. The small portion of the head in which the horns were fastened squeaked a little, then moved slowly outward until it was an inch beyond the deer's muzzle[94]. There, the hardwood peg on which it was sliding stopped short, and, a moment later, something metallic clicked.

Gordon pulled the right antler in line with the deer's muzzle. Nothing happened. He swung the left one over. There was a sound as of a screw turning. He whirled the antlers twice. A crack began to open just behind the deer's ears.

Swiftly, yet with anxious care, Gordon whirled the antlers. A moment more, and he could see that there was a small door in the back of the head.

Hope leaped in his heart with a wild, glad throbbing. Perhaps Edwin had hidden a key behind that tiny door. As soon as dark closed down, he could escape. Edwin would help him find loyal clansmen.

---

[94] The forward part of an animal's face including mouth, nose, and jaws; the snout

He whirled the antlers with shivering fingers. Now he could reach the knob of the door. Now he had it open. In went his hand. Something there, something wrapped in silk, but not a key. He drew it out—a book, only a book, nothing but a book. He flung it sailing through the air until it fell on the bed.

Surely, there must be something worth finding hidden in such a secret place. Walls—top, bottom, back—he felt carefully. There was nothing but polished wood.

Bitter disappointment, dizziness, a heartbreaking nausea struck him. Slowly, wearily, Gordon shut the tiny door and screwed the antlers back into place. He worked his way down to the floor, stood trembling a moment, put on his shoes and socks, and dropped into the old armchair.

The wag-at-the-wall began to jeer at him again. "Tick-tock, tick-tock, Ed-win, did not, did not, did not!" He sprang up with a wild desire to tear down the clock and fling it at Edwin's helmet.

Then his eyes rested on the silken bundle lying on the bed. "Edwin must have thought that would help me in some way," he reasoned. "Perhaps he has hidden something in the book."

With dogged[95] step, he went over to the bed, picked up the bundle, and unwrapped it listlessly.

"Oh, beautiful!" he whispered.

The book lay there in his hand, soft brown buckskin with his own coat-of-arms tooled in gold. The three boars' heads of Gordon and the crowned heart of Douglas, they seemed to cry out to him as do the trumpets that blow for the battle:

"Son of a Gordon and a Douglas, can pain wear you down

---

[95] Stubbornly persistent; unyielding

like this? Are you flinching in your first real grip with the foe? Are you faltering in the charge, you that pledged Stephen Douglas this morning to stand for God and our Lady, you that like Sir James, your own father, are sworn to follow even to the death a Leader Crucified?"

The Gordon's sagging shoulders straightened. A shiver ran through his sturdy frame. The book in his hand trembled, opened a little, and a bit of folded parchment fluttered to his feet.

My Son,

In prayer, the thought often comes to me that as you were sent out all alone to learn your Faith, so you shall stand out all alone on the day when your Faith is tried.

What will that trial be? Pain of mind? Of body? Of both? I do not know, but always I feel I shall not be near to blunt the jagged edge of that pain. Yet I can tell you, my son, you are not the first Gordon who has suffered. These tales will show how knights of Christ do win their golden spurs.

Courage, then, my son. Whether I am living or with the dead, my prayers shall plead for you in that hour; and accept this small gift. It is all I have to give, child, save the heart's deepest love of

Your Mother.

11

RETURN OF LANG-SWORD

I n the great room of the seaward tower in Castle Ravenhurst, Lady Anne stood beside the window and gazed
on the surging waters below. Her arm encircled a fair,
strong-limbed boy; and now he spoke, pointing one wee finger through the bars, "My father, the great Lang-Sword,
comes today. Welcome, most noble Lord, your heir salutes
you!" He spoke slowly, essaying each phrase with energy,
lisping his way through with difficulty. She laughed and
kissed his rosy lips and cuddled him. With waggish[96] grace,
he made his mighty speech again. They had stood in that
place a thousand times, looking across the narrow, tossing
bay to the bold headland of Ben Ender around which the
pathway ran that led to the war-racked world beyond the
rampart[97] of the mountain. All his little lifetime they had
waited there. For Lang-Sword had been in France on the
King's business, and the child had never seen his father's
face. So long had Lady Gordon hoped and watched and

---

[96] Humorous
[97] An embankment for protection or defense

prayed, standing beside the window with Angus, her child.

On the shoulder of Ben Ender where the faint line of the path came into sight rode horsemen outlined sheer against the sky. A flash of light sprang toward the watchers, touching the window, dazzling their eyes. Lady Gordon drew her boy close.

"It is my Lord!" she cried. "He has caught the sunlight on his sword to signal us. Who else would know to touch this window with the light? Wave, darling, wave! Thy father comes!" and two white kerchiefs fluttered at the window.

The heavy masonry around her trembled as the cannon on the seaward tower saluted the returning commander. Above the noisy joy of the garrison[98] boomed the castle bell. The folk were hastening from the village; plows paused mid-furrow in the fields.

Now Lang-Sword and his retinue[99] were returning through the town: knights in mail[100] on armored horses, pennants of red and gold and azure, glint of sun on spears and helmets—all the gay riot of sound and color that marked the height of chivalry[101]. To right and left the Earl flung largess[102]. The cheers of the crowd echoed among the turrets[103] even to the seaward tower where Lady Gordon waited with her child.

Then a look came over the face of the woman, an expression of cold and stately grace, as if she had hidden her deep

---

[98] An established military post where troops reside; may also refer to the troops themselves

[99] A group of servants or assistants who accompany an important person

[100] Flexible armor made of small overlapping metal rings

[101] The ethical code, customs, and principles of knighthood

[102] Gifts and/or money

[103] Small towers extending above the buildings

emotion under a courtly mask; for in the hall below, she must be Anne, Countess of Ravenhurst, receiving with gracious welcome her Lord, the Earl.

An hour passed. The formal welcome was over, and the three sat alone in the great room in the seaward tower. Ever since the Holy Three made blessed the home in Nazareth, God's benediction[104] has been upon the love of father, mother, and child. They sat on the couch by the window, Lang-Sword and Anne and the child, the baby finding a thousand shining playthings upon his father's armor and laughing in high glee at the strange distortions of his dimpled face wrought by every polished curve. The mother spoke, telling the many nothings that the little son had said or done. The father feasted his eyes on the two that were his heaven on this earth.

A question gleamed in the eyes of Anne. A hundred times it had almost crossed her lips, but she feared to ask it. And just as often he had seen the look and tried to turn her thoughts away as if he feared to answer. Lang-Sword was still in full armor. In the court below, the troop sat in their saddles; but surely he had come to stay at least a few short weeks? He had been gone so long. Trembling, she whispered:

"Were it not better that you lay your armor by?" She paused, for he had suddenly raised the child before his face, tossing it till it screamed for the very pleasure of the thrills. Anne could not see her husband's eyes, and his words gave no answer to her careful question.

"The friars will sing Te Deum[105] *for my safe return. We*

---

[104] A divine blessing or protection

[105] Ancient hymn of praise and thanksgiving to God; name derives from the first words of the hymn, *"Te Deum Laudamus"* or "We praise you, O God"; originates from around the fourth century

shall go there presently."

Then came the ride under the ancient oaks. Crimson and brown of autumn arched the bridle path. The woodland's cloth of gold was spread beneath their feet. The Lady rode at her Lord's right hand. A groom at his left bore the child. They were alone—almost—the troop keeping a respectful pace apart; yet each knight was alert in his saddle, and the question bit at her heart.

Like some saint's relic[106] set in a jeweled shrine lay the gray old friary,[107] now but a pitiful ruin in the oak wood near Ben Ender. Lengthening years had watched its growth since the day when Fire-the-Braes made the beginning. Wild marauder though he was, lover of the moonlit uproar and the daring raid, after his conversion he was prompt to deeds of good as he had been prompt to deeds of ill. Now a full two hundred years he had slept in the shadow of this sanctuary, clad as a humble Tertiary[108] of St. Francis; and at every daybreak, a Mass was said for the repose of the wild Gordon's soul.

Chief after chief had added to the foundation as his means or piety suggested. Lang-Sword's eye rested on the quaint minster chapel. This was his gift, and he said to his Lady: "Here God is praised, and the poor of Christ are fed."

"And ever shall be," she responded.

But Lang-Sword drew his keen claymore from its scabbard and scanned its blue-gray edge.

"And ever shall be—if Highland steel ring true," he an-

---

[106] An object connected with a saint; something they used, part of their body, or something they had touched

[107] A community of friars, or the residence in which they live

[108] Member of the Third Order Secular which includes members of either sex who live in the world and do not wear a religious habit, but follow a religious rule of life

swered. He looked away from her as he spoke, and Anne drew a swift breath that held a hidden sob.

* * * * *

Lang-Sword had come into power in time to face the dangers that Fire-the-Braes had feared. The centuries of family feuds had left Scot so bitter against Scot that it was impossible to present a truly united front against any enemy.

In past generations, at least in moments of national peril, family quarrels would be forgotten. In the bloody circle of Flodden Field[109] around the royal standard of James IV they stood: Border spears and Perthshire men, Fife and Gordon, Merse and Argyll—feuds forgotten and hearts aflame for Scotland while rank by rank the red English bills cut them down. Grim death clutched them man by man, but none faltered and none fled. Yeomen, spearmen, archer, knight, and earl twisted in one mass of dying men; till, with a crash which shakes the soul of Scotland yet, the King charged—and charging fell, his lifeblood flowing on the silken banner of our land, down trodden on Flodden Field.

So were the Scots from before the days of Fire-the-Braes till James IV—ruining Scotland by their endless petty feuds yet loving Scotland to the death, while among them, stirring up strife at all times, went traitors paid with foreign gold.

Beside this strong spirit of national loyalty, or rather causing it and continually reviving it as the feuds killed it, was the one great source of unity—the Church in Scotland.

---

[109] Battle fought between the forces of King James IV of Scotland and King Henry VIII of England on September 9, 1513 in Northumberland; the Scots were defeated with ten thousand Scottish men killed including King James IV

All Scots were still of the one true Faith.

There are sincere men on all sides of all great controversies, but Henry VIII of England stands in history as an infamous, treacherous, and most cruel tyrant. Though victorious at Flodden, his taste of Scottish steel was so bitter that he preferred to conquer by fraud rather than by war. He saw a way to break the one great bond of national unity—the Church in Scotland. Constant civil war had left many Scottish lairds poor. The lands of the Church, left in comparative peace for centuries, were prosperous. Henry whispered in the ears of these impoverished nobles to enrich themselves by stealing from the House of God. Some took Henry's path to wealth. More would have done so, but they feared the anger of the young King of Scotland, James V. Though of that passionate nature which has often many sins to answer for, James had that strong faith in God and in eternal truths that makes a man repent and try to atone.

James loved his native land and bent every energy to heal the feuds that sapped her life. Justice was the only road to this. Many nobles were but titled and jeweled murderers who lived on spoils[110]. James put these men in order, and they went hotfoot to Henry's side. James would hear no word of robbery, whether of the war-impoverished common people or of the House of God. The royal expenses were covered by rearing sheep upon the crown lands. He bade the nobles follow his example, and Lang-Sword was the first to obey.

* * * * *

The gentle old Friar Warden[111] stood by the gate of the friary to welcome Lang-Sword, his Lady Anne, and their

---

[110] Goods or property taken by violence
[111] The superior of a religious house; now called "Guardian"

son, Angus Gordon. Behind him, row on row, reaching back to the door of the minster, were the souls beneath his care: files of scholarly men with saintly faces; lay brothers, rude and simple toilers but students of the lore St. Francis learned from Sister Earth and Brothers Storm and Sunshine; the orphan boys and the sick from the lazaretto[112].

All the eyes of this holy hive were turned on Lang-Sword with simple, gentle confidence. In the wild outer world, convents might be destroyed and the work of centuries obliterated; but here beneath the strong, kindly rule of their Earl, all must continue to be well. Such was the thought behind the gaze.

In the deep currents of his soul, Lang-Sword felt the keen joy of their trust in him, and it was with reverence that he dismounted and came forward to receive the welcome of the Friar Warden.

"It is with great gladness that we hail your return, my Lord," said the old friar. "We have prayed long that God may make you wise in council. Only this very fortnight it has been brought home to us that we should give great thanks to God that we are living on Ravenhurst lands and under our good King James; for Friar William and eight of our brethren have fled to us from the ruined convent in Northumberland. A horrid tale they tell of theft and murder and sacrilege; they say—but may Christ prevent it—that King Henry's men are marching toward our borders and intend war upon Scotland."

"And King James will meet them on the border!" The Earl's voice had in it the clank of steel. "It is for this reason that I come to ask Your Reverence to bless our banners this morning after Holy Mass. Also, I bring presents to you from

---

[112] A hospital where those with infectious diseases are treated

our Lord, King James—a most beautiful window of fine Flanders glass—and bid you in his name to have the orphans say daily an Ave[113] for our success in battle and for the birth of a royal prince. For myself, if I should fall, I ask some small remembrance in your prayers."

So Anne learned the answer to her question; her face expressed neither pain nor fear, but her lips grew deadly white.

With reverent pomp, the ceremonial pageant passed. These were days when friars went bare-footed and toiled long hours, were coarsely clad and slept on straw; but nothing was too rare, too costly, too magnificent if it were meant to adorn the temple of Almighty God, or bring before men's minds the daily renewal of Christ's Sacrifice on Calvary.

To Lady Gordon, crushed in the wine press of her pain, the music of chant and beauty of symbol spoke of Mary standing by the cross. Silence filled the minster. Then sounded the clink of steel as armored knights bent low before the King of kings. Strength stole through the soul of Anne. She made her sacrifice: offered her husband for the cause of Scotland and of God.

* * * * *

November's winds made desolation of October's beauty. The Lady Gordon took again her never-ending watch, standing beside the window with her child. Below them, the frith tumbled along the gloomy shore, angry, menacing, a sullen white tip on every groveling breaker. The skies dripped with fog through which the dim bulk of Ben Ender glowered. Many days they had been the sentries of endless waiting. Suddenly she clutched the child. On the shoulder of Ben

---

[113] *Ave Maria* is Latin for Hail Mary

Ender where the path should be, a misty something moved through the fog, a long and winding something. Faint, far-sounding on the wet air, came the notes of the pibroch[114] wailing:

The Gordon's awa'
The Gordon's no more!
Alack an' a woe for the Highlands!

The cannon above her boomed. The castle bell clanged with backward stroke, clanged and paused, and clanged again. Anne grasped her child with the fierceness of her agony. She watched. The winding, wailing something had reached the village. Through the mist she saw a broken rank of staggering men with spears reversed and ensigns[115] trailing and in their midst a black-draped thing, and they that bore it stumbled as they came. The voices of the village rose to her—tumultuous agony, high-sounding, wild— Clan Gordon in despair.

The Countess turned from the window. There was a fearful quiet in her face, an awful silence surrounding her. An esquire[116] advanced, bowed, and lifted the child.

Softly, he followed the Lady out of the room and down the stairs till she stood at the head of the great hall. Around the outer edge of the room, the garrison and the inmates[117] of the castle ranged themselves quietly, as if they dared not intrude themselves upon her grief. The harsh jangling of the drawbridge chains grated on her ears. Then the rattle of

---

[114] Military music played by highland bagpipes; often a traditional dirge (mournful funeral hymn)
[115] Military banners, standards and/or flags
[116] Attendant and shield bearer to a knight
[117] Persons living with others in the same building

*bolts on the outer doors, the heavy tramp of buskined feet[118],
and through the arch at the lower end of the hall came that
woeful company.*

*The pibroch was hushed. In silence, the bearers marched
up to the feet of the Lady. There they laid down their burden
and drew back the bier-cloth[119]. Lang-Sword lay under the
eyes of Anne—a bruised and sallow face beneath a broken
visor. A groan passed over the assembled clan like a winter
wind through the oaks of Ben Ender, but the Lady made
no sound.*

Then Tarn, the armorer[120], addressed the Countess:

*"Flodden Field was lost and every orphaned bairn was
proud to say, 'My father fell at Flodden.' Solway Moss is
lost and every Scot shall hang his head forevermore, for
Scottish lairds were aye traitors! May the word burn my
lips that I say it!—Scottish lairds wi' honor bought an' paid
for wi' English shillin's! Chiefs o' Highlands an' Lowlands
soft steppin' it hame at the first charge o' the Southerns!
The yeomen? A-weel for the yeomen that didna flee—but
where were the leaders? Back steppet the lads to get fight-
in' room and bogged doon i' the morass—helpless! The
Southerns butchered them like pork at a fairin'. Esk Water
was a-choket wi' blood an' wi' bodies! The English came
swarmin' o'er the milldam. Clan Gordon had not faltered
yet, though a' around us roared the tumult o' yon traitors'
flight.*

*"Then rose the cry, 'Lang-Sword's down!' But the Laird—
I saw him my ain sel'—he wrenches him free from his dyin'*

---

[118] Feet covered with thick-soled, laced boots that go partially up
the legs; also feet that drag due to tragedy

[119] A cloth that covers a corpse or coffin

[120] A person skilled in making arms and weapons; someone who
is in charge of the upkeep of small arms

horse, plucket oot the arrow from his ain wound, catches the bridle o' a riderless beast an' drags himsel' to the saddle, yellin', 'Who said that Lang-Sword is down? I'll split the coward with my claymore! Rally! God for King James! Forward! A Gordon! A Gordon!'

"Then, Lady, the Laird went down, six English bills[121] piercin' his body. I leaned o'er him as he writhed on the blood-sodden clay an' heard the gasp o' his deathword— 'Tell her,' the Laird said, 'bid my son, Angus, be a man. God's mercy on my soul!'

"An' worse yet must I tell ye, Lady. Scotland is down! The Church o' God is down, for James, bonny King James, laid him out an' died after the battle.

"An' worse an' worse must I tell ye. The heir o' the throne is born—the curse o' God, it be upon us—the royal bairn is a maid-child, namet Mary!"

The armorer ceased, and a groan passed over the clansmen. Well did they know the woes of civil war that would be during the long minority of a queen.

Then Anne of Gordon spoke. Somewhere in her deep soul, she had hidden her widowed heart. Her voice rang like a bugle call.

"No cause is lost while true hearts live! We have a Queen! Long live Mary, Queen of all true Scots! Ye have a chief. Step forward, Angus, Lang-Sword's son!"

The child, dimly conscious that great things were being done, stood out before them. His grave baby eyes traversed each rugged face, then fixed themselves upon his mother.

"Angus Gordon, lay your hand on the heart of your dead father."

The child obeyed. Slowly, word by word, as they fell from

---

[121] Weapons with hooked blades mounted on short staffs

his mother's lips, he repeated:

"I, Angus, Lord Gordon, Earl of Ravenhurst, do vow allegiance to Mary, Queen of Scotland! I swear to defend my lawful liege Lady and God's Holy Church from all their enemies, even at the cost of my life."

The lisping words died out over the silence of that hall. Then sounded the command of Anne of Gordon:

"Let each man do obeisance[122] to the Earl."

One by one, the war-scarred clansmen knelt before their chief, and his baby hand was wet with warriors' tears.

Short rang the Lady's order:

"Each man to his post. We have a Queen. We have an Earl. Castle Ravenhurst never shall surrender!"

---

[122] Bowing or bending of the knee as a gesture of homage or submission

12

LAST STAND OF THE OLD EARL

A ngus Gordon rode in the teeth of the March wind. Full seventy winters had whitened Lang-Sword's son; yet, like the oaks of Ben Ender, he stood snow-crowned and strong. Seventy years of storm, civil war and chaos, famine and plague—Scotland had scarcely known a "Shrovetide[123] peace" in all that time, and Clan Gordon had been in the thick of every fray. Sir Angus had kept the pledge his infant lips had made there in the feudal hall among his warriors with his hand on his dead father's heart. He had been true to Mary Queen of Scots through the wars that raged around her cradle, the tumult of her reign, the years of her captivity, true till she ended her peerless life on the scaffold—a martyr in fact if not in name.

Now it was her son that reigned, sixth James[124] of the old Stuart line, a man like and yet unlike the kings that had

[123] The few days preceding Ash Wednesday
[124] King James VI of Scotland and King James I of England who reigned Scotland from 1567-1625 and England from 1603-1625

gone before him. He had the same high and headstrong pride, the terrible and untamed passions of that race, but into his life the gentle influence of the Faith had never come. He was greater and yet less great than they. His scepter[125] swayed two kingdoms, but to gain the English crown, he made allies of those who murdered his own mother.

Between the two nations there was peace after centuries of conflict, peace on the old border, in the debatable land, in the rebellious Highlands—such peace as the conquered know under the tyrant's steel-shod foot.

When James crushed the Highlands, he thought it hardly worth his time to drive the old Earl of Ravenhurst into exile. He had one foot in the grave as matters stood. Why spend powder and ball taking that strong fortress which in time must fall into the royal hands like a ripe apple? His Majesty contented himself with confiscating land after land till the old Earl had but the empty title of greatness left to him: Lord of massive buttresses and stately halls wherein dwelt poverty, almost starvation—chief of a clan but clanless. This was the plan of that most gracious sovereign, James VI of Scotland, James I of England, but leaders will be followed. As the Lowlands have ever brought forth riches, so have the Highlands given the world men. The clan had pledged itself to Angus Gordon. They who made that vow had long been the food of ravens, but the sons and grandsons of those men were Clan Gordon and they knew no thought but loyalty. In the wild fastness of Ben Ender's glens they lived, rugged as the thunder-splintered crags of that mountain and as true.

So the Earl rode in the teeth of the March wind. He rode a-hunting. Not that the weary old man loved the sport, but

---

[125] Ruling power or authority; a staff held as a symbol of such authority

the orphans wandering in the ancient halls were many; and, tired of salt fish, they were begging for meat. The men were at work in the barren fields, so Sir Angus saddled his own warhorse and went a-hunting on that bleak March day.

The old Earl was returning toward evening with a deer across his saddle when he thought he heard a moan. It was very low, but he was so sure that he had heard the cry of a being in distress that he searched the bushes for some time. Finding nothing, he was about to proceed upon his way but he could not bring himself to do so and searched again. At last, he saw a man lying in the shadow of a log and hurried to him.

"Mother of Mercy! Can this be you, Friar Walter of Alnewick?" he cried.

"Your ears are sharp, my Lord," answered the friar with a faint smile, "and it is a kind heart that makes them so; but go, most noble sir. You know that I am outlawed."

"The King's men have done worse than outlaw you! It is on the rack[126] you have been!"

"Go, my Lord, you must not be seen speaking to me."

"Do you think I will leave you here? You are not the first outlaw that has found refuge at Ravenhurst. It is in my mind that you have been racked for not telling that Holy Mass is offered in my castle. It is for sparing me that you have suffered."

"Let it pass, Sir Angus. Leave me here. You are risking your life uselessly. All will be over by sunrise, and heaven is as near here as elsewhere. For yourself you never think, but remember that the clan and the orphans are depending upon you."

"Father, to Ravenhurst you go whether you will or no.

---

[126] Instrument of torture upon which a victim's body is stretched

Had I the strength of other days, I would carry you. That I cannot do now, but there are those who can." He raised his battered bugle to those kind old lips and the sweet notes rang out, *"A rescue! A rescue!"—fitting notes, in truth, for the last call ever blown upon the war horn of that veteran in the cause of God.*

Some workmen in the fields came in answer to the bugle. They made a rough litter[127] of boughs and, spreading their plaids[128] upon it, carried the friar to the castle. For days, the good priest lay between life and death. Sir Angus would not leave his side. At last, he was better. He could walk about, but the racked arms were still so sore that it went to the heart to hear him moan when the bandages were changed.

The old Earl took a trusty lad—the grandson of Tarn the armorer, called Muckle John-o'-the-Cleuth—and sent him to find a friendly sea captain who would take the friar to France. Not that the priest intended to give up the Scottish mission; he was to return when strong again. Before going, Friar Walter determined to say Mass so that the faithful might receive their Easter Communion[129]. He could not move his arms, but he asked Sir Angus to stand behind him and move them for him.

"Ah, Father," remonstrated the old Earl, *"how can you bear the pain of that?"*

"Do you fear for the Blessed Sacrament, Sir Angus?" the priest said quietly. *"I can control my fingers fairly well now, and I think I have strength enough not to faint. Re-*

---

[127] A stretcher for carrying sick or injured persons

[128] A rectangular woolen tartan (scarf) worn over the left shoulder by Scottish Highlanders

[129] The reception of Holy Communion (accompanied by the Sacrament of Penance and Reconciliation) as required by the Church each year between Ash Wednesday and Trinity Sunday

member, we can count upon the assistance of God, for this Mass is necessary to fulfill His law. It may be a year before I can return, perhaps longer. The faithful must receive Holy Communion at Easter time, and there is no other way."

Mass was said in the great chamber of the seaward tower. The fireplace in this room served more purposes than one in those wild days. The mantel could be drawn out twice its width and lowered to form an altar. Within the carven figures were hidden the sacred vessels of the Sacrifice. Behind the mantel was a hole large enough to conceal a man. In truth, a cunning piece of Flemish woodcarving was the fireplace in the great room of the seaward tower. All could be hidden in the space of an eye's twinkling: sacred vessels, holy vestments, even the priest himself. But the best-laid plans sometimes fail. Judas was one of the Twelve, and Bertrand was the Earl's most trusted servant. He owed his very life to Sir Angus. A starving, hound-tracked outlaw, he had fled to Ravenhurst; and, as with all in sorrow and need, the old Earl had been a father to him. But the Master washed the feet of Judas and that same night was betrayed by him. Christ's nearest followers have ever found the same fate.

Sir Angus sent Bertrand to tell the outlawed Catholics that Mass was to be said at Ravenhurst on Easter Sunday. Bertrand did that, in truth, and then ran posthaste to Russell to tell him the same. The clink of gold was more to him than gratitude or honor, friend or God.

It was three o'clock on Easter Sunday morning. The great room was nearly filled with the folk kneeling about on the floor. In the corner knelt four children. They were dear to the old Earl. James and Roger were his grandsons. The other two, Stephen and Margaret, were orphans of the Douglas line, and to them Sir Angus had been more than a father. It was to be the children's First Communion day, and the old warrior had prepared them well for the coming of the King of kings. But the little ones could not say their prayers. They were watching the face of the priest. It was so thin and white, yet wonderfully beautiful. The lines about the mouth drew in so sharply when Sir Angus moved his arms this way and that. They could see the drops of cold sweat shining in the candlelight. His voice, as he said the old, old prayers, had a strange sweetness in it that sank deep into their hearts.

Then sounded the little bell that warns of the coming of the Lord. Again the silence. The silver bell's low music once more. The Sacred Host raised high in those thin, white hands. The sweet-toned bell through the stillness. The golden chalice with the Precious Blood. The Lord blessing them as they adored.

There was a clank of armor in the outer hall. The door swung open. Something flashed from the doorway through the candlelight and struck Friar Walter in the side. He lowered the chalice, set it gently upon the altar, and sagged against the old Earl. Sir Angus clutched the stricken priest.

Bertrand had warned the King's men. Bertrand had passed a rope to them over the wall—Berrand, the trusted servant, the one left on guard.

The soldiers were everywhere. Men and women fled helter-skelter through a side door while the four frightened children crawled back under the old Earl's great bed and lay still.

By and by came a silence, and they ventured to peep from the hiding place. Some twenty troopers were standing at the end of the room with drawn swords. They stood as if waiting an order, and the captain was slow to give it. Twenty-three in number, but they were in downright terror of the lang-sword in the Earl's right hand.

Friar Walter lay across the hearth. He was dead. On the altar, the chalice gleamed in the candlelight. Beside it lay the Sacred Host. Just in front of his God stood the brave old Earl. It was a strange sight: the white-haired warrior in the surplice[130] of an acolyte[131], the light of battle in the old blue eyes, and clenched in his right hand the lang-sword that had named his father, that had been the ances-tral blade of the knights of Rock Raven since the days of Fire-the-Braes. By his side was the young lad who had served the priest at Mass, Muckle John, grandson of Tarn the armorer. In his hand, he held the dirk[132] that had pierced the heart of the priest. Twenty-three against two, and it was the twenty-three that were afraid: the Earl's swordsmanship was a toast in two countries.

The officer took a step forward. One could see he had lit-tle liking for his work.

"Captain John Brent," said Sir Angus slowly, "I was your godfather in baptism. By the vows I took that day, I tell you that you have committed a grievous sin this day. The pun-ishments of God Almighty are terrible."

"My orders, sir," growled the officer. "A soldier must obey orders."

"And since when do the orders of a king make it lawful to break the laws of the King of kings?"

There was a struggle on Brent's face. He was too good a man for such a trade.

"Come," he growled, "let's go. We have done enough of

---

[130] A long-sleeved tunic; a liturgical garment
[131] A person appointed to minister to the needs of the priest by assisting in the service at the altar and as needed in the celebra-tion of the Holy Sacrifice of the Mass; an altar server
[132] A short knife with a pointed blade; a dagger

the devil's work for one day!"

The men seemed only too willing to obey. They had no wish to match swords with the great Sir Angus Gordon.

But Bertrand sprang forward.

"You white-livered cowards!" he roared. "Twenty seasoned veterans against one old fool and a fisherman's gilly[133]! A thousand pounds' reward for the priest's body! The rubies on that chalice are worth rattlin' guineas! Here you stand like whipped curs[134] in fear o' the lang-sword! Don't you know the old cutthroat has reached his doddering days?"

"If fight you will, fight I will!" shouted Brent. "But I draw for the other side! Perhaps God may forgive me the sins of this night!"

"He will forgive you," said Sir Angus.

The captain sprang forward, but paused and dropped on his knees as he passed the altar. He looked at the Blessed Sacrament, one sorrowful, pleading look. Then he took his place.

Two troopers tried to follow him.

"Down with the turncoats!" cried Bertrand. Half a dozen swords pierced them before they could take another step.

Something struck the altar. One candle went out. The blue light of the lang-sword shot in quick flashes through the semidarkness. There were curses and wild cries. Swords clanged as they struck each other.

"Brent's down!" It was Bertrand's voice. "Finish him! That's a clean stroke! Now back and rest a bit! There's only the old fool left!"

The troopers drew off a few steps. Sir Angus stood in a pile of dead. Brent and young Muckle John were among them. The old Earl was straight still, but there was a wound above his temple, and the blood trickled over his thin white

---

[133] A boy or young man; a young, male assistant
[134] Mongrel dogs; cowardly persons

hair. The good right arm hung limp by his side. The lang-sword was clenched in his left. Age was beginning to tell, for his breath came in quick, short gasps.

Then Stephen grasped his sister's hand, "Hist, Margie!" he sobbed, "look at the altar!"

Some sword had struck the chalice. It was lying on its side. The Precious Blood was dripping, drop after drop, from the cloth down to the hearth and mingling with the blood of the martyred priest.

Bertrand's voice snarled again, "Once more, and the job is done! Up, lads!"

The lang-sword flashed. A trooper went staggering back toward the wall. Another fell with a wild curse across that dark pile at the Earl's feet. Then Bertrand's sword caught the old man's wrist. The lang-sword sprang high in the air. Sir Angus was down. They were dragging him along the floor. Others had the body of Friar Walter.

Then the old Earl saw the altar, the overturned chalice, the Precious Blood—and Bertrand reaching one greedy hand for the chalice with the gems that were worth "rattlin' guin-eas[135]." The chief's voice rang as in the battle days.

"Bertrand, have a care! You have spilt the blood of man this night, brave John's, and Brent's, and the blood of a holy priest of God; but have a care, Bertrand. If you touch that chalice, the blood on your hands will be the Blood of God!"

The traitor turned as if to answer, but a trooper broke in.

"Come on! Let it alone! There'll be bad luck with a chalice along. There always is. We had plenty o' it the day! Five a-livin' out o' twenty, and all o' us wounded! It'll be na ladies' job to get the dead one an' the live one up to Castle Russell

---

[135] Gold coins worth one pound and one shilling each

and the old Earl jailed before sunup. Matt an' Dave canna help at all."

Bertrand snarled but he followed them muttering under his breath, "I can see to that later. They're worth guineas, rattlin' guineas!"

13

GUARDIANS OF THE KING

The struggle was over. The children were alone. Trembling, they crept from their hiding place, sobbing, clinging to one another in their fear. The terror of the battle was still upon them, the horror of the sacrilege[136] before their eyes.

"We must not leave the altar so," whispered Stephen, stepping forward.

"No, Stephen, no." James drew him back. "We daren't. It is only for priests to touch holy things!"

"But there isn't any priest here now. Friar Walter was the only one we ever saw."

"There must be one somewhere. I'll go. I'll never stop till I find a priest."

"The fear has taken your wits, Jamie. Can you go miles in minutes? We must do something now. Let me be. Stop holding me back."

---

[136] A deliberate violation or desecration of sacred persons, objects or places; a sin against the virtue of religion

"It's you that have lost your wits. We must not, Stephen. You know it is a sin to touch holy things."

"At times like this we can, when there isn't any priest!"

"No, Stephen, not at any time. Don't pull away. It'll be a sin on you, Stephen."

"But, Jamie, Friar Walter said so."

"He said so?"

"Yes, he said so. I heard him, I tell you, and Sir Angus said it, too."

"Well, if you have Father's word for it." The two boys took a step forward.

"Don't go," whined Roger. "Aren't you afraid to pass those?" He pointed to the dead.

"Stay where you are!" blazed James. "Stay where you are. Margaret will take care of you."

Roger followed for a step or two. He was afraid to go and afraid to stay. The other two had picked their way over the dead, and now they knelt before the fireplace.

"Oh, Stephen," cried Jamie again, "do you know that you are sure? That you heard him right?"

"But I did hear him right!"

"Well, what did he say for us to do?"

"Oh, that's what I don't know. We must do whatever should be done, but I don't know what should be done!"

Stephen looked with trembling reverence on the Sacred Host lying there so white and still. "O Lord" he prayed, "don't You see how it is? We don't know what we ought to do, and we must do something. We cannot leave You like this. Please forgive us if we make mistakes, and forgive us our sins so that we shall not be too bad to touch Your Sacred Body and most Precious Blood."

From that moment, both boys lost their fear and knew that the good Lord would reward with His eternal gratitude *whatever poor, little, clumsy service they might render Him, now lying as if helpless, as if needing their care.*

Stephen took a clean finger towel and raised the chalice with it. Then he cut out from the altar cloth the linen stained by the Precious Blood and laid it gently in the chalice. With a little linen, James absorbed the pool upon the hearth. He passed the cloth to Stephen who placed it in the chalice. Then he lifted the paten[137], slipped it under the Sacred Host, and placed it over the chalice, covering all with the corporal[138] and a piece of linen cut from the altar cloth. James laid a piece of clean linen upon the hearthstone and over it a shield. That was the only thing at hand. The lads turned from the altar. The dead lay all about them in the cold, gray light of the dawn.

'We must get these bodies out of here," whispered Stephen. "Things ought to be tidy. This room is the same as a church now."

The bodies lay as they had fallen about the old Earl's feet—a tumbled, ghastly pile with a great trooper's face upward on top. The look on his brutal mouth made them shiver and turn their eyes away. There was another face just below. It was peaceful, almost beautiful.

"That is Captain Brent," whispered James. "I wonder whether God forgave him."

"Oh, surely! He was sorry right away and he died defending the Blessed Sacrament. Maybe he's looking at us from heaven this minute, but that other one—is he suffering for his sin right now?"

---

[137] A saucer-like dish of the same material as the chalice—gold-plated and consecrated by a bishop; holds the bread to be consecrated and later the Sacred Host

[138] A square, white linen cloth upon which the chalice and paten are placed on the altar during Mass

"Didn't get much by sinning, did he? Thought he'd have a lot of money, and instead got a slash from the lang-sword."

"Say, we shouldn't be talking. We're forgetting this is a church in here."

"What's that?"

"Nothing but a board creaking."

"There it is again!"

"On the stair!"

"It's a step/"

"Maybe it's Bertrand!"

"He said he'd come back for the chalice!"

"There it is again!"

"Quick! How do you open that place back of the fireplace?"

"That won't do! Bertrand knows the hiding places better than we do!"

"Here, hand it to me! Wrap the linen tightly! The soot will get in!" Stephen had stepped into the fireplace and was clambering up the chimney on the rough stones. James passed the chalice to him, then ran back to where Roger and Margaret were standing. They crawled into their old hiding place under the bed and huddled close, their eyes fixed on the door.

A board creaked in the hall. The children scarcely breathed. The door swung open silently. Bertrand crept in.

"Gone!" he snarled. "Gone, as I am a living man. No wonder they were for leaving it for luck. Came after it themselves. No, they couldn't have beaten me. They had to take the old fool down to the dungeon. There must have been someone left in the house."

He slipped back into the hall. Under the bed, the tense little muscles relaxed a moment, but the next instant Bertrand was gliding back through the door. He seemed intent on beginning his search with the secret places of the great *fireplace.*

"Oh, let me get behind you," whimpered Roger. "You are bigger." He tried to crawl over Margaret but his foot slipped. There was a scraping sound.

"What's that?" Bertrand was beside the bed in a moment. He caught James by the foot and drew him out. "Where is that chalice?" he snarled. "Don't deny that you know!"

"I'm not denying it."

"Where is it, then?"

"Do you think I am going to tell you?"

Bertrand gave him a cuff[139]. "Might as well argue with a mule. There's no time to lose. Who else is underneath?" He stooped down to look. "Margaret? Not much better. Stubborn piece of baggage. Roger, come out here, you." Bertrand reached in and caught the little coward by his long curls.

"Ouch! Ow!" he squalled, but the man drew him along without mercy. "Where did you put that chalice?"

"I didn't touch it. I—I—I didn't do anything. Ouch, oh, don't! I say I didn't—I even told them not to!"

"Who?"

"Oh-o-o-o Ste—!" began Roger.

"You dare say a word, you little coward! Is there no drop of Gordon blood in you? Were you changed in the cradle for a swine driver's child? A traitor's no brother of mine," blazed James. "Let the baby alone, Bertrand! He had nothing to do with it. If you want to take spite out on anyone, take it out on me."

"I'll give you enough before I go, enough and to spare, you mule-head!" Bertrand gave Roger's curls a savage twist. "Answer me, booby! Who took the chalice?"

"Ow! Please let me go," wailed the child, looking from

---

[139] An open-handed blow

Bertrand to his brother and back again. The poor little weakling did not know whom he feared more. "Oh, don't! You hurt so!"

"Where is it?"

"They'll tell Mother on me if I do say who!"

"Your mother is in prison. Small harm or help can she be to you!"

"Ow! Please stop, Bertrand! I'll give you fine things when I grow up if you do."

The servant laughed derisively. "Fine gifts of young Laird Landless!" he mocked, still twisting the child's hair with savage cruelty.

It was too much. Pain had triumphed. "Ow, don't! Ste— Stephen. He—he's up the chimney with it!"

Bertrand dropped the sobbing boy and ran over to the fireplace. He looked up into the black hole. A foot scraped. A cloud of soot fell. He sprang back in time to miss it.

"So that's your game, my lad! Soot works two ways, boy! Better come down before the fire is lit!"

No answer from Stephen save another gift of soot.

"There's kindling in the hall. Get it, Roger."

The sobbing boy turned to obey.

"You just dare!" yelled James springing at him, but Bertrand caught the elder boy by the collar.

"Do as I bid you, Roger! I'll attend to this meddling brother of yours and settle him!" Then he rained kicks and cuffs on James until Roger returned with the wood. "Take that for the stubborn mule that you are and always will be!" Bertrand snarled, striking a blow that sent the boy spinning across the room. James struck with his head against the stone wall, but he was on his feet in a moment.

"Come on, Margaret," he called, "we've got to keep him from starting that fire. It'll kill Stephen. He'll never give up."

Blood was streaming from the boy's temple, but the pain only roused his spirit to madness. The two children sprang upon Bertrand. James caught him by one hand and Margaret by the other. The boy made a battering-ram of his head while he kicked with all his might. It was little so small a girl could do. Her teeth were sharp and she used them. Between the two, they held the servant for a time. If Roger had helped, they might have overcome him, but he was no help at all.

"Roger," cried Bertrand with a foul oath, "light that fire!"

"If you do!" yelled Jamie.

The poor weakling stood sobbing. The fighting midgets seemed to be holding the man. So, Roger obeyed his brother, though he grew white at Bertrand's muttered threats.

The strength of the children began to fail. Bertrand caught Margaret's hand, then Jamie's. He tied the wrists together with a cord wrapped many times around, and swung them up over the high carven back of the bed. There they hung on agonizing muscles, for the little girl's feet could not touch the cushions, and the boy was dangling down the smooth back. James made matters worse for his small comrade without realizing the fact. Being much the heavier, he had dragged her wrist over to his side of the top, and the weight was on her tender flesh.

Roger fared little better than they. Bertrand now beat him for failing to obey him. Then they lit the fire.

"Oh, pray, Margie, pray!" sobbed Jamie. "Stephen will die! He'll never give up! Oh, he'll die!"

There was a scraping in the chimney. Poor Stephen was trying to climb from the flames.

"Get a little water, Roger," sneered the brute. "Smoke will reach him anywhere."

The scraping within the chimney seemed still in the

same place, and Bertrand laughed.

"Put the water down. We do not need it yet. He cannot climb. Let him stick there and roast a while."

Again a frantic scratching in another place and higher up, then silence in the chimney.

"He is out of reach of the fire," said Bertrand. "Pass the water pail to me, Roger. That's a good boy. We'll give him a smoking."

Bertrand dashed water on the fire. Smoke rose in a white cloud; no more sound came from the chimney.

Suddenly Roger screamed. The trooper on top of the dark pile of slain was moving. There was no doubting it. Broad daylight had come now. He was slowly rising. He could not be living. No man alive ever had such a gash across the throat, but moving he was. His head rolled this way and that. His arms rose and fell again. Bertrand's face whitened with terror. The trooper raised his head till the staring eyes were full upon him. Then the head nodded and dropped back.

Bertrand waited for no more. The children heard his swift steps echoing through the vacant halls below, then silence. James was the first to come to his senses.

"It's not the trooper at all. It's Muckle John down underneath, moving him. Come out and cut us down. Aren't you hurt?"

"I canna get oot," replied the young sailor. "I canna lift the body." Then, with a bit of a chuckle, "But I lifted him so as to give the laugh to yon Bertrand."

"Here, Roger, help us down," called James.

"You won't hurt me? Promise you won't."

"No, you booby. I wouldn't dirty my hands by touching you. Hurry, you poor little sneak! Stephen can't get out of the chimney and you know it. Maybe the smoke has killed

him."

Roger freed his brother and Margaret as swiftly as possible, probably hoping to curry favor[140] and save later trouble. James sprang toward the fireplace as soon as his feet touched the floor.

"Margaret, you roll the trooper off John, can you? I'll help Stephen," he called over his shoulder as he raked the smoking embers from the hearth out on the stone floor. "Throw water on them, Roger. You can do that much maybe. Hurry! The smoke is mean!"

Laying a shield upon the hot hearth, James stepped into the fireplace. "Slip down, Stephen. I'll catch you," he called.

There was no answer. James looked up into the black hole. "Get me a stool," he called. "Stephen must have fainted. Be careful. Don't set your dress afire. Thank you, Margaret. There, hold it steady!" James had climbed on the stool and was standing with his head in the chimney, trying to loosen Stephen's body. "Catch him, Margaret! He's slipping! Easy! The chalice—be careful! I have it—Steady! Hold Stephen! There, you have him. Take him out on the floor, can you? That's it! Roger, help, will you? Lift him past the coals."

Roger and Margaret managed to lift Stephen over the smoking embers while James was climbing from the stool, holding the chalice reverently.

The cloth was still in place. Not a speck had touched the Sacred Trust. Stephen had guarded his Lord at a bitter cost to himself. He lay where his sister had placed him—his eyes, nose, and mouth filled with soot.

"The young gentleman's done for, my Lord," groaned Muckle John, dragging himself up on one elbow. "He'd be

---

[140] To seek to gain goodwill

chokin' or gaspin' if there was a breath o' life in him."

"Oh, no!" cried James. "Drowned folk are limp like that when they're not dead yet. You fishermen work their shoulders some way. Tell me how."

"Turn him face doon. Na! Na! Do na let his face bang the floor. If I could but help ye a wee!" John strove to drag himself up and fell back among the dead. "I'm near done for my own sel'. Hald him up a bit. Work his shoulders. Na! Na! More round-about like! They be no pump handles. Aye, if I could get the lead oot o' me and help ye a wee. Yer doin' better, but no right yet."

James worked desperately. Still there was no sign of life. Margaret had her brother's burned feet in her lap, sobbing over them, trying to loosen the stockings without breaking the blisters.

"If he would only cough or something," wailed James, weary with his struggle. "Or if I had sense to do what you tell me, Muckle John." Suddenly dropping his friend, the boy turned toward the altar. "O Lord," he cried, "Stephen was hurt taking care of You. John can't do anything. We haven't Mother or Nurse or anybody. Won't You help us?"

The trustful prayer of a child is an arrow that pierces the Heart of God. Stephen moaned faintly and twisted. Then came a sudden coughing, which seemed to tear his little lungs asunder[141], and he spat out quantities of soot. For an hour or more, he lay in his friends' arms, racked by the maddening cough and faint from exhaustion. His eyes were dazed, but slowly they cleared, and he staggered up saying, "Who put that dirty rag over the Blessed Sacrament?" He stumbled over to the altar. "Oh, yes, the soot from the chimney."

He lifted the cloth reverently and, taking the cleanest

---

[141] Into separate pieces; apart from each other

bit of linen left, laid it over the chalice. Excitement seemed to have made the child unconscious of his burns; but now that the Sacred Trust was safe, his face grew sick with pain, and he sat down on the floor, rocking himself back and forth in his misery.

Suddenly Muckle John raised his head and whispered, "What be that? I heard it twice afore. A step! In the lower hall."

Stephen staggered up on his burned feet. Not even the fear of more pain could daunt his soul. He was on the point of climbing back to his post in the chimney, but Muckle John whispered, "No' so quick, my Lords. 'Tis no' Bertrand's step. 'Tis light, more like a lassie's."

"Sounds like Nurse!" James dashed into the hall and they heard his joyous shout, "Oh, Benson!"

The maid was in the room in a moment—a simple, homely country lass; but the angel Gabriel could scarcely have been more welcome than Benson. A babel[142] of tongues greeted her. The tale was told in a child's jumble, but whatever of horror the sight of death and sacrilege might have made her suffer, she spoke cheerily and her calmness quieted their fear.

"Poor John, I hope the cut is no' so deep as you say. Never mind, we'll fix it. Bless us, what a wrist, my little Lady! And such a brave woman she is—hasn't cried at all! And Stephen—ah, those burns, laddie! But it's the spirit o' a Douglas your Lordship is showin'. Sir Angus will be that proud o' his bairns! But you and your sister must suffer in patience. John has lost overmuch blood. He is most in need. I must care for him first, dears."

Benson's deft fingers had kept pace with her words. She

---

[142] A confusion of voices and other noises; from the Tower of Babel in Genesis 11:1-9

had found linen and torn it into bandages, and now she addressed James and Roger.

"Your young Lordships are unhurt. Will you please bring me the salves from the buttery[143], a pan of water also, warm if there be any? Then these bodies must be removed. Such things canno' lie before the Blessed Sacrament. By the time you are back, I'll have poor John that I dare move him. Whiles I'm carin' for the hurt, your Lordships make this room fit for Him that's abidin' in it."

But Roger drew himself up with much dignity for so small a person. "Benson," he stormed, "do you forget your place? To whom are you speaking? Those are servant's duties."

"The honor due to your noble blood did no' trouble you overmuch whiles you were playin' servant to yon Bertrand. My Lord, your mother, Lady Isabelle, bade me take charge of all things durin' this black time while she lies in prison; and I am to be punishin' of you, Master Roger, whenever you stand in need of the same. Well she knew the other three would no' be givin' trouble in such a day o' sorrow. They know what is becomin' o' noble blood, and their honor has no' the queer quirks in it that yours has—Lord Roger Gordon!"

Roger was white with anger, but one glance from his irate brother made him cringe, and peace reigned under the government of Nurse Benson. At noon, James leaned over the chair where Margaret was dozing.

"Come, my brave comrade-at-arms," he said half-tenderly, half in mischievous remembrance of the minutes that they had hung upon the high carven top of the bed. Together they passed down the hall.

---

[143] A small room for storing foods or wine; a pantry

The door of the Earl's room was ajar and they tiptoed in. It was the most beautiful place the little girl had ever seen. Benson had not left a spot anywhere. Evergreens had been brought up from the castle yard. The chalice, draped in white linen, stood between rows of shining candles, and there at the good God's feet were many new-blown violets smiling up at Him, simple, beautiful, like the faces of loving children. Stephen was in prayer. The lines of pain were still upon his face, but over it there was a look unspeakably holy—the light of the joy that shines on those who have suffered for the Lord our God.

14

GLORY OF THE BITTER END

Days dragged themselves into weeks and months. One by one, the clansmen and the household came back from prison or from their hiding places. Life went on almost as before save for the constant worry over the old Earl and the Lady Isabelle, the mother of James and Roger.

At last, in May, a carriage swung round the shoulder of Ben Ender on the old road from the outer world to the little world sheltered behind the rampart of the mountain. A bit of white fluttered from the window.

"It is Mother! Oh, I know it is," cried James.

Then the castle bell pealed joyously. Down to the great gate ran the three children. The old keeper's hand trembled so for very gladness that he could scarcely let down the drawbridge. At last, down it came with a jolt and a clang, and the carriage rolled in. James had the door open before the footman could reach it.

"Oh, Mother, how well you look!" he cried as he helped her down. "I never saw your cheeks so red!"

"God bless you, my son," she whispered as her hot lips touched his forehead. "Where is Roger? Ah, my dear little ones of Douglas!" She stooped to kiss Margaret and Stephen but turned away coughing, and they knew that she was in pain.

"Come inside, Mother," said Jamie anxiously. "The wind is blowing. You have a cold, haven't you?"

"Yes, dear," she said with strange gentleness.

Jamie kept close beside her all afternoon. He was troubled. He had a fire lighted in the grate, although it was a warm day, and brought a little shawl to put about her shoulders. At last, Lady Isabelle sent them all out while she spoke with the steward[144]. Then James went straight to Benson.

"Mother is sick," he said. "I mean she's very sick, isn't she?"

The good nurse turned away. There were tears in her kind eyes.

"The damp o' the dungeon! Oh, I knew it, my lambs, I knew it!"

"Can she ever get well?"

"I think she be nigh the gates that be made o' pearl, but play the man, my little Laird Jamie. The more cheery we keep her, the longer she'll bide with us."

Before the last June roses were in bloom in the castle yard, James and Roger were motherless.

News came now and then from Sir Angus. In one of Lord Russell's dungeon cells, he was awaiting his trial. At last, the House of Lords sat upon the case. They found him guilty. Of what? All his life the Earl of Ravenhurst had been a traitor. That was why his lands had been given to the loyal

---

[144] One who manages the household affairs of a large estate

Henry of Russell. It was but owing to the extreme clemency of His Majesty, King James, that Sir Angus had not been beheaded long before. Now his most treasonable conduct had become more than the patience of so mild a monarch could endure. He had harbored—aye, harbored with direct will to displease the King, knowingly and with full consent, within his own castle—had harbored an outlaw, an accursed Catholic friar. He had permitted—nay, ordered to be celebrated—the foul and abominable[145] Sacrifice of the Mass. He had drawn the sword against the King's dragoons and had slain twelve of them with his own hand. No one spoke of the honor due the twelve bold warriors that let one old man lay them around his feet like sproutings clipped from a hedgerow. In truth, the Earl of Ravenhurst was guilty of death. He deserved to be drawn and quartered like a common villain; but, in consideration of his great age and the loyal deeds of his father, Lang-Sword, King James would be satisfied that he be merely beheaded, the sentence to be executed upon the popish[146] feast of Our Lady in Harvest[147].

Sir Edward Gordon, an old knight whom the Lady Isabella had appointed the guardian of the four noble orphans, said that they should go to see the execution. Others said no, such sights were not for children. They were too young and would never be able to forget the awful spectacle.

"Forget it? No!" cried Sir Edward. "I want them never to forget it! They are the children of martyrs. They must stand for the Faith though it cost them their lives. Aye, sirs! Let them see a martyr win the palm! Let them see and never

---

[145] Thoroughly unpleasant and disagreeable; loathsome
[146] Of or pertaining to the popes or the Roman Catholic Church; usually a derogatory term
[147] A feast day of the Blessed Virgin Mary celebrated on August 15—the Feast of the Assumption or Dormition

forget it!"

The stern Scot had his way. The four children rode with him. On the way, he spoke to them of the glory of dying for God and for native land. Roger listened eagerly. He seemed to think some great honor would be shown him as a martyr's kinsman. A base nature cannot understand the kind of glory of which Sir Edward spoke. As they drew near the throng that gathers at such a time, a man turned his head and nudged his companion. The other laughed.

"Yes, I see—Ravenhurst crest—the traitor's family, no doubt. Not so much as one retainer[148] with them. They are in beggarly poverty, you know."

"Aye, an' so it should be!" The speaker was a mighty, broad-shouldered Scot of the Covenant[149]. "Root an' branch, out w' all idolaters[150]!" he shouted.

"Now, my father," boasted the first speaker, "he was always tellin' us aboot the doin's o' his grandfather that was at the burnin' o' the convent i' the wood. Aye, that was a lootin' worth goin' to. The Catholics ha' nothin' now, but in those days they were grand an' fine: silver an' rubies, silks an' cloth o' gold—a pile like a haycock[151]! That was for the great folk: Laird Russell, the fine gentlemen, an' Queen Bess[152], down in England, an' all that! But the poor common soldier didna' come off w' nothin'. My grandfather had the smashin'

---

[148] A servant or attendant who belongs to a family of high rank
[149] A member of the National Church of Scotland, which opposed the Roman Catholic Church
[150] A derogatory term for Roman Catholics stemming from the mistaken idea that Catholics worship the Blessed Virgin Mary and the saints
[151] A conical pile of hay left in the field to dry before storing
[152] Daughter of King Henry VIII, Queen Elizabeth I of England reigned from 1533-1603

o' the big window wi' the Virgin on it. 'Twas give to the lazy friars by King James that's lang dead—a barrel full o' fine lead my grandfather got oot o' that same; but 'tis na good setting the hounds on Catholics now. They all be as poor as field mice in famine year"

"Keep still," whispered Sir Edward, noting the flush of anger that rose on the faces of the children. "We are the kinsmen of a martyr. We must share his glory with him. Poverty and shame the dear Christ bore. Keep that before your eyes and be brave."

"Make room!" called a brutal voice. "Here be the fine Catholic nobles! Give place! Let them see the old fool pass."

The crowd opened, and Sir Edward's party pressed close to the roadway down which the Earl must pass. Roger let his horse slip behind his brother's as they moved forward. James saw him crawling from the saddle.

"Where are you going?" he asked.

"I will not be called a traitor's child!" Roger muttered. "They are pointing at us!"

"You are not ashamed of grandfather, are you?" whispered James. "Don't be a coward this time. Words can't hurt when we know they are not true!"

But Roger had slipped from his horse and mingled with the crowd. A coarse fellow jostled against James, then bowed in mock apology.

"Be throwin' your bonnets in the air, lads!" he shouted. "Mates, this young gentleman will be Earl o' the Raven's Roost before he's an hour older!"

"Hald your tongue, bully!" called the great Scot of the Covenant, shouldering his way toward the speaker. "Leave the poor bairn in peace. Sorrow enough he has afore him! But mind ye, lad, let the ald Earl's death be a lesson to ye. When ye be top at Ravenhurst, give good riddance to Catholics."

James flushed. Then suddenly he turned. His child's voice had in it the ring of a man's determination. "When I am Earl, I shall take up the battle where my grandfather lays it down!"

A jeer rose from the crowd. But in the eyes of the Scot, there was admiration, and Margaret leaned toward the lad and whispered, her eyes bright with pity and pride, "No cause is dead while true hearts live."

Quick gratitude shone in Jamie's glance. "Aye, little comrade-at-arms!" he said.

But the words were not heard by the crowd. A sound floated toward them. Heads were craned, and brutal jests broke forth. Then into sight came the prison cart, and standing in it, butt of ridicule, sport of the mob, was Angus Gordon.

The dungeon had shattered the Lang-Sword's son. He could scarcely hold himself erect in the jolting cart, but erect he was and a soldier still. The old man seemed but the more beautiful for the marks of the dungeon upon him. He was looking straight at the crowd, a joyful smile was on his lips. The noise died. The mighty Scot of the Covenant turned menacingly toward the fellow who seemed to be the leader of the jeerers.

"Ye can hald yer gibin' tongue!" he roared. "Na doot, Russell paid ye weel to stir up the mob, but chew yer cud on this: I'll pay ye wi' my fists if ye do." Then, turning to the crowd, he spoke his mind like an honest Scot: "Ye all know me. I be no Roman Catholic body. I ha' fought the abominations o' Rome afore, and will again; but, mates, I fight a man's battle. I would na be one o' a pack o' hounds besettin' a lone sheep or one o' a mob o' cowards jeerin' an ald dungeon-broken man."

There was a change on those wild faces, for the will of a mob is the will of the wind. Sir Edward's party moved for-

ward, and a whisper went through the throng.

"Give place! Let them pass. They are the old Earl's kinsmen."

There was pity in the tone, and the crowd followed in silence, perhaps thinking over their own wrongs. Many among them were Covenanters; they were men who had suffered from the cruelty of the King almost as greatly as had the Catholics.

The cart rattled up to the scaffold. As it stopped, a dozen hands went out to help the old Earl down. Lord Russell, who stood on the platform, seemed a trifle uneasy. He whispered a moment to a knight beside him, then came a curt order. The soldiers drove the crowd back from the foot of the scaffold.

A muttering rose from the mob. They began to move as if to join a second throng that was coming up the road from the opposite direction. Another whispered consultation between Russell and his aids. The action of the Covenanters seemed puzzling to them. A troop of cavalry was swiftly placed between the two crowds.

'Well planned, Sir Henry of Russell," muttered Sir Edward. "That second throng are from the Ravenhurst lands. They hate their new master as they loved the old. They have never had the courage to join the outlaws of Ben Ender, but will they stand tamely and see Angus Gordon die?"

The knight's eye flashed with quick fire. "Ho, my bairns, we may save him yet! The Covenanters are now more for the Earl than against him." Sir Edward's trained eye ran over the field. Then he shook his head. "Six hundred men, I take it. Weapons? Sticks, stones, a few swords. The other side? Two hundred horse, three hundred foot, well armed. No, my children, it would be folly. A sheer waste of life. We could never reach the scaffold."

Angus Gordon stepped out beside the block. He raised his hand as if about to speak. A hush fell on the mighty throng. His voice was faint—that voice which in years gone by had rung above the din of battle. It was feeble now and low, yet piercing-sweet, like the notes of some far-off bugle.

"Sir Henry of Russell asks what I wish to say in answer to the charge of treason which now stains my knightly honor. There are stains that tell of shame, and there are stains that speak of glory. When they brought the standard[153] back from Flodden Field, there was a stain upon it. Aye, a dark blot upon the fair silken banner from Dun Edin, but that stain was the lifeblood of a King. That torn and bloodstained banner is a sacred thing. Aye, a sacred thing. Now the Faith of the King who fell on Flodden Field is called treason against Scotland. This Faith is that stain which lies on my honor as a Scottish knight. This stain is my glory as it was the glory of those that are no more. Would I were worthy to fall under the banner of the King of kings, worthy of my place in the red-robed army led by Stephen[154]. Thank God for the honor done me, and stand for God and our Lady till we meet again. My Lord of Russell, I thank you for your courtesy."

Sir Angus knelt by the block and laid his white head upon it. Sir Henry turned to the headsman[155], but the brawny fellow was sobbing like a child.

"Go find a knave[156] that will do your foul work for you," *he said. "I'll no' have innocent blood on these hands."*

Russell's face whitened with anger. A sympathetic growl

---

[153] A flag, banner or ensign of an army or country; the colors of a military unit
[154] A reference to St. Stephen, the first Christian martyr
[155] An executioner who beheads condemned prisoners
[156] An unprincipled, deceitful servant

rose from the mob.

"Allen," said the old Earl gently, "the sin of this lies on the judge, not upon the executioner. You will be merely doing your duty according to law. Do not bring trouble on yourself through love of me."

"It may be no sin in the eye of the law—queer laws they do be havin' these days! Was it your duty accordin' to law to send a cow to my brother's wife? They were no' your tenants more. If the widow and her wee bit bairns were starvin', what was that to you in the eye o' the law? But you sent the cow!"

"It is little I gave them, Allen. Do your work, lad. I shall bear you no ill will, nor will the good God lay this to your charge. Sir Henry is angry. He wilt make you suffer, my poor fellow."

"Sir, you gave the best you had and you gave it wi' kind words. If there be men in yon crowd, Angus Gordon does no' die this day! I set my foot on the scaffold for that I have given my word to all true clansmen that I am not to kill our chief, but to see to it that he is no' killed!"

"Aye, aye! Hald to it, Allen! There speaks a Gordon!" came from strong though scattered voices in the throng, for the handful of Ben Ender outlaws was sprinkled through the mob.

"Strike or rot in my dungeon!" hissed Russell.

"I'll no' have a good man's blood on these hands!" retorted the headsman.

A roaring applause from the Ravenhurst men.

"Stand your ground, Allen! You are no' alone the day!" It was the voice of the big Covenanter.

"The Gordon!" The first shout was faint and fearful, but it was caught up on the instant. Then the old war cry burst like thunder. "The Gordon! Clan Gordon to the rescue!"

The mob surged madly forward, catching at anything that might serve as a weapon: sticks, stones, clubs, and here and there a sword. Sir Angus rose to his feet and raised his hand. There was silence.

"Sticks and stones against powder and shot! It is folly, pure folly! You cannot save me. Do you think I shall die easier for knowing that more Gordon wives are widows, more Gordon orphans wail for bread!" He knelt again. "Let the ax fall, Allen. 'Tis an easy way to heaven, lad. The clan will suffer for this attempt to save me. Let it fall, Allen, let it fall!"

"Never!" cried the headsman. "Are you men that you dally so?"

A maddened roar came up from the people, and an echo, faint, solitary, yet distinct, from somewhere among the soldiers.

"Quick, or we are lost!" whispered the knight at Russell's elbow. "The troopers are siding with the mob!"

"Run a sword through that mutineer!" howled Russell. A dozen soldiers sprang upon Allen and dragged him from the scaffold. There was a sharp struggle.

Allen wrenched himself free and joined the mob, yelling, "The Gordon! The Gordon!"

"Gordon for God and our Lady!" thundered the mob as the stones began to fly.

"Fire on them!" rang Russell's command.

"Do you see that?" roared the knight in Sir Henry's ear. "Half of them are firing in the air! They let Allen go! Quick! A headsman or we are lost!"

Russell's voice rang above the roaring of the mob.

"A headsman! Fifty pounds for a headsman! One hundred! Five hundred!" A stone struck him. He dodged back under cover.

Allen was almost at the scaffold again, his club crashing to right and left among the soldiery.

"Down wi' them! Why should we stand for King James? Russell's a Lowlander! Scots are we all!" It was the big Covenanter at Allen's side. The two throngs were one at last.

Someone was climbing the ladder. Russell passed him a purse. He clutched it with eager, trembling fingers and sprang to the ax. His face was turned and the sun shone full upon it. The man was Bertrand. A wild cry from the mob, a sudden hush. The steel flashed in the morning light, and the grand old man was with his God.

15

SPLINTER OF THE LANG-SWORD

A sound struck on Gordon's ear. His mind reeled between living thought and living fact. Before his mental eye, the mob still surged around the blood-soaked scaffold with its sacred dead; still Russell snarled, defiant, guarded by his lords, the traitor Bertrand cringing in his shadow; still over all hovered the martyr's soul, just catching the breath of Heaven's welcoming: salvos[157] of angel hosts, trumpets of seraphim[158], hosannas of the myriad[159] ranks that bear the victor palm, and echoing through the courts of bliss the Voice from the white throne of God, *"Ave, Martyr Christi!"* But jarring up from the world of fact came a key that grated in a lock, the dull pain of the chair in which he sat, the familiar things crowding on his sight, and the stunning sense that enemies were near. His own battle horn was blowing.

---

[157] A sudden outburst of cheers or praise
[158] The highest rank of the nine choirs of angels; sit before God's throne, praising Him in their cries of "Holy, Holy, Holy" as in the *Sanctus* of the liturgy
[159] Large, infinite number; innumerable

The door creaked as it opened. Sir Roger was there with Godfrey at his elbow. The tutor drew in his breath with a hiss. Disappointment darkened Sir Roger's face. He had thought to find a lad worn weary with pain, petulantly[160] defiant, but breaking. Gordon's hot words of a few hours ago had shown his self-control to be weakening. Here, strengthened from some unknown source, the boy stood before them. His face was swollen and twisted with pain, yet in his eyes there was no fear, no yielding, no weariness, but a look of joy deeper than the wrongs of earth, sweeter and stronger than human. Godfrey would have slipped out again. Though his soul was too grossly formed to comprehend the boy's exaltation, yet his mind was too cunning to start a battle lost from the beginning.

Sir Roger sprang forward. There was that in the boy's look which made his soul writhe along the burning ways of memory. His clenched fist drew back menacingly. The Gordon looked calmly, almost pityingly on the man's fury. It was as if the boy had suddenly become the elder. He spoke with a half-stern yet sorrowful kindliness.

"Roger, Uncle Roger, why are you the only traitor, the only weakling in the House of Gordon? Has Bertrand's son led you to this shame? But you can throw it off even yet, Uncle Roger. Even yet you can be a man and not a traitor!"

Blows like an avalanche were the weakling's answer. Roger's lean hands were gripped about the boy's throat, throttling him, pounding his head against the sharp moldings of the chair. One more fearful blow and Gordon plunged forward. The heavy oaken chair had come upon them both. A maddening crash upon his temple, something warm and wet between his cheek and the stone flagging, a creeping

---

[160] Ill-temperedly; irritably

dullness . . .was this death? Death for God and our Lady?

A scuffling sound came faintly. Godfrey had pulled Sir Roger off. He was forcing the frenzied man from the room. The lock grated.

Gordon lay still and waited. In a moment, he would hear the songs of the angels. His heart went out in a great swell of joy that soon died away into a terrible dread and then to a bitter disappointment. The dullness was passing. Death with its freedom from pain, with its joy beyond all earthly compare, was not there; but pain was.

Hours before, Gordon had thought that he had suffered all a boy could bear. Now bruise had been added to bruise. In his head, a hundred hammers seemed pounding. Hunger was gnawing, and thirst like a fire burned high over other woes. He was alone in his pain, as his mother had said, pitifully alone. The great exaltation of some minutes before had died, and even God with His beautiful heaven seemed far, very far away.

Gordon drew himself up slowly, painfully on his elbow and wiped the blood from his temple. Then he crawled to his feet and stood a bit unsteadily, holding to the overturned chair.

Once again, he read his mother's note. "Whether I am living or dead, my prayer shall plead for you in that hour."

"At this moment my mother is praying for me, and she herself is suffering below in one of those terrible dungeons!"

The thought gave him new strength. Slowly straightening himself, as if by so doing he could the better shoulder his cross, Gordon walked over to the fireplace and looked long and searchingly at the pictures above the mantel. Was the martyr Gordon smiling at the lad? It seemed so as he stood there beneath the crossed swords, and that the square-jawed boy by the Earl's knee was looking straight into

Gordon's eyes.

"You held out to the end and it was the rack, the dungeon, the scaffold. I'm a coward if I give up, and I won't! But you had better pray for me so I won't ask for water! I'll stand, as you stood, for God and our Lady!

The words were brave, but the noble head was bowed on the mantel, the square jaw set. The brown fist clenched was by his side. Then the shining silver spot on the hearthstone caught his eye, and he knelt down beside it.

"The Precious Blood fell here long, long ago," the lad whispered. "Father Cornwall said It fell on the stones all around where they scourged You! Oh, how it must have hurt! Uncle Roger brought the blood only a few times on me, and You were covered with blood all over."

Gordon stooped down and kissed the spot on the hearthstone. A strange, deep joy came trembling through his soul.

16

ESCAPE

Evening had come. The wag-at-the-wall agreed with Gordon at last and chimed its slow-toned *Angelus*[161]. The shadow of old Ben Ender lengthened across the meadows. From lane and field, the tinkle-clinkle of returning herds floated up to the weary boy. It was evening, but never had so long a twilight followed so long a day—never since the world was made. The boy stood by an open casement[162]. The wind blew about him, cool and damp, bearing the mist from the sea on its wings. He opened his lips and drank in deep draughts, vainly hoping the cooling air might do what cooling water could; but the raw wind only made the bruises ache with a more sickening throb. The fiery thirst burned on. Gordon turned and walked back to the

---

[161] A devotion to the Incarnation, commemorating the angel Gabriel's annunciation to the Blessed Virgin Mary; recited at six in the morning, noon, and six in the evening; the Angelus bells were rung nine times with a pause between every third ring for the space of one Our Father and one Hail Mary
[162] Window that opens by means of hinges on one side

fireplace with a restless yet lagging step. Then he stood as he had done a hundred times, fists clenched, head bowed upon the mantel, staring at the silver spot on the hearthstone. Strength came with that appealing look —strength, not joy. Joy had been given once that he might have stout courage to fight this battle. This was a day on earth to win heaven—not heaven come down to earth.

"Jesus!" Faith had grown in the land of pain. The boy seemed looking into those eyes beneath the crown of thorns, filled with blood and dust and tears. "Jesus, I am tired. Uncle Roger means what he said, I must stay till I give up—till I die. If it was only die and be done with it—but I shall live for days. I am wearing out, Jesus, and if I slip— oh, I don't want to go back on You—but if I slip, if the thirst gets more than I can stand, You won't let me say those words, Jesus, You won't let me fall."

A drop of blood splashed on the silver spot. Gordon started, opened his hand, and looked wonderingly at a nail-cut in his palm.

Then he stooped to wipe away the blood; as he did so, a thought stirred in his mind, dim, uncertain, an echo from that strange first night. Hadn't his mother said something about flying from the castle? Hadn't she told him to go to someone? Whom? Oh, Muckle John! He remembered it now. She said to go from this room, but how? A secret passage, that was it, and Uncle Roger didn't know about it. It started at this fireplace and ended near the fishing village. Why hadn't he thought of it before? But his going would leave his mother alone. Yet, what good could he do her by staying? Muckle John would help him to save her. Certainly, it would be better to go.

Gordon drew a chair toward the mantel and climbed on it. "The soldier on the right hand, and twist the handle

of the sword twice—but it won't move. Perhaps it was broken during that changing. The blade went farther down into the handle before. There is the mark. Why won't it slip down?"

The lad twisted the handle sharply, then pushed the blade downward. It slipped into place with a metallic click. "That's it! Now round it goes—one, two."

Springing from the chair, he ran to the left side of the fireplace. The panel moved under his fingers, sliding silently into the wall and disclosing a black, cob-webbed hole. Running back again, Gordon pushed the chair into its place, wiped the dusty footprint from the seat, straightened the rug, and looked about him.

"There is nothing to show them what I've done, so far as I can see. Uncle Roger will spend some time tomorrow guessing how I got away. If I can find this brave John, he will help me get Mother from the dungeon."

The lad hurried to the passage and climbed through the opening. His fingers sank in powdery dust, a thousand cobwebs clung to him. Beyond, the hole seemed full, and the must[163] in the air choked him. Gasping, he thrust his head into the room again to draw one more deep breath.

"Well, it's go! Find John, get Mother and—oh, surely—there will be some little stream near the outlet in the forest. That means a drink. I would go through anything for one drop of cold water."

Drawing back his head, Gordon slipped the panel over the opening. The last ray of light died. His groping hand touched a bar; as it slid into the socket, he heard the lock click far up in the soldier's extended hand.

Gordon felt about in the darkness. The passage was

---

[163] Staleness; odor

small, scarcely large enough to crawl through, and seemed to run along in the wall. His groping hands found the floor level for some twenty feet, then came a rough stone stairway. Turning around, he crept down backward for a dozen steps, and again the way was level. A sharp turn to the left, and a radiant, fan-shaped light shone far ahead in the darkness.

"Why, there is the end! It is not so long after all."

Gordon hurried forward, but the bright spot was not the end. It was only a small hole in the side wall. There was a faint hum of voices. Scarcely daring to breathe, he crawled on till he was within the dancing, mote-filled[164] light. Oh, how small the hole was, not half so large as his own eye. He looked through—then drew back in terror. Not a dozen steps from the wall sat Sir Roger.

Surely, his uncle must have seen him. No, the hole was too small and too far away for anyone in the room to look through. Gordon laughed softly; it was funny to be able to see so well and yet to remain unseen. There sat Godfrey by the table, shaking his finger at Sir Roger as if laying the law down about something. Gordon could not catch the words, but he distinctly heard his uncle's snarling answer.

"The foolish child will yield in the morning. You are always finding fault."

"My Lord, Gordon has a brain; he will not be twice fooled by any man. Yet there is one way. . . ."

"And that?"

"Tomorrow we shall go to him—you and I—tell him his courage has won our hearts, we must respect a Faith that can make so young a lad so great a hero, give him full liberty to practice his religion—privately—"

---

[164] Full of specks; full of dust particles

"Of all the follies? Are you mad?"

"Mend the folly, my good Sir Roger, mend the folly with this."

The tutor held up a vial[165] that gleamed red in the candlelight.

"You mean—"

"Oh, its action is very gentle, my Lord. As the warm days come—a paleness, a weakness, just a slight malaria; yet in the autumn all the gentlefolk of the countryside will come to the funeral of this promising boy, and the mourning uncle—well, it will all be very sad—but, of course, the mourning uncle will be Earl of Ravenhurst."

---

[165] A small glass or plastic container used for storing liquids; the small neck can be plugged or capped

17

SECRET PASSAGES

For an hour or more, Gordon crawled on. The passage was straight for a time, then it dropped to a lower level and ran on again. Each room had its little spy-hole hidden in some carving. As he crept along, the levels became shorter and the stairs longer. He had not found a spying place for a long time. The darkness grew even blacker. He could not see his hand before his face. The stones were cold, so cold and wet. Then came more stairs, and down, down into the blackness he went.

"It has to sink so low to get under the moat, that must be it," and as he spoke he splashed into a puddle at the foot of the stairs. Oh, how sweet that water tasted, muddy though it was!

He crawled over the mossy stones of the level. Now he must be going under the moat. That was why it was so wet and slimy. The end of the passage could not be far away, at least not much farther, for he had been crawling such a long time. When once he got outside, what if Uncle Roger did take the castle? They could have a little farm of their own or a fine fishing boat like—

Gordon's right hand shot into space. He tried to grasp the stones, lost his balance, and fell—down—down—down into never-ending blackness. Something cold! Water! And down, down, down again. He was rising. One hand shot out, then his head.

Gordon drew a quick, deep breath and floated as he had done many a time when some chance slip had plunged him into the old fishing pool beneath the alders while he and Joel were playing in the Maryland woods.

"Thank God, it is water. I should have broken my neck if it had been stone. Well, the joke is on me! All day long, I have been praying for a drop of water. Now the good Lord has given me a drop into it, instead of a drop of it."

Then Gordon's right arm glided out in a cautious over-hand stroke, but the water was cold, very cold, and his left leg felt queer. It would not follow suit. The lad struck out with all his might, and the struggle sent him under again . . .down, far down, till the roaring in his ears deafened him. He had fasted in bitter pain since early morning, and a boy's strength cannot last forever.

As the body rose for the second time, one hand touched something floating and clutched it as only the drowning can. A plank, short, water-soaked, and slimy, it could bear but little weight, yet that little was much to him. He drew it under his armpit, and his lips were above water. Ah, how sweet is God's own air! Gordon never knew before how much one breath is worth.

Then the lad tried to paddle with his free hand, but the weight of his cramped legs was too great for so feeble a stroke. Still he kept on paddling. He must have been making headway without knowing it, for at last his hand touched the mossy stones. He pulled the plank nearer. They seemed to form the wall of the passage. He drew himself along beside it for a dozen strokes. The plank stopped abruptly.

"I have struck the other wall, I guess. This must be a corner." Gordon felt about in the blackness.

Floating along beside the plank, half resting on it, half drawing himself onward by the stones, Gordon tried to loosen the plank from the unseen snag which held it. A sharp push—too sharp—the slimy wood slid into the water again but out of the boy's hand. He groped in black air and blacker water. It was gone. Search was useless. Clinging to the stones, he dragged himself onward once more.

"This cannot be a corner," he muttered a moment later. "There is another side to it, just over there; but it doesn't come over to make the point. Oh, I wish I could see for a minute, only one!" Suddenly his cramped, dragging feet struck something hard. Crying out with pain, he sank, but not far. The rough stone floor was just beneath him.

Crawling, dragging himself, feeling in the blackness ahead before each onward movement, slowly, slowly he struggled on.

"The water is more shallow," he muttered. "I am going uphill just a little bit now. This must be some other passage. I wonder where it ends. Oh, well, when I am outside, I can see Ben Ender and tell by it which way to go."

Hard work was warming his weary, cold body, and the cramp came out of his legs by and by. At last, he could crawl, and the water was soon behind him.

This passage was crooked and narrow. After crossing that first rise which had shut out the water, it went winding, winding, with a constant downward slant. Gordon could touch the roof with ease. The air, long-imprisoned, had in it something which sucked his breath. He was sure he had crawled onward for an hour or more, but it is hard to tell how quickly time passes when a boy is weary yet dares not rest. Then he cheered himself by planning.

"It cannot be much farther now. I wonder what that John is like. He must be a big man, or folks would not call him Muckle[166] John. When we get Mother, we shall have to go down into the dungeon. How shall we manage that?"

One hand dropped into space again, but this time he did not fall; he was a wiser lad now. Gordon groped about in the hole below him.

His fingers touched something a couple of feet lower. It felt like a step. Were these more stairs? Dared he drop so far without knowing what came next? He sat on the edge and explored the thing with his toe. It was a step, but one end was broken off, and the stone wiggled. How he hated to climb down upon such a wobbling thing there in that blackness! What if he should fall again? Still, he must go on for he had no choice. Could he pull back if he must? The rocks about him were slippery with slime. How could a boy cling to them? At last, he found one that had something like an edge.

Slowly, cautiously Gordon lowered his weight to the dangerous step below, rested a moment, steadied himself, dropped on his knees, then sat down, clinging all the while to the mossy stones of the wall. A breath of less foul air was coming from somewhere, and the lad drew a deep draught. With one wary toe, he explored the lower blackness. There was another step, wide and solid near the wall, but broken off halfway across. The boy slid down on it. He was gaining courage now. One more step was tried. It was better, and the dozen forming the rest of the stairs were broad and firm. Gordon stood at the foot of the stairs and

---

[166] Much; a large amount or number

felt about. The arch of the passage was just in front of him. It was low, perhaps even lower than the one from which he had come, and the stone floor was more deeply bedded in moss and slime. The air was somewhat better, and this encouraged him. Surely, God's good out-of-doors must be drawing near. He crawled on eagerly and had gone a dozen yards or more when one groping hand came upon a little pile of small, rough stones scarcely larger than pebbles. He held one in his hand, wondering.

"These have no moss on them at all, and this one is dry," he said aloud.

As he spoke, something caught his foot. Pull as he would, he could not loosen it. The thing had clenched around his ankle and was holding him fast. "Snakes!" he gasped, struggling wildly. Weak and weary, the lad could make but a small effort at best. The thing only tightened more and more. Catching up a stone, he reached back cautiously and struck a sharp blow. It yielded a moment but tightened again. A second blow. The slimy rock slipped and he touched, not a snake, but fingers—a man's fingers, rough-skinned, long, and thin.

A muffled voice whispered, "Who are you?"

18

SIR JAMES OF GORDON

Gordon did not answer; he was searching for the stone lost a moment before. His left hand groping along the floor found nothing loose but the pile of dry pebbles. His right hand, outstretched and trembling, waited to guard against the next attack of this unseen foe. The man made no further movement, yet he kept whispering, "Who are you?"

Now Gordon's left hand began to creep up the wall, vainly hoping to loosen some small rock, but the stones on this side of the passage were uncommonly large, square-cut, and well set in mortar. A moment later, the boy's fingers touched the man's arm. Gordon shivered, drew back, waited an instant, and felt again. The arm came through a small, rough hole in the wall.

The muffled voice repeated, "Who are you?"

But the lad still kept silence. It was only a hand, not a man, with which he must deal; so he tugged at those clenched fingers with all his feeble might.

"Speak out. You may as well obey now as later, for you cannot go until you do," the muffled voice insisted.

Gordon had no breath to waste on words. He must unclasp those fingers—thin fingers, so thin the lad was almost sorry he had struck them. Something dampened the boy's hands as he struggled—the man's fingers were bleeding. Such fingers must be weak. Why could he not loosen them? His own strength was almost gone. The fingers held him prisoner.

"Are you of the old Faith or the new?"

"I am a Catholic, sir."

"No brass in the ringing of that coin, boy! Well spoken! Who are you? Speak out, child; it is a friend that you have met in the darkness."

"If you were a friend, you would let me go—"

"Let you go on following Blind Duncan? Aye, that would be kindness!"

"Duncan, sir? You are mistaken, I have not seen him."

"Nor will you. When boys follow Blind Duncan, they go down a passage that winds, winds, winds. For a long, long way it has come downward; for a long, long way it will go upward, though never to the light of God's day. By and by, the little boy will find again that the air sucks his breath; by and by, he will lay his head down on the moss and—"

"You mean there is no way out of this passage!"

"No way that you would find without—"

"But there is a way?"

"Yes, yet one so dangerous that it would be tempting God to send a child through it were you not in need—"

"In need?"

"Would you be here if you were not in need, aye, and sore need? But answer my questions now, lad. Afterwards I shall give you what help I can. First, the old question, who are you?"

"I do not like to talk to strangers, sir. What is your own

name, please?"

"I told you, 'a friend', but come, child, you waste time—"

"Friend! A mean sort of friend you are!"

Gordon had never ceased tugging at those clenched fingers; now, disappointment and weariness made him wink back the tears.

"A friend would not torment me. Why should I think that you are one? I do not know you."

"It would indeed be a very wicked man that would not

befriend a little boy lost in the wicked Blind Duncan passage. Let it pass at that. Now tell me who you are."

"Well, I guess I have to."

"In truth you must."

"I am the Gordon."

"That you are not."

"Sir!"

"It is the chieftain alone who is called the Gordon. You are not yet Earl of Ravenhurst, my lad, but you are a Gordon, a small splinter of the Lang-Sword." The deep voice grew strangely tender. "You are he that was born ten years ago on the feast of Our Lady in Harvest."

"Sir! But how in the world did you learn that?"

The muffled tones sank lower. Gordon could scarcely hear the words. He put his ear near the hole, almost touching the man's forearm, and listened closely.

"All day long there has been that old foreboding thought: 'The boy is in danger.' All day long down here in my dungeon I have prayed. Now, sweet Mother, you bring him to me." Then the voice broke sharply, "And . . . and. . . Margaret your mother, lad . . . did she live or die?"

"Why, sir, she is alive. I mean I hope—"

"Hope? You hope? Why don't you *know?*" The man's hand gripped Gordon's ankle till the pain shot through him, keen and sickening. "Answer me!" Agony, not anger, was in the muffled voice.

"Sir, I can't talk of these things to a stranger! Who are you? Why do you want to know so much about me and my mother? You are hurting my ankle; it's sore."

"Poor little one! There, it does not pain now, does it? No, surely you could not speak of these things to a stranger, but you need fear no longer. I have the best reason in this wide world for asking about you and your mother, my son.

I am your father, James of Gordon."

"My father!"

Gordon caught that thin hand and kissed the damp spots. "My own father! Oh, why do I always get things wrong? I hit you and made you bleed and—"

"You struck only to defend yourself. There is no pain, laddy, none whatever; but if there were, the joy in my heart would drown so small a thing. I know now this son of mine will never make my heart bleed. That is the pain a father dreads, my boy. If you knew the joy it gives me to learn it is my own son's voice that rang out so true and clear as you told me your Faith, here in the face of darkness and danger. Such joy is worth these long years of suffering. The Blessed Mother of God has watched over you. But your mother, Son, where is she? Tell me what you know or fear about her. What new harm has Bertrand's spawn done? Your own heart seems full to bursting. Come, pour out all this trouble, Son." The fingers trembled as if caressing the boy though still holding him a prisoner.

"I don't know. Betsy thinks she is down in the dungeon, and Uncle Stephen—"

"Uncle Stephen? You have spoken with him? What did he say?"

"He thought Mother must be in some part of the castle, perhaps in the north tower."

"Probably. That is the prison tower. But what reason did he give?"

"Uncle said Mother broke some law or other when she told me about you and spoke of the Faith."

"And Roger took full advantage of his legal right as guardian, no doubt. God help me if evil has come to Margaret! But speak on, tell me all you know."

Then the whole tale was told for the second time that

day. There is a blessing in confession. Telling the story to Stephen had brought the boy near to his God, and now, when it had been all poured out again, peace filled his soul though he still sobbed in the darkness, clinging to his father's hand.

"Well, Son, if Mother is in heaven, she knows all this; or if, God willing, she is still alive and we find her once more, you shall tell her the story just as you have told it to me and to that saint of God, Stephen. Then do as she will—forget it."

"Could we begin to hunt for her right now, Father?"

"That is impossible. This hole still is too small for me to crawl through."

"Maybe the passage you are in meets this one farther on."

"I am not in a passage. I am lying on my face in a tunnel that I am making. My feet are a yard or two from my home, cell eight, third level of Fire-the-Braes' dungeon beneath the north tower. Even now my legs are cramping."

"You in a cell of this castle!"

"That I am."

"Mother told me the king's dragoons took you years and years ago!"

"They did, but they let me go after six months of rack and dungeon. I staggered home to old Ravenhurst one rain-swept night. Godfrey found me, too weakened to offer resistance. He was for giving me a merciful sword thrust, but my gentle brother could not quite bring himself to risk murder. Instead, Roger gave me this pleasant chamber for the rest of my days. He told me about you. He said you were a fine healthy babe, and that he would teach you to curse the very name of Catholic. He swore that Ravenhurst should rise at the cost of the old cause; gold was far better than martyr's blood, and fools were all those that put trust in God's grace above the favor of kings. Of your mother, Roger would tell me nothing. I had left her at the point of death, and the longing to know which way the tide of life had turned came near to—ah, well, God's hand has been over us."

"But you—you have been alone here in a dungeon cell ever since I was a baby? How did you. . . ."

"When a man faces life imprisonment in a doorless pit thirty feet below the land where God's sun is shining, he has the choice of three things which he may do: despair, and become a sullen madman; brood over his wrongs, and become a fiend; or find some work, some business which will save both soul and reason."

"But what work, what business? Oh, I know, you made this tunnel to get out. But that wouldn't take ten years."

"Would it not? Grinding out a hole through blocks of granite with one small diamond taken from a ring and fastened to a rusted spur—such work is swiftly done!"

"But you have been here in this dark night, you—my own father—here alone through all the jolly days when I used to play with Joel!" With one finger, the lad explored the smooth yet uneven edges of the hole through which his father's arm was thrust.

"Joel? Ah, that Maryland farmer—Abell's son." Sir James paused, thinking. "Perhaps, my son, this sorrow may have taught you some things. 'Jolly days' you called your old life; perhaps you have learned that there are worse fates than the hard work of a farmer's home."

"Worse fates! I wouldn't give one log of Daddy Abell's cabin for all of Castle Ravenhurst! Oh, Father! I didn't mean that to hurt! Of course, if you and Mother had been here all winter! But folk like Uncle Roger don't make home.

It's the old log house that's in my mind whenever I say 'home.'"

"And you would be willing to go back to that simple life again?"

"Willing to go back to Abell's? Do you mean that there is any possible way?"

"Yes, there is. But one great sacrifice will be necessary if ever we go to Maryland."

"What, Father?"

"The coronet[167] of Ravenhurst must be given up forever. Long titles and log cabins do not go together."

"Oh, is that all? I thought you meant I must go without you or Mother."

"So? Who taught you that lesson?"

"Lesson? What lesson? Godfrey has been teaching me Latin and things, but—"

"No, this is not one of Bertrandson's tasks. Sir Angus strove to write it in my mind, or rather in my heart; but I learned it, my son, on the day when my treason was proved —or declared to be!—before the peers of Scotland. I knew the forfeiture had passed. I saw the escutcheon[168] of Gordon riven[169]. Then I learned it; and here in this dungeon when through the black hours I knelt alone with God who had decreed this sorrow for me. Here, imprisoned by my own brother, under my own strong battle tower—a branded outlaw whom it were a favor to Scotland to kill, spurned from the presence of Scotland's king—here I found the presence-chamber of the King of kings."

"Don't worry about the escutcheon any more, Father.

---

[167] A small crown worn by princes, princesses, and other nobles
[168] A shield or shield-shaped emblem upon which the coat of arms is displayed
[169] Torn apart; split into pieces

Uncle Roger told me a lot about it, but he used such big words I understood only that he had straightened everything between the Gordons and the King. The lands, most of them, are ours again, but Uncle Roger paid for them with his soul."

"So! My good brother has been letting it appear that I am dead. He could not have succeeded with that plan otherwise. Very well, when we go to Maryland, it will be to his interest to let us remain there in peace, provided he finds no means to kill us before we set sail. Such a course would let him slip into the earldom with small trouble. Poor weakling, God pity him! Now, we must face the present. Roger is hunting for you or soon will be. It would take a month to grind this hole large enough to be crawled through, but a strong man with a pick or a crowbar could take out this block of stone in less than an hour. You were seeking John-o'-the-Cleuth when I caught you, and he is the man we need."

"But, Father, how shall I ever find Muckle John-o'-the-Cleuth? I have been seeking him so long it seems like always." A feeling of hopeless weariness surged over him, born of hunger, thirst, exhaustion, and the endless aching of his wounds. In the excitement of the last hour, these had seemed to dwindle, but now a wave of sickening misery swept over him.

"Small wonder you think so, Son! You have traveled on your poor knees around Castle Ravenhurst just six times and were on the point of beginning your seventh trip. Margaret had sent you by the fireplace passage safe and direct without cross tunnels or danger, but it cannot have been repaired these ten years since the floor above the cistern[170] rotted through. God's angels must have guarded

---

[170] A receptacle for holding water; a tank for catching rainwater

you—a full twenty feet you fell. If the best passage is in such a condition, what of the worst? Yet through the worst I must send you—the wicked Death-Trap of the Blind Duncan. It was pitted to catch men; God pity the child that should fall into one of those holes. They are ten feet deep with mossy sides and paved with pointed spikes. And you are already worn weary till your brain must be dizzy. How long have you been without food?"

"I do not know. But never mind, Father, the hunger did hurt all day but I have not half so much pain now."

"No, you are living on the excitement and the good red blood in your veins. That sort of strength does well while it lasts, but it comes to a short end sometimes, my child. There is a small crust in my cell. I had thought of giving it to you before, yet did not, for it is badly molded. Still, there is some strength in the bread."

Gordon heard the stealthy movement of the Earl crawling backward through the narrow tunnel. In a moment, Sir James returned, and the boy reached eagerly for the pitiful fare. Then the Earl spoke again, his voice low and clear.

"Begin at the stairs you descended a while ago. Count along the floor thirty blocks of stone. At this point, stand, scrape off the moss where the roof joins the wall, and pull down the iron ring you will find there. Twist it sharply three times and pull down. A door will open into the upper passage. Go forward past a staircase. Two tunnels open there in a 'Y'; take the right-hand one. Would to God I did not have to say that to you! You will be in the Death-Trap of the Blind Duncan.

"Now feel along the floor with care. Count ten stones. Change sides in the tunnel. Count ten stones and change sides in the tunnel. Count ten stones and change sides again. Do this ten times. You will come to short stairs. Go up. You will be in a large tunnel and safely out of Blind Duncan.

"There will be more light and better air if the ventilators are not clogged with old leaves. Five hundred feet from the stairs, you will come into the main passage, which you would have found hours ago but for that hole in the floor above the cistern. Follow the large passage to its end in the woods near Ben Ender.

"Go north to the frith. Follow the shore to the fishing village in the Cleuth and ask for Muckle John. Tell him to come with what men and weapons he can muster. Tell him to bring a pick, shovel, and crowbar.

"Now repeat the instructions."

The boy did so once, and then again.

"Another thing," resumed the father, "leave small strips of your plaid along the tunnel to mark the returning way. Now go, and may God our Father keep His hand above my boy."

The lad's back ached from stooping; his head from hunger and weariness. Often one trembling hand slid into some black abyss, and he would cling to the mossy stones, quivering.

Little by little, the slime on the floor gave place to moss and damp stone. He climbed the last stairs. Air—God's sweet air—was drifting from somewhere, and with it came a dim gray in the blackness. He could see the floor and the walls at last, and before him, only a few yards away, an arch outlined against a stronger light.

This was the main passage. Oh, such a long main passage! Did it run beneath all the fields and meadows from Rock Ravenhurst to Ben Ender? On and on the lad crawled, for even here there was not space to stand. The dull ache of weariness drove all reckoning of time from his thoughts.

One thing only he knew clearly: Mother and Father were there in the dungeon; he must seek John-o'-the-Cleuth.

Something was shining near him. Gordon leaned against the wall and looked. Light, an arch of real light from God's own out-of-doors, and across that light a branch was swaying in the breeze, a branch full of buds just bursting into leaf. He staggered out into the moonlight.

Gordon stretched every muscle in his tired body, then shivered. The north wind pierced his damp clothing that stiffened as he hurried on. Last year's leaves about his feet were white and glistening, the pools frozen. The lad tried to run, beating his arms wildly, but the cold could not be thrown off so easily. Suddenly he stopped. There came a long-drawn whoo-hoo-ah-oo-o!

"Wolves!"

Gordon dashed up the bank toward the big oak tree at the top of the hill.

The lad ran as if he were not weary, ran as he had never run before; but down in the glen, three lean gray bodies leaped. They had seen him.

He reached the tree, the wolves still a few leaps behind. Gordon caught a branch. It slipped from his numb fingers, and he fell. They were almost upon him. He caught the branch again, climbed it, from that to another. They were springing at him wildly. He could not reach the swaying branch above. Higher, still higher leaped the crouching forms, their white teeth gleaming in the moonlight. Then a gust of wind swayed the branch above down toward him. He clutched it, drew himself upon it, crawled back to the trunk, and clung to the oak. Safe! No wolf could jump so high.

They would go away in the morning, and it must be almost dawn, thought the lad. But hours seemed to pass, and

still no hint of coming day. The wind blew fiercely through the wood, the oak wood on the slope of Ben Ender. Those small, numb hands found it hard to hold the lad in the tree crotch. The frozen clothing rattled when he moved, and a quick, sharp pain shot through him with every breath. Down below, the wolves waited, snapping at him now and then with long white teeth, their red eyes glowing in the darkness. Would there be a dawn for him?

At last it came, a faint flush far off on the waters of the frith. But the boy did not see it. He was wondering why the blackness about him whirled round and round, why the three pairs of red eyes were dancing, dancing and whirling round and round.

Two arrows hissed from the bushes. Two gray watchers leaped high in the air and fell with guttural howls. Another shaft flashed through the dawning light, and the third fell across his mates, kicking wildly.

"Well-sped bolts, Muckle John!" someone shouted, springing from the bracken. "Three gude wolfpelts afore sunup!"

"What's treed? A bairn! Quick! Lend a hand! He be fallin'! There, steady, easy, lay him doon."

"The wee Laird o' Gordon!"

"Na doot o' that! Hald him easy whiles I wrap him up in my plaid."

"Would ye see the welts on his face? God's mercy on the laddy! Clad in rags, muddy, stiff wi' cold, beaten bloody— what make ye o' that?"

"It be the work o' yon devil in the castle. An' the Gordon up an' fled to us! God's blessin' on our wee chief!"

19

MUCKLE JOHN

Dawn had come at last. A red light was dancing far out on the water. The clouds were all afire. Gordon lay in a bed, looking out through a doorway, puzzled. Where was he?

He tried to raise his head. It was oddly heavy. Something seemed to be weighing it down. He lifted his hand to remove the thing, and stared. Long fingers, thin and white, blue veins winding in and out among bones—this hand was not his; it must belong to a sick girl.

Someone was speaking in a low tone. Turning his head was too wearisome, but his eyes followed the sound. A man was standing near a fireplace, a rough giant of a seaman with a scarred face. The woman beside him came swiftly forward as she heard the lad stir.

"Ha' a wee drop o' soup, my lamb, would ye?"

"No, madam," he answered; but why did his voice sound so faint and queer? "No, madam, I cannot stay to eat. If you will unfasten that thing which is holding my head down. . . ."

"Bless the soul o' my bairnie, nothing be there save a damp cloth. Yet if the weight troubles ye, I'll—"

"It does not trouble me, madam. It holds me down, and I must go to find Muckle John-o'-the-Cleuth."

"An' what would my chief ha' me to do?" The burly fisherman bent close to hear, but Gordon's eyes grew suddenly wild. Weakness seemed to vanish. He sprang forward, staring at an old collie that had slipped in, snatched the bowl from the woman's hand, and flung it at the dog, crying, "I hit him! That's one wolf done for! But there are so many eyes, red eyes going round and round . . . and the dawn, will it never come? I can't . . . hold on . . . any. . . ." His voice trailed off into silence as he sank back on the pillow.

"Aye, there he goes off again," moaned the woman. "If we do na get yon fever doon, there'll be no wee chief a-ravin' come sunset."

"Na, Na! Jeanie. The wee Gordon can no die! All the hope o' the clan be in him."

Muckle John sat by the lad all day. Now and then, he sponged the hot body gently, so gently that the boy did not stir, or he roused the lad to give him a drink of soup. Hour after hour, he watched for a glimmer of returning consciousness. And all the while, the beads slipped through his iron-muscled fingers as he pleaded with God's Mother for his chieftain and for Clan Gordon.

The sun was setting. Long shafts of light glinted along the heather, under the oak branches, and through the cottage window until they danced over Gordon's face. Then the deep-blue eyes opened, clear and quiet. The moment had come.

Muckle John leaned forward. His rugged face was gentle, his voice low as a mother's crooning a lullaby, yet in his eyes was the coming fury, still controlled, like the sea along the Highland coast rolling its oily billows before the storm. "I be yer Muckle John. Who beat ye?"

"Uncle Roger. But it is not for that I came, my big John. Mother, she's gone. I don't know where. Father, he's living. . . dungeon . . . north tower, and he said. . . ." The voice was dying low, yet the words fell one by one before the eyelids drooped again.

Muckle John took down his old claymore and tiptoed out into the sunset. Men sprang up from doors half-hidden in the heather[171] and sped toward him.

"Aye," he growled, "I ha' news for ye. Roger beat the wee chief an' would ha' murdered him. God give me strength o' arm till I deal the weaklin' his portion. Wi' a galley whip, blow for blow, will I pay him afore I fling him fra' the seaward tower's tip, oot, far oot, till he falls on the wave-beat rocks below. More! Hear ye! Sir Jamie be alive an' callin' the clan. Speed ye all to Rock Raven!"

The red had not left the waters of the frith when all that were loyal still of Clan Gordon were flying hotfoot to the rescue: Muckle John, grandson of Tarn the armorer; his six bold sons; his crew of fishermen, rude[172] fellows with gnarled hands and shaggy beards; Ald Donald, last of those trained to war by Angus Gordon; Davie, trailing the scabbard of his father's sword and panting to keep pace with the men.

They had been crawling a long while in the tunnel when a whisper floated back, "No signs o' the plaid yet, and here be the three arched openings."

Donald slipped forward. He felt along the arches and

---

[171] Low evergreen shrub; grown in the northern hemisphere in dense masses; scale-like leaves and small purplish-pink flowers
[172] Vigorous; sturdy

reported: "Thra crosses—na, na, that be the Blind Duncan. Keep oot! Twa crosses—I ha' no mind o' that. Ain cross— na, it be the way what ends up on the south front o' sea- ward tower nigh the fireplace, too far fra' the north tower."

"By the twa-cross way we'll ha' to go," decreed Muckle John, and the clan crept on.

To the crawling men, it seemed hours later that Muckle John's voice drifted softly back, "Light ahead. Na' a sound that a rat could hear! Dirks oot!"

The light drew near, a bar of yellow darting out from the side wall. A voice ripped up the silence: "Tell that lie again, Betsy, and I'll—"

"But it's the truth, Master Godfrey!"

"Truth? Don't think to fool me! That boy did not fly out the window or crawl through the keyhole. You opened the door or you know who did. Mind, I saw you whispering at the crack."

"Sir, I did but say—"

"Lie again and I'll bash your head in!"

Muckle John hurled his bulk against the wall. The pa- nel crashed. Struggling through, he caught a beam by one hand and dropped. Godfrey whirled to face the giant fish- erman's dirk gleaming in the candlelight.

"Give a sound an' I'll drive my dirk through the black heart o' ye, devil's bloodhound that ye be." Then, glancing at Betsy, he said gently, "Ha' no fear, child, we be more rough in look than in deed. Lang Andrew, care for the lass. Let no ill befall her. Now, as for ye, Godfrey son o' Bertrand, if ye love yer foul life a wee, ye'll answer me true: Where be the keys o' the dungeons?"

"On a peg in Sir Roger's room."

"He's lying," whispered Betsy.

Godfrey snarled, looked at Muckle John's knife, drew

the keys from his doublet[173], and handed them to John.

"Where be the cells o' Sir James and Lady Margaret?"

An ugly smile crossed Godfrey's face. "I'll tell that gladly: the Earl's, third level, second corridor, cell eight, Fire-the-Braes' Dungeon; the Lady's, second level, fourth corridor, cell three. I'll even say what you can find there. In my Lord the Earl's apartment is a hole, a sort of tunnel, leading into the Blind Duncan. In the boudoir[174] of my Lady the Countess is a hole similar to the one through which you have just come. As to the Earl and his Lady, we had thought they were with you; now we know exactly where they are. You have the boy. Keep him. Can you prove before the courts of Scotland that he is the heir? His parents will not aid you because 'dead men tell no tales.' Tomorrow we shall drag the cistern for their bodies. Their residence in the pool does not make the water too wholesome. Stay for the funeral, and bid the brat come from the glen to be chief mourner. You are quite welcome." He ended with a curse and a laugh.

"Keep the name o' God off that foul tongue o' yers! If ye be tellin' a lie, I think I'll dirk[175] ye. If ye be tellin' the truth, I know I will. Ye be so o'er wise an' all-knowin' it be a bitter pity ald Satan ha' no gived ye a seat on his council bench afore now. Wat and Will, keep this devil's darlin' under yer wings. Dirk him if he makes a sound."

From the lower end of the hall came a sentinel's[176] tread. Muckle John crept out of the room and crouched in the shadow.

"Noon o' night, an' all is weel." The deep voice echoed

---

[173] A close-fitting jacket

[174] A woman's bedroom

[175] Stab with a knife

[176] Belonging to someone employed to keep watch; a lookout man's

through the empty corridors.

"Do na be so sure o' that!" Muckle John whispered as he sprang on the sentry's back and clasped one mighty hand over his mouth. A short struggle, a fall, their faces met. "Edwin!" gasped Muckle John.

"At yer service! What brings ye here? Be they all safe wi' ye in the Cleuth?"

"The boy is, but—"

"Then where be the Laird and his Lady? Whiles we were searching the secret ways, I found Sir Jamie. I helped him oot, an' we got the Lady an' Benson oot. Then I went for food, came back, and could no find them at all."

"Halt or I fire!" Ald Donald's voice rang out.

Muckle John whirled. Godfrey was halfway up the corridor, running for his life.

"Halt!" The timeworn hackbut[177] blazed, but Donald's aim was not what it had been in bygone days. The bullet flattened against the wall. Godfrey dodged behind a pillar, around a corner, and was lost. His voiced echoed back, sounding the alarm.

Edwin whispered: "Quick! This way! The kitchen stairs! They'll be afore us!"

The outlaws dashed for the stairs, plunged up, and stopped short. Arms were clanking in the upper hall. Sir Roger's voice spat an order, "Shoot the first head that comes above the step."

"Bottled in the stairway!" came Godfrey's yell. With it was the sound of hurried marching in the lower corridor.

There was a faint, scratching sound near Muckle John's head. He glanced up. A crack was slowly widening as four slender fingers strove to slide a panel back. They heard

---

[177] Firearm with a long barrel; a matchlock gun

Lady Margaret's low, "Quick, John, open it for me!"

The fisherman's mighty shove sent the panel back. Swiftly, silently the men of Clan Gordon crowded into the dark passage. Muckle John slid the secret door shut, and they lay still.

"Fire!" Godfrey's voice snarled from below. A volley of shots spat up the stairs.

"Fire!" Roger echoed from above. A volley spat down.

"Charge!"

Footsteps thundered above and below.

They stopped uncertainly.

"No one here, sir!"

"Aye, sir, nobody here!"

20

GORDON FOR GOD AND OUR LADY

The clanking tramp echoed in corridors above and below, then died away.

"Muckle John," came Lady Margaret's agonized whisper, "my boy? Did he reach you?"

"Aye, my Lady." The fisherman paused. How could he tell her of that wasted, wounded bairn gasping on the cot at home? "Aye, my Lady, he did."

"Speak out, Muckle John. True kindness will make you tell me the worst. It is much, so much, to be sure he reached you and Jeanie."

"Aye, my Lady, he ha' been wi' us fra' the first. Do na fear o'er much. We still ha' hopes. He was all wounded, wetted an' weak an' weary; then the bitter north wind struck him. I did not find him till mornin', an' he was oot o' his head by then. Lung fever[178] do get a bairn flighty so fast. He did no get his wits till this eve at sundoon; so we did no hear Sir Jamie's orders till then. Ten days on the

---

[178] Infection of the lungs; pneumonia

187

way, he must think us grand an' fine laggers[179]!"

"No, no! The Earl knows you too well to doubt your loyalty. He feared that Gordon had never reached you, and he has been searching the death pits of the Blind Duncan ever since."

"Be the Laird there?"

"No, Muckle John. He and Stephen went to—hark! I hear them coming . . . James?"

"Who is with you, Margaret?"

"Muckle John, Donald, Edwin, and the rest of the brave lads from the Cleuth. Gordon is safe in Jeanie's care, ill with lung fever."

"Thank God they have my boy! Muckle John?"

"Aye, sir."

"Stephen has the sacred vessels, but it cut to the heart to leave the sacred stone. We could not lift so great a weight. Take your sons and get it."

"Aye, sir."

"Donald?"

"Aye, sir."

"If I put you into the fireplace passage, do you know how to lead out without crossing the cistern?"

"Aye, sir."

"Do you remember where we hid the chest of gold?"

"Aye, sir."

"Guide Muckle John, and then get the chest."

"Aye, sir."

"Edwin?"

"Aye, sir."

"Could you get the dungeon keys?"

"Aye, sir. Muckle John has them."

---

[179] Stragglers; those who hang back or proceed with extreme slowness

"Are any of the clan in dungeon cells?"

"Aye, sir, no a few. There be Peter, skipper o' the *Saint Andrew*. Roger ha' a guess that Peter helped to hide the bairn. An'—"

"I trust you, Edwin. Release all innocent men of Clan Gordon. But how will you manage it?"

"Godfrey's men be chasin' o'er the north tower, the kitchens, wine cellars, an' such for us. I can lead the lads oot by the Death-Trap o' the Blind Duncan, for I know the tricks, an' he'd as lief[180] search in the pit o' the Ald Black Hornie[181] as there."

"Good. We shall all meet where the three arches open into the main tunnel."

"Aye, sir."

Dawn's arrows began nipping the wave crests of the frith, but down where the three arches opened from deeper to lesser darkness, the clan was still awaiting late comers.

"If we bide longer in the silence, we shall be hearin' the spiders a-spinnin'," growled young Davie.

"Na, na," laughed Peter, "ye never do hear their shuttles clack; but, my lad, ye'll soon feel how weel the ald granny o' the weavers do bite. See yon muckle lassie crawling nigh yer hand?"

"See? Be ye stark mad? Who can see here!"

"Shut yer eyes, Peter," came Edwin's swift command. "Sir Jamie as weel an' all the lads fra' the third level dungeon, ye ha' lived o'er long in the black night. Can ye ladies give me kerchiefs? I must bind their eyes now. Full sunlight, that we'll go into as we pass oot the tunnel, would turn them stone blind."

---

[180] Willingly; readily
[181] The devil

"God bless you," whispered the Earl as Edwin made the bandages secure, "God bless you, for 'tis little else but wishes your poor chief has to give. Let Donald lead. He knows the way."

As the last comers arrived, Clan Gordon crawled forward. Slowly the light grew until, at long last, the arching end of the tunnel was near, and across it a nodding spray. "Oh, James, I wish you could see this: only one tossing branch of heather with dewdrops glistening on half-open buds and God's own glad sunshine over all."

"And so I shall, comrade-at-arms, so I shall one day when we three, you and our boy and I, wander through the wild green forests of our Lady's land beyond the sea. But, hark! Not so fast, Donald. Something is clanking among the oaks. Move that heather with your claymore but keep under cover."

Donald touched the root sharply. Crack! A bullet flattened against the arch. Then a laugh floated in from that outer world and on it Roger's snarl.

"Come on, and a warm welcome to you! Godfrey is waiting where the passage opens near the old ruin. The seaward opening is well guarded. Come out, and a dose of lead to each. Crawl back, and pass the other two if you dare. Stay where you are, and die. Those old pitted rat-holes make fine graves."

"We shall have to tunnel out." The Earl's weary voice had still in it the ring of steel.

"Hark! What be that?"

"Stephen Douglas!"

"Na, na, that can no be!"

"But it be!"

"See the ald gray cloak o' him! Oh, he must no! There be a thousand pounds on him dead or livin'. It'll be his death, for Roger sees—"

"Hark! He be speakin'."

"Lads," the voice of Stephen Douglas rang clear and steady, "lads, your guns are leveled at Sir James and Lady Margaret. What harm have they done you?"

"It can't be the Earl; he's dead!"

"But it is the Earl! See!"

The heather branches were parting, and the prisoner, clutching the stone with one hand, was drawing himself erect before them.

"The Earl! This, the Earl!" jeered Sir Roger.

"Stephen Douglas never lies!" It was the captain of the guard speaking.

"The Gordon!" That old cheer was scarcely more than a murmur somewhere in the ranks; then it came in a long peal of thunder: "The Gordon! The Gordon! Welcome home, kind Laird! Thrice welcome!"

"Fools!" gasped Sir Roger, dismayed because he had no Godfrey to prompt him in this extremity[182]. "Fools! Can that wandering beggar make you believe a lie? That madman of the gray cloak! That hounded outlaw! Do you believe him? Would you call this old wretch by the rocks the Earl of Ravenhurst? Were my brother James of Gordon living, he would be a nobleman in his prime. Fools! Can you call that vile, dungeon-rotted criminal an Earl and my brother?"

"Sir," the captain spoke curtly, "Sir, the valets of your dungeons are not over careful of the personal appearance of prisoners. This is the Earl. Stephen Douglas has said it. See, Lady Margaret is stepping out beside him to lay her hand on his arm. Sir, you can command us no longer. Our allegiance is to the Earl. Aye, lads, the cheer!"

---

[182] Grave necessity or distress

Then the roar broke from a hundred throats until Ben Ender re-echoed the old war cry: "The Gordon! The Gordon for God and our Lady!"

Sir Roger turned swiftly and strode up the path. Not even the stiffness of wounded vanity could hide the writhing of his sallow face. He knew—when had he ever forgotten it?—the very scullions[183] of Ravenhurst had nothing but contempt for the weakling of the House of Gordon.

The Earl drew his hand across his eyes. The bandage was wet with tears. "God bless you. You are Gordons and Clan Gordon was ever true. Do not judge poor Roger overhard. He has not the strength of will that goes with the Gordon blood. Poor fellow, he has gone down with the evil tide."

"More than he have done that," admitted the captain. "Not all of us, though. Edwin never failed to make his Easter. Others risked it. But most of us up at the castle, sir—myself among them—most of us have gone down with the evil tide. Still, now that you are again with us, my Lord, we will—God helping us—we will stand with you again for God and our Lady."

"Aye, my Laird," cried Edwin. "Give us the word! Only give us the word! We'll ha' Rock Raven for ye afore the sun's at the noon o' the dial."

"No. Roger may have Castle Ravenhurst and whatever of this world's goods goes with it."

"Sir!" broke in Muckle John fiercely, "ye will no give yer rights to yon traitor!"

"Let it pass, you brave-hearted clansman. Is it so much that is given to him? Even here in this world, is there nothing better than piles of ivy-mantled stone and heaps of

---

[183] Kitchen servants; those employed to do menial tasks and hard labor

golden treasure?"

"Weel, Sir Jamie," Edwin raised his hand in the old salute, "if ye dinna care to take Rock Raven fra' yer brother—blood be thicker ner water an' ye ha' a forgivin' heart—we could make ye a snug hold on a high crag in the heart o' Ben Ender."

"I have a better plan to offer. Erecting a fortress means the beginning of a feud and the end of that we all know. More Gordons would die in battle. More orphans wail for bread. The cause for which our fathers stood is dead in Scotland, though not forever. It is to the New World we should turn our eyes. There the old cause lives anew."

"Aye!" shouted the captain of the guard, "aye, my Lord, would ye lead us there? That is a plan worth hearing if sailors' tales be true: red men roaming the wildwood and trading you furs fit for a king's robe to the tune of a few glass beads—aye, lads, and Spanish gold!"

"No, no! I am not promising fortune in the New World. It is not a land where gold is picked up by the handful and jewels shine like drops of dew on a May morning. These are but sailors' tales. Those who follow me to Maryland must go for one reason: to find a spot where we can be free to worship the Lord our God.

"There are few priests now in Scotland. Soon even these will be gone. Without priests and sacraments, the Faith must die among our children.

"Years ago, Baltimore[184] told me much about his colony. Do not hope for gold, for you will find hardships instead. On the way, we shall suffer. We may face starvation. In Maryland we shall suffer much, at least during the months before the first harvest. Even after the worst is over, there

---

[184] Possibly George Calvert, First Baron Baltimore (1580-1632) and founder in spirit of the colony of Maryland

will be hard work and grinding poverty all our lives.

"But we shall be free men in a free land. We shall adore God as our souls cry out to do. We shall rear our children in the Faith.

"How many are willing to follow me?"

"Sir," Ald Donald's trembling hand rose in salute, "Clan Gordon ha' ever followed the chief. I be at yer service. Muckle John, do na be all day wi' yer 'Aye, sir!'"

The fisherman drew a bit of heather through his fingers and looked off across the sea.

"Never to know Scotland more; never to smell the wind o' mornin' blowin' fresh fra' o'er the heath[185]; never to watch the sun a-risin' oot o' the waters o' the frith, glintin' along the whitecaps, reddenin' the snow on the head o' Ben Ender, callin' an' callin' the fishers home!"

"Muckle John Tamson o' the Cleuth!" cried Donald, "ye be the last man I'd take for a lagger!"

"Lagger? Who be laggin'? All the clan be goin', save Edwin. His ald mother be past ninety and bedridden. He can no come till he lays her in the kirkyard[186]. All the clan be goin', but it cuts, man, it cuts."

"And I have a greater burden to lay on your shoulders, my brave Muckle John. You are the best seaman among us. It falls to your lot to be skipper of the ship that bears Clan Gordon overseas."

"Sir, I be no fit for that. I'd land ye all in Davy's locker[187]. You need a deep-seas man—"

"By the time we found such a captain, what would Sir Roger have done?"

---

[185] Small evergreen shrubs; heather

[186] A churchyard; a cemetery situated next to a church

[187] Davy Jones' locker; a fictional place at the bottom of the sea; a resting place for those who die at sea

"Got twa brigs[188] or more to guard the mouth o' the frith. If go it be, go we must wi' the mornin' tide afore sun-up. Peter could take the *Saint Andrew* wi' the seasoned crew, the women an' bairns an' goods o' most value. I could take the *Nancy Kitts* wi' the landlubber crew. Then we'd run-it for the Irish coast where we might pick up a deep-seas captain, food, an' such."

"Well planned, Muckle John. There we could get your altar wine, Father Stephen."

But the priest was shaking his head. "No. My duty is here. The few Gordons who cannot go with you must not be left without the sacraments."

"You! Oh, do not stay!" Lady Margaret paused. It would be useless to plead with her brother; she knew his noble heart too well.

"Muckle John," called the Earl sharply, "what are you doing beyond that heather bush?"

"The dungeon ha' gived ye eyes in the back o' yer head!" growled the fisherman under his breath. "My Laird, I ha' a wee bit o' business to be done."

"And that business is?"

"I'd as lief not tell ye, my Laird."

"Out with that business, John! Your blood is up!"

"Weel, then, Sir Jamie, ye may ha' settled scores wi' yon traitor, but I ha' sworn afore the clan to—"

"Put the sin of vengeance on your soul the day before you face death on the high seas!"

"Sin? It be no sin! But—" He strode to Stephen Douglas and like a giant boy knelt at his feet. "I ha' sworn to give the traitor what he gave the wee chief, blow for blow, wi' the knouted lash o' a galley whip; and then, I ha' sworn to

---

[188] Two-masted sailing ships

fling him fra' the tip o' the seaward tower. Weaklin' o' the House o' Gordon, coward, traitor to the Faith, he what ha' traded kith an' kin[189] for gold, put his own blood brother to dungeon-rot for ten long years, broke the heart o' Lady Margaret wi' waitin', he what would ha' murdered the wee chief—but ye did no see the bruised an' bleedin', gaspin' laddy! It be I what took him in my arms to Jeanie. Sin to kill yon Roger? It be no more sin ner to crush a venom-spittin' asp under my heel!"

"Vengeance is sin, Muckle John," said Stephen Douglas gently. "Because Roger has wounded the heart of Christ by sin, need you sin also?" He laid his consecrated hand on the shaggy black head. The rough hair parted. He ran his finger along the white line from crown to forehead to cheek. "Where got you that scar, my son?"

"Ye know weel, I be prouder o' yon scar than o' all the marks o' a Laird's shield."

"Proud because once you fell guarding the Body of Christ, and now you would wound His Sacred Heart by sin?"

"Na! Na!" The giant shoulders quivered. A tear splashed on the sod. "Na, if ye say it be truly sin, na, I would no wound the heart o' Him what bled for me. I'll forgive the poor weaklin'. I'll forgive."

---

[189] Friends and relatives

21

ROCK RAVEN NO MORE

J ean stood in her doorway, now watching the group speeding down the Rock Raven path, now running back to the couch where Gordon lay.

Was there a sound or the lessening of a sound? Jean sprang to the lad. There was no light in the half-closed eyes. His head rolled limply, and he sighed.

"But it be a sigh! He ha' no gone yet. Mother o' Mercy, let him hald oot till she comes. If I could get the wine on the mantel. . . ."

A hand slipped under the boy's head. A mug was pressed to his half-open lips. Jeanie knew those firm, slender fingers.

"Thank God, my Lady, ye be come. I'll run for Father Stephen. He may yet be in time."

Jean sped up the path. "Aye, that be Lady Margaret for ye," she murmured, "quiet and steady always, even when her heart be a-breakin'."

"Quiet and steady!" Jean did not see her now, the white head bowed on the rushes of the couch, the thin, bent shoulders quivering under the silken plaid, the hot words springing from her heart, swifter than her tears.

"O God! O my God, I cannot! Only in baby days was he mine. O God, remember the years of fear and waiting. Then You gave him back. He was mine, mine for a few hours. How the memory of his brave young face has sweetened the long months of darkness! Now, are You taking him from me—now when we three might be together? I cannot! O God, forgive me! I cannot, my God, I cannot!"

The voice of Muckle John came from the doorway. "Lift yer foot the breadth o' a hand, my Laird. Now, ain step or twa to the right an' yer by his side."

Then the fisherman slipped away again.

Sir James pressed his fingers on the lad's wrist. "The little barque[190] is far out toward the eternal sea," he whispered.

"No, no! We can hope! We must hope still! But I am glad your eyes are bandaged, James. You cannot see where the lash cut so many times, wounds that do not heal, fretted with fever. If we could let him rest only a few days before going on shipboard—"

"He will be at rest in a little while where no man shall trouble him more."

"No, James, no! If we could wait only one day—"

"But that cannot be. We must face the truth together, comrade-at-arms." Slowly he pushed his rosary beads cross foremost over the quilt, blindly groping for her hand, but she did not see them.

Her eyes were on her boy's face, the dark bruises, the pinched, half-open lips. "And he was alone when he suffered. So I knew it would be." Then her eyes went upward to the Calvary on the cottage wall where stood that other Mother beside that other dying Son.

---

[190] A sailing ship with three masts

The cross in her husband's groping hand touched her fingers. She started and saw the mute struggle in his lips, the will of the House of Gordon forcing out the words: "Suffered under Pontius Pilate, was crucified, died. . . ." She shivered, picked up the cross, and finished the words of the Creed.

Prayer and response ebbed and flowed, growing ever more and more pleading.

"Holy Mary, Mother of God, pray for us sinners." Over and over the brown beads slipped by.

A change came. Gordon had not stirred, but there was a light in the half-open eyes. Slowly, very slowly, the waxen lids drew back. The right hand fluttered, a weary load to lift; but it rose one, two, three inches until it touched her hair. "White?" he breathed. "This is my own mother, for her hair is white."

A shadow darkened the doorway. Jean tiptoed in, lit the candles, and knelt. Father Stephen entered and laid his Sacred Burden on the linen cloth.

"Gordon," he said in his clear, low voice, "I am going to give you Extreme Unction[191]."

The eyes brightened, then grew puzzled. "Confession first—"

"If there is anything to confess. You have nothing to tell, have you?"

"Can't remember . . . maybe I haven't had time . . . to be bad."

"Blessed are the days when we have no time to be bad!

---

[191] For centuries, the term used for the Sacrament of Anointing of the Sick; extreme as it was used when death seemed likely and unction as the person is anointed with oil; when death seems imminent, the Sacraments of Penance and Reconciliation, and Holy Eucharist (Viaticum) may also be given

So, do not worry. Say in your heart, 'My Jesus, I love Thee. Forgive me.'" Then Stephen anointed the boy. Not much of evil had he ever known. Not far had his feet gone astray. And then, Gordon's eyes rested on the Sacred Host. Nothing else he seemed to see.

"Aye," murmured Muckle John, "an' tell Him yer father an' mother an' all o' the clan ha' need o' our lad. Mayhap He'll leave ye bide wi' us, for sure the good Lord be kind."

The eyes closed. Margaret's head sank on the couch, her hand clenched on the cross. But Stephen whispered softly, "Sleeping, only sleeping with the good Lord in his breast."

* * * * *

The day fled swiftly. Inside the cottage, the ebb and flow of the rosary still beat on the eternal shore, but the song in those waves was of hope. Outside, the silent folk sped on errands to and from the boats or went on noiseless feet through Ald Donald's door to pour into Stephen's patient ear their sorrows and their sins and to come out again with hope-lit eyes and firm-set lips.

A little after midnight, the altar was prepared. The Holy Sacrifice was offered, solemnly, silently, lest some sacrilegious band steal upon them through the darkness, and to each was given the Bread of the strong.

The sentinel on the seaward tower of Castle Ravenhurst watched the fishers putting out to sea in the dawn. "Fair day coming," was all he thought.

He did not see the tall, gaunt figure in a long gray cloak standing on a cliff and holding out his crucifix in blessing until the ships rounded a headland and could see Rock Raven no more.

Then Stephen Douglas turned and strode back into the forest to wander, hound-tracked, starving, and alone, happy if he found a soul who even in the last dread hour would make its peace with God.

No man knew when the good Lord called him home.

But one year when the snows of Ben Ender were slipping away in merry, tinkling rills[192] over the stones and under the mosses, Edwin found him. His face was strangely beautiful, lying there host-white on a corporal[193] of virgin snow.

---

[192] Small brooks

[193] A white linen cloth on which the Host and chalice are placed during the celebration of the Eucharist

22

IN THE HOLLOW OF GOD'S HAND

But into the west sailed the *Saint Andrew* and the *Nancy Kitts*. For three months, waves raced with a singing wind. Watchers hoped hour after hour for a glimpse of unknown shores. Folk chatted gaily of Mary's Land beyond the sea.

Then, with a snarling roar, the storm swooped down, snapped the mast of the *Kitts* short off, leaving her a helpless log tossed hither and yon by the waves, and wrenched the old timbers of the *Saint Andrew* till she sprang a leak. Yet when the storm drew back grumbling, both hulks were afloat.

The *Kitts* had held her calking[194]—she was of Muckle John's making from the toughest oaks of Ben Ender—but the doomed *Saint Andrew* floated only until her living freight was shifted to the lugger[195]. As she lurched under, Sir James said, "Let us thank our Father 'who ruleth the waves and

---

[194] The waterproof filler applied to make a watertight seal
[195] A small fishing boat with two or three masts and several jib sails

holdeth the sea in the hollow of His hand.' No lives were lost. Only our treasured goods and our chest of gold are gone. God's Mother will provide."

Then followed weeks that were a stern test of that Faith. The derelict[196] of the *Kitts* floated on sun-bright waves. Water was doled out in spoonfuls.

Then the bloodhounds of the air were unleashed again. Muckle John had stood at the wheel through all the raging darkness of the night and the wilder tempest of the day. Now, once again in the howling night, the winds fought with the *Nancy Kitts,* driving the sleet over her in hissing sheets. All about her, long writhing lines of foam moaned as they rose and fell.

Peter, clinging, sliding, stumbling, forced his way to the skipper's side. "Give me the wheel," he panted.

"No."

"Give it to me or I'll take it from ye!" His hand gripped the spokes.

"Take yer hands off or ye'll know who be skipper o' the *Nancy Kitts!*"

Peter stepped back. "Ye be Muckle John, but there be an end o' what ye can do, muckle or no muckle. Yet I may as weel go argue wi' the mast. Ye will na give in. Fit to fall fra' sheer weariness! Ha' a pint o' common sense, John. Give me the wheel afore ye faint."

The grim lips were motionless, the giant frame tense, only the eyes moved following the seething lines ahead.

"John, lad, give me the wheel an' go rest. Six months and more since ye had a night's sleep. Be it restin' to fling yersel' doon on the deck, only to spring to yer feet every time a spar[197] creaks? Will ye never trust me more since I

---

[196] That which has been abandoned
[197] A wooden or metal pole used to support rigging and sails

lost the *Saint Andrew*? Give me the wheel, man, give me the wheel!"

"No."

"Ye be killin' yersel', John! Give me the wheel!"

"Pray more an' prate[198] less. God be lookin' doon on us, be that true? Weel then, He knows what we ha' to face: the ship aleak; the sick dyin' in the hold; the water spent; the last chest o' mouldy bread all but gone. God knows I must ha' strength to steer the *Nancy Kitts,* an' He will give it."

"Steer where? God may will for Clan Gordon to go to Davy instead o' America."

"If that be so, so be it."

"God ha' mercy! What now?"

A writhing, screaming whiteness rose out of the sea before them. The mighty frame of the skipper bent, clenched upon the wheel. The *Nancy Kitts* sprang like a living thing, slipped into the trough of the wave, righted herself, mounted the next, bow to crest. The booming, seething whiteness swirled by on the starboard bow, sending a wilderness of foaming waters tumbling across the deck.

The thunder of a hundred cannons bellowed to larboard[199]. Not a cable's length from the bow, a wild thing groveled, fierce as the spirit of the tempest, soft, fleecy, shimmering as the froth of moonlight.

"Reef to larboard!" shrieked Peter.

The grim skipper clenched the wheel and reversed. The *Kitts* swung to starboard again and, groaning in every wrenched timber, plunged madly onward.

"O God! The rocks o' an unknown coast on such a night as this! But the wind ha' fallen!"

"No. We ha' turned a headland."

---

[198] Idle talk; rapid speech; chatter
[199] Port; the left side of the ship facing forward

"Hark! Do ye no hear yon ugly slushin' sound? A growler[200] to larboard!"

The *Nancy Kitts* struck.

Peter lurched forward. The roaring swirl carried him out. He clutched the rail. Waters above, below, around, booming in his ears, yet he clung. The fury grew less. He struggled to his feet on the trembling deck. Muckle John still clenched the wheel.

"Speed ye weel—to Davy!"

"No. We be anchored in America, bow wedged 'twixt a reef an' one horn o' a jetty[201]. The tother[202] be rammed into the stern. Get word to Sir James. We be on a reef in the lee o' rocks wi' the tide nigh to the turn. If we can float half an hour, we be safe."

Peter began to crawl toward the hatches. The waves broke in sheets over the larboard rail, seething across the deck. The eddy caught him and whirled him like a bit of driftwood over the starboard rail. There he clung till the waters passed, crept back to the slippery deck, caught a rope, began dragging himself hand over hand. He had won ten feet or more when the hatches opened.

A man stumbled up, grasped a rigging line, staggered, fell, gained his knees; but the billows roared over the rail again. Peter, clinging to his rope, spun like a trout hooked in the rapids. Someone was coming toward him through the surging waters. Peter stretched out his hand. The other clutched it. Together they swung in the blinding swirl for a moment. The wave was passing. Peter could see dimly the straight-shouldered frame and the white hair of Sir

---

[200] A large mass of ice floating at sea
[201] A structure that sticks out into a body of water to influence the tides or protect the shoreline; a wharf or pier
[202] The other

James. The Earl gained his feet.

"Boats, Peter!" he shouted. "Water pouring into the hold! She can't float an hour!"

"She can float a half-hour, then. That puts us all safe, for the waves will no beat the *Kitts* to bits afore her job be done. Muckle John made her, an' she will hald to her wheel till the end."

Hour by hour, the fury of the waves grew less and less, for the storm had spent itself, and the tide left the *Nancy Kitts* high and dry. In the gray dawn far out beyond the headland, the cannons of the surf were still booming; but within the cove, the war of wind and wave had ceased.

The morning sun burst through the banks of cloud, flushed the foam, and set a thousand rubies gleaming a-long the reef where the *Nancy Kitts* was perched with Clan Gordon crowding out on deck to see the brave New World. The wet rocks of the headland behind them had each a golden crest. Swift rays of trembling light danced across the mile of shallow, tossing sea lying between them and the beach.

But what shore? New England? Virginia? The Spanish Isles? The forest-crowned steep beyond the sand was silent, solitary.

"Aye, Muckle John," laughed Peter, "when be the dories goin'? The waves are scarce even choppy now. I be fit to go wild wi' longin' to set foot on yon invitin' sand."

"The dories be goin' when Sir James gives the word. Can ye no see he be takin' in the lay o' the land afore he makes a start?"

"Father!" A thin yellow hand touched the arm of Sir James. Joyous eyes looked up at him, joyous though the black circles beneath them were deep. The old merry laugh rang out from lips pale and cracked, rang and then stopped, for pain almost choked it. The Earl smiled at the eager boy.

"Well, Son?"

"O Father, if you will let Davie and me have a dory, we'll get some oysters. I know how to rake for them, and there must be plenty in a cove like this. If you will let us—"

"By and by, my son. The exploring party must go first." Then, seeing the disappointment in the lad's eyes, "Both of us cannot go in the first dory. That would leave Mother alone. She must feel cold down in the damp cabin, but the sun has already begun to warm the deck. Suppose you ask Jean and Davie to help you make a couch for her up here."

Gordon ran gaily toward the hatches, that is, he ran a dozen steps. Then, with a hand upon his side, he leaned against the stump of the broken mast for a moment, straightened himself with a shiver, and went slowly, very slowly, down the ladder.

"God's blessin' be on him!" murmured Ald Donald. "There he be at the pumps last night beggin' to help, an' that pain a-stabbin' his side wi' every breath. He ha' more grit ner twenty men."

Sir James turned from his study of the shore.

"Muckle John."

"Aye, sir."

"Are you sure the large dory is still seaworthy?"

"It be, sir."

"Lower it and put in five muskets with powder and shot, a spyglass, and a compass. You will go with me in search of a suitable place for a camp."

"Aye, sir."

"Wat and Will."

"Aye, sir."

"You will climb that point, the highest on the bluff yonder, to scout. Silence and caution before all things. We cannot fight Indians or any other enemy now. If any sign of human beings be seen, give warning at once. If not, stay as sentries."

"Aye, sir."

"Peter."

"Aye, sir."

"You will guard the dory. Be ready to push off at a moment's notice."

"Aye, sir."

"Silence as soon as the dory leaves the ship. No unnecessary noise on land, such as shooting game. We must know first whether or not this country is inhabited."

"Aye, sir."

A few moments later, the dory slid into the choppy waters. Sir James was standing amidships[203], scanning the beach, the clay bluffs that walled in the cove, and the forest edge above them. Peter was at the helm, Muckle John's brawny sons at the oars, and the skipper on guard.

Gordon, perched on a coil of rope near his mother's couch, reported events.

"They will be on land in a little while now. All the birds up there in the trees will be singing like a bagpiper's band because the rain's over, the sun has dried their feathers, and they can see the makings of fine breakfasts everywhere. O Mother, don't you wish you were—but you're asleep!"

Lady Margaret opened her eyes and smiled. "No, Son. How warm the air is! You love America, laddy, and so shall we." Clasping the boy's yellow hand in hers, she closed her eyes again.

An hour later, Peter and the skipper came back. The place for a camp had been chosen. No Indians or other human beings had been seen, in fact, no living thing save

---

[203] Near or towards the middle of the ship; between the stern and bow of the vessel

the birds. Then came the hurried unloading. Time must not be lost. The next tide would strew the shore with the broken timbers of the *Nancy Kitts.*

The sick were brought from the ship and placed on rough couches made by piling branches on empty casks and covering them with mats and coarse bedding. A shelter from the wind and sun was rigged up from canvas fastened to poles.

This would seem scarcely a fitting couch for Lady Margaret of Douglas, Countess of Ravenhurst, daughter of Sir Wilfrid Douglas of the line of old Sir Archibald Bell-the-Cat; and yet, perhaps it was most fitting, for the ballads of ancient days call the women of that famous name, "The Ladies of the Bleeding Heart." More noble by nature than by blood, Lady Margaret whispered, smiling faintly though the deep-blue Douglas eyes were dark with pain:

"You have been so gentle in carrying me, Muckle John, may God bless you. But see, John, this soft quilt. Benson needs it far more than I. Lay it on her couch. No, but you must, John. See, they are bringing her now."

And the giant skipper, wiping his eyes with his great hairy hand, did as she bade him.

Down by the water's edge there was bustle and haste. Pale women and meager children were searching among the rocks for clams and crawfish. Dories were plying[204] to and from the wreck. Gaunt men were carrying the sick or dragging bundles above the reach of the tide. Weary, miserble, starving, yet a smile lit every face, a smile of thanksgiving for solid earth beneath their feet, a smile of gratitude for freedom to worship the Crucified.

Gordon came hurrying from the tent toward his father.

---

[204] Working steadily

"Well, Son, how is she?" Sir James asked.

"I just gave her a drink of cold water, but what she needs is something she can eat."

The Earl's face flushed painfully. It was hard to bear such poverty as this. "Son, we must not complain. The best has already been given to us. We must remember, Son, that we are really beggars depending on the charity of the clan. They are too loyal to speak of it, even to think of it, but it is true. I am a worn-out man and penniless since the bit of gold I had saved went down with the *Saint Andrew*. We must face the truth, Son."

"I did not mean that, Father. Anyway, what if the gold did go to Davy's locker? There is nobody here from whom to buy. But if Mother had a little soup, a bit of venison, even a rabbit stew. . . ."

"Son, the men have been watching for game all day."

"Sure, there's none down here on the sand. The storm has sent the game into the thickets."

"The men must unload the *Kitts* before the tide comes in. None can be spared for hours."

"They won't let me help, so let me hunt. I could get a few rabbits with a sling even if you do not want a gun fired."

"No, Son, no! You must not go into these strange woods alone. If you were lost—"

"But I won't get lost. I was bred in the woods."

"Near Abell's farm in Maryland, perhaps you could find your way, but we do not know where we are in America. From the trees, I judge we are not far to the north nor in tropical land, but this forest may stretch to the vast South Sea for all any of us knows."

"But Father! Daddy Abell taught us how to find our way in unknown woods. Every boy had to know things like that. I know how to blaze a trail, but on short trips he said to

211

find a good landmark and not get out of sight of it. Oh, Father, I do know how to take care of myself. Mother needs the soup. Oh, please, Father! Don't say no!"

Sir James looked at the pleading boy, then at the canvas stretched above the sick. "You give me your word not to get out of sight of your landmark, even once, even for a moment?"

"Yes, Father."

"You will come back in an hour whether you find any game or not?"

"Yes, Father."

"It is a great risk, but the sick need food. Well, you may go and God bless you, Son."

Gordon walked over the sand and made his way steadily up the steep clay banks that bounded the beach. A year ago, he would have climbed for the very joy of the struggle. Now it was slow and painful work. A half-dozen times he sat down to rest, head against the hard clay of the slope, hand upon his throbbing side, but the memory of that gentle mother under the old sail brought him wearily to his feet again.

At last, the climb was over. He stood under the first of the forest trees. Before him, they stretched in endless leafy arches. He turned and looked back. A dwarf in a toy dory coming from the *Kitts* with a load; that was Muckle John. Someone struggling with a heavy burden; that was Sir James. A lump burned in Gordon's throat.

Now for a landmark! Not a good one in sight. He might get one from a treetop.

Climbing a tree was fun a year ago, but not now. His head throbbed with dizzy pain as he struggled from branch to branch, not daring to look down, resting often when the pain shot through him with sickening misery.

"I must be almost at the top now," he panted. Gordon

raised his head, leaned forward, gasped, and stared again at a little bluff outlined against the blue October sky.

"Sutter's Knob! It's Sutter's Knob! We're not five miles from Abell's!"

23

OUR LADY'S HOME

How he reached the ground, Gordon never knew. His next memory was of trees flying madly and that stabbing pain telling him he could run no more. The lad was walking steadily in spite of the pain, looking straight ahead, thrusting aside the long sprays of blackberry vine, fruitless in the bright October sun, crashing on through burrs and goldenrod, sending the milkweed fairies fluttering before him as he passed. The way had been uphill, endlessly uphill, but for how many hours had he been struggling? Had he failed to sight trees and so let his treacherous left foot lead him in a circle? What were those whirling black things dancing in the air before him? Were they crickets that chirped so loudly through the silence, or frogs, or was it only the blood throbbing in his temples[205]? His foot caught in a tangled vine, and the dull pain of the fall relieved the stabbing in his side at last.

---

[205] That part of the face in front of the ears and above the check bones; the sides of the forehead

The sun climbed the blue October sky, slipped behind a white mare's-tail of cloud, and stole slowly down again before Gordon's pain called him back to aching reality.

Grasping a twisted grapevine, he rose wearily. Where was he going? His head felt like a windmill. Abell's, he was going to Abell's, wasn't he? Which way was it? He had been climbing uphill? No, that could not be right. The morning sun would be in the east, but this sun seemed to be in the west. But if that was east, then going uphill would be going south when he should be going north if he were going from the cove[206] to Abell's.

"Maybe I was going up the hill to get a better view of Sutter's Knob."

Gordon stepped forward with dizzy uncertainty. This climbing was weary business; but at last, he gained the spot, and his glad shout sent all the squirrels on the hill slope scampering.

"The pool! That's our fishing hole under the alders! There's the tree we climbed when the bear was after us! And . . . whether I'm going north, south, east, or west . . . there's the path to Abell's!"

The lad sprang forward only to sink with the pain. Struggling up again, he staggered onward. The old path followed the endless winding of the creek. Was ever the way so long? Were ever feet so slow?

"Is it dark under those trees, or am I going blind?" Gordon muttered as he stumbled on. "There never was a bat more stupid. The trees are thinning out ahead. It must be where the valley widens into the slash[207], and the clearing's just beyond. Surely! Yes, between the oaks—that's the new

---

[206] A small sheltered bay or inlet on the shoreline
[207] An open area of land in a forest that is littered with debris from clearing

field. Daddy has it stumped already. That cloud . . . fire? No, but the sky's all red! The sun—oh, it couldn't be going down now, it's not noon yet."

The lad broke into a staggering run. Hardly a dozen more steps, and the old scene burst upon him: the long, low cabin nested among trees, the orchard and the wide stretch of stubbled field, the shocks of corn and the fodder[208] stacks, the pasture land and fallow[209]—over all, red clouds afloat in the glowing sky.

"Sunset!" he gasped, leaning against the great oak. "Sunset! I must have lain in the grass all day, and Mother has had no food."

On again, down the slope from the woodland, over the bridge in the hollow—the path seemed weedy—was it that Scottish lanes were more often trodden and better kept? No sound came from the farmyard. The wide barn doors were closed, the yard empty, the bucket overturned near the edge of the well. A stifling horror gripped him. Had things gone wrong at Abell's also? It had never been still before. A dog sprang from the bushes with joyously wagging tail.

"O Shep! Old Shep!" Gordon slid through the bars, and the dog was upon him. "Don't, old Shep, don't! I can't roll around like I used to, it hurts me in my side." The friendly brown eyes were full of pity; dogs understand so much. "What's the matter, Sheppy? Why is everything so still?"

But the dog only smiled dog smiles, casting uneasy glances toward the house. Along the side of the cabin and around toward the kitchen door the two friends passed together. A sound floated to them, low, murmuring. The door

---

[208] Feed for livestock; coarsely chopped hay or straw; the stalks and leaves of any cereal plant

[209] Land left unplanted during a growing season; may be plowed

was open. Gordon stepped noiselessly on the worn stone sill. Then a smile sweetened his troubled face as he knelt on the step, whispering softly, "Bead time, only bead time, and even you, old doggy, know we must be still at prayers."

Daddy knelt by the fireplace with the rosary in his blunt, scarred hand. Joel was just behind him close to Which and Tother, and all the rest of the red-headed dozen knelt, each in the same old place. One change there was. Mammy no longer rocked the cradle with her foot, keeping time to the murmur of the prayers. He that used to crow within it knelt beside her, wobbling from side to side on his little knees, chewing her homespun apron string, his shrill voice sounding above the Abell chorus, "Muver uv Dod, p'a 'er ut 'inners."

The last "Glory be to the Father" came from Daddy's fervent lips. Rosary was over. No, he drew the cross back again beneath his broken thumbnail, and his voice was deep and low. "Second rosary in honor of our Lady, Star of the Sea, for the eternal well-being and safe return of our George."

A choking sob clutched Gordon's throat.

"They never forgot! Oh, I knew they wouldn't!"

Then the shore rose up before him—the weary, starving folk, the sick and dying sheltered by that ragged sail—and all the pain and sorrow welled up in the old, old cry, "Holy Mary, Mother of God, pray for us sinners."

Joel twisted on his knees, and Daddy, hearing the sound, turned with one hand upraised to punish the offender. But the hand dropped. The rosary fell clinking on the hearth. John Abell sprang to his feet.

"Mother of Mercy! Would ye look at the doorstep! But come in, boy, come in! Lizzie, get a stool, girl! Don't stand starin'! Can't you see he's fit to faint!"

"Never mind, Daddy, I'm all right. But if you can help—"

"Who?"

"The folk at the cove!"

"What folk?"

"Oh, they're all on the sand—the clan and my father and mother. The ship ran on a reef last—"

"Hold on a bit! How many be there? And where?"

"About fifty, not counting the ten that are sick."

"You mean fifty draggin' yet and a dozen dyin'! Now where?"

"The cove where Alder Creek comes in, but not far up there. It's about four miles south from Sutter's Knob, I think."

"Get the bays[210], Joel! You ought a' had them out a'-ready! Haven't you any sense at all? The light wagon! The heavy one'd stick in the sand. D'ye hear?" he shouted after the flying boy. "Tom, that haunch of venison's in the smoke-house, three or four hams and a bacon or so. Matt'll help you. Ed, run up to the windmill and sack some of that fresh corn meal. I'll help you carry it down."

"But, Daddy, how did you know? I hadn't told you yet."

"Lord bless you! Starvation written on your face. Lizzie, is that you starin' there? Get the boy some supper. Haven't you any wits?"

But Mammy's bony hand was on the boy's forehead.

"No, Lizzie, heavy food won't do. There's fever—"

"Wait a minute," broke in Daddy. "Are they on the shore or up the bluff?"

"Down on the sand but out of reach of the tide."

"Might have a hard pull through the sand. You, Which and Tother, get out the mules! You can ride them till they're needed. Don't leave no straps flapping, and watch out the

_____

[210] Reddish-brown horses, usually with black manes and tails

219

gray don't kick you. He's been skittish all day, consarn him. You, Sam, come to the root house with me. Get a couple of potato sacks."

Mammy's voice could be heard at last calling through the trap door for someone in the cellar.

"No, the last pan's the jersey's. Them's the fresh eggs in the basket. Got the blackberry brandy yet? Annie, yes, bring it here. Molly, run up in the loft and get my herbs and my sunbonnet. That's a good girl, Lizzie. Now hand me the cup. Fine eggnog. Couldn't have made it better myself."

"O Mammy, don't worry about me," cried the boy as her homely face turned toward him. "I'm all right, but if you could fix something good like that for Mother—"

"For the land's sakes! Don't you think there's more than one cup of milk and one egg on the Abell farm? You drink this, and don't fear Mammy won't take care of any folks of yours, least of all your real mother."

"But Mammy!" A spasm of terror crossed his face. "I forgot! I promised Father to be back in an hour—that was early this morning—but I saw Sutter's Knob and—"

"You clean forgot everythin' but to run like a deer for yer mammy. Never mind, I'll stand 'twixt you and a switchin' for once in yer life."

"Oh, it's not that, but their worry . . . ."

"Will be over mighty soon, laddie. See, the wagon's at the gate. Lizzie, you'll have to stay at home and see to things while I'm gone. Yer turned fourteen and should have some sense. If the little twins goes to pesterin' or playin' off on you, well, Daddy will be round to settle them. Molly better come along with me. It's time she learned to nurse anyhow. We'll be gone a good spell likely; ship fever ain't no fun to cure. The rest of you—hear me now—yer to mind Lizzie and help her, and not be pesterin' the calves ner climbing the windmill. She'll have work enough and bother to spare without you little uns layin' yerselves out to be mean."

"Mary," came Daddy's voice from the gate, "we're ready if you are."

The sleek bays swung into a bouncing trot down the lane and out into the highroad, but the talk rattled even faster than the spinning wheels or the clicking hoofs. All had to be told and retold. Many times Mammy cried, "For the land's sakes!" and "Who ever would ha' thought it!" Many times Daddy said, "Thanks be to God and to His holy Mother!"

By the time they reached the shore, food and rest and joy had given the lad his old spirit. He would have walked with the others while the double team strained through the heavy sand, but Daddy carried him as if he were a babe.

At last, a shout came from the cliff above them. A mighty figure stood out against the stars, and the voice of Muckle John came ringing down.

"Seen a boy? A boy! Lost boy!"

Abell lifted the lad in the air and bellowed joyously, "Safe and sound! All is well!"

A light came and went among the rocks.

"There's the tent!" shouted Gordon. A moment later, he was lifting the tent flap to bring the glad news to his mother.

From outside, Mary Abell's voice came in that strong, quiet, cheery tone that makes the sick better by its very sound, and John Abell's welcome rang over the camp:

"Sure you're safe. Our Blessed Lady is not going to turn stepmother to you in her own land."

EPILOGUE

When at long last, old Edwin was free to join Clan Gordon overseas, he gave them these jottings of God's finger on the shifting dunes of time:

Sir Roger tied his fortunes to an earthly king, but that monarch's head rolled from the block while Puritan soldiers glared[211]. He might have escaped had not that staunch Puritan, Godfrey, betrayed him. Guilt-stained, cringing, a coward to the end, Sir Roger went to the block; but he may have been a repentant coward, for Edwin heard him mutter as he climbed to the scaffold, "Fool, fool, fool!"

Then Godfrey had his little day of crush-all, grab-all success until Cromwell[212] caught him playing one last game of double-dealing and set his iron heel down on him as if he had been a viper in the path.

---

[211] The successor of King James VI of Scotland (King James I of England) was Charles I who reigned from 1625 until his execution in 1649. Throughout his reign, Charles I fought with Parliament as well as the Puritans

[212] Oliver Cromwell (1599-1658), controversial Lord Protector of England, Ireland and Scotland from 1653-1658

AIDS TO APPRECIATION
FOR
OUTLAWS OF RAVENHURST

Aids to Appreciation

In order to deepen your family's appreciation for *Outlaws of Ravenhurst* and to utilize this work of Catholic historical fiction as a catechetical tool, several areas of study are provided below. The discussion questions for each chapter are intended to increase critical thinking skills. Scripture references are presented in the hope of connecting God's Word with daily living and to better familiarize families with God's great gift of Sacred Scripture.

Additionally, lessons on Christian living and the virtues have been created, especially for those preparing to receive the Sacrament of Confirmation. One virtue is studied with each chapter. The virtues include the theological virtues (faith, hope, and love), the four moral virtues (justice, prudence, temperance, and fortitude), the seven gifts of the Holy Spirit (wisdom, understanding, counsel, fortitude, knowledge, piety, and fear of the Lord), and most of the twelve fruits of the Holy Spirit. Matching exercises (with corresponding answer keys) on the corporal and spiritual works of mercy and the Beatitudes are also included.

Instructions for use: After each day's reading is complete, discuss the questions provided for each chapter. Use the Scripture connections as desired. Consider memorizing some of the referenced Scripture passages.

To utilize the virtue study, briefly study and discuss the definition of each chapter's virtue. Then re-read the passage given in which a character from the story demonstrates this virtue. Complete the virtue study by conducting a short discussion on the given virtue in action. One possible format for this discussion is provided, but be willing to vary the conversation from chapter to chapter. Utilize the matching exercises on the works of mercy and the Beatiudes upon completion of the book.

Chapter 1 – The Gray-Cloaked Stranger

Discussion Questions

1. There is an air of mystery and secrecy in this first chapter. Speculate on what is happening. What do you think the plan of the "gray-cloaked stranger" is?
2. Consider who or what the man is who had "the appearance of a missionary passing from one Mass station to another." (page 3)

Scripture References

1. Read the story of another child who traveled under the cover of darkness due to danger in Matthew 2:13-15.
2. Read the story of Moses, another child purposely placed, in Exodus 2:1-10.

Virtue – Kindness (Benignity): The expression of sympathy and concern for those in trouble or need; can be shown in words, deeds, or acts of forgiveness for injuries sustained; one of the fruits of the Holy Spirit

Virtue Passage

Although the gray-clocked stranger was firm in his mission, he conducted himself with great kindness: Begin reading with the first full paragraph on page 2 through the first paragraph on page 3: "Keen and marrow-searching. . . through the stinging sleet."

Virtue Discussion

1. Discuss this passage. Can you recall any incidents from the lives of the saints that demonstrate kindness?
2. Consider a time in your life when you or someone you know practiced this virtue. What was the effect of this action? Discuss at least two specific things you can do differently in your daily life to improve your practice of the virtue of kindness. Do them!

Chapter 2 – Brown-Head Goes Fishing

Discussion Questions
1. Relating this chapter to the first chapter, speculate on how these "twins" can look so differently.
2. "There was nothing in his tone to show which boy was his son." (page 13) Explain this statement.

Scripture References
1. Read about the birth of the twins Esau—a red-head—and Jacob in Genesis 25:19-27.
2. Like George, in his youth King David killed a bear. Read 1 Samuel 17:32-37. Read and discuss Proverb 17:12.

Virtue – Goodness: the exercise of the will to keep the divine commands and the precepts of nature; those actions consistent with God's nature, and suitable and befitting a Child of God; one of the fruits of the Holy Spirit

Virtue Passage
Read about George's goodness to his twin brother Joel beginning on page 8 with "Joel gave a sharp cry" through "and fastened it securely" at the top of page 9.

Virtue Discussion
1. Discuss this passage. Can you recall any incidents from the lives of the saints that demonstrate this virtue?
2. Consider a time in your life when you or someone you know practiced this virtue. What was the effect of this action? Discuss at least two specific things you can do differently in your daily life to improve your practice of the virtue of goodness. Do them!

Chapter 3 – Uncle Roger

Discussion Questions
1. "No man can lead you into sin if you don't follow him." (page 17) What do you think this means? How can you apply this quotation to your own life?
2. What characteristic did Roger recognize in Gordon's eyes that caused him concern? (page 20)

Scripture References
1. George obeyed Mary's quiet voice when she asked him to obey his uncle. Read and discuss Colossians 3:20.
2. Read Proverb 16:8. How can you apply this lesson to what you know about the Abells and Roger Gordon?

Virtue – Piety: Honor or reverence given to someone in any way responsible for our existence or well-being such as God as our Creator and constant Provider, our parents, or our country; leads to devotion to God; one of the seven gifts of the Holy Spirit

Virtue Passage
Although upset and confused, George demonstrates the virtue of piety by unwaveringly obeying his mother—and defending her. Begin reading with the first full paragraph on page 19 and conclude at the chapter's end: "Ah, if a man has a cabin. . .the Abell's are my folk."

Virtue Discussion
1. Discuss this passage. Can you recall any incidents from the lives of the saints that demonstrate this virtue?
2. Consider a time in your life when you or someone you know practiced this virtue. What was the effect of this action? Discuss at least two specific things you can do differently in your daily life to improve your practice of the virtue of piety. Do them!

Chapter 4 – When Men Play Marbles

Discussion Questions
1. What might change in your family if "the word 'I cannot' is not said" (page 26) in your house?
2. Just as Lang-Sword gained royal favor by jumping into the sea to deliver a message, what might we do to gain good favor with our Lord, Jesus Christ?

Scripture References
1. Read what our Lord says about "cannot" in Luke 14:27.
2. Read and discuss what Proverbs suggest regarding gaining favor with the king or the Lord: 8:32-36, 14:35, 16:12-15, and 19:12.

Virtue – Justice: The cardinal (moral) virtue that consists of the constant and firm will to give to God and to neighbor their due; giving to others what by right belongs to them

Virtue Passage
Begin reading near the end of the second full paragraph of page 23, "Now, Fire-the-Braes was a bold and bloody man" through Gordon's comment about him, ending with "cried the boy" at the end of the page. Notice how Gordon does not hesitate to profess Fire-the Braes' behavior as unjust.

Virtue Discussion
1. Discuss this passage. Can you recall any incidents from the lives of the saints that demonstrate justice?
2. Consider a time in your life when you or someone you know practiced this virtue. What was the effect of this action? Discuss at least two specific things you can do differently in your daily life to improve your practice of justice. Do them!

Chapter 5 – Castle Ravenhurst

Discussion Questions

1. Discuss Godfrey's idea of "ridding" Gordon of the Catholic faith. (pages 32-33) How can we nourish our faith?
2. Why did Roger inform Lady Gordon of the "laws concerning the imparting of knowledge on certain dangerous subjects to youth of our land?" (page 39) Why would the Catholic faith be considered a dangerous subject? Who or what might it endanger?

Scripture References

1. Read and discuss the following Scripture passages: Wisdom 16:20, Sirach 15:1-7, and Ephesians 6:16.
2. Regarding Lady Gordon's portrayal as "a mother eagle guarding her young" (page 40), read Exodus 19:3-6 and Psalm 91:1-4.

Virtue – Modesty: Grounded in humility, that fruit of the Holy Spirit that moderates our behavior toward others and inclines us to recognize our own worth in true light; purity in words, actions, and dress; helps us to avoid what is offensive to others as well as those things that are unnecessary

Virtue Passage

Gordon has not let his rank go to his head. Begin reading on page 35 with the first full sentence, "From the seaward tower came," and end with "are welcoming you, my Lord."

Virtue Discussion

1. Discuss this passage. Can you recall any incidents from the lives of the saints that demonstrate this virtue?
2. Consider a time in your life when you or someone you know practiced this virtue. What was the effect of this action? Discuss at least two specific things you can do differently in your daily life to improve your practice of modesty. Do them!

Chapter 6 – By the Old Fireplace

Discussion Questions

1. "The Earl of Ravenhurst must always stand for God and our Blessed Lady, let the cost be what it may." (page 43) What are some costs of practicing the Catholic faith and being devoted to our Blessed Mother today?
2. Discuss the following quotation: ". . .saints do not reason as worldly people do." (page 50)
3. Against what and whom did Margaret warn her son?

Scripture References

1. Regarding the "great white throne" (page 48), read Revelation 20:11-12.
2. In reference to "Holy! Holy! Holy! Lord God of Hosts!" (page 47), see Revelation 4:1-11 and Isaiah 6:1-4.
3. Gordon's mother refers to his soul as a pearl. (page 50) In many cultures, a pearl is a symbol of great worth. Read the parable where Jesus compares the Kingdom of Heaven to a pearl of great price: Matthew 13:45-46.

Virtue – Faithfulness: The fruit of the Holy Spirit that allows us to constantly submit our will and intellect to God and to the truth the Catholic Church proclaims

Virtue Passage

Read six paragraphs on page 43 from "Oh, why did everyone hate the Faith" to "let the cost be what it may."

Virtue Discussion

1. Discuss this passage. Can you recall any incidents from the lives of the saints that demonstrate faithfulness?
2. Consider a time in your life when you or someone you know practiced this virtue. What was the effect of this action? Discuss at least two specific things you can do differently in your daily life to improve your practice of the virtue of faithfulness. Do them!

Chapter 7 – My Friend Godfrey

Discussion Questions

1. How can you explain the discrepancies between Godfrey and Roger's description of Gordon's mother with Gordon's memory of that first night at Ravenhurst?

2. Godfrey accuses Gordon of being a dreamer with a dream-mother and a dream-church. (page 62) What are the advantages and drawbacks of seeing things in a positive light—of being a dreamer?

Scripture References

1. In reference to Gordon's statement that his mother's hair was snow-white (page 56), read Proverb 16:31.

2. Godfrey compares the Church to a tree. (page 62) St. Paul compares the Church to a living building in Ephesians 2:19-22, and portrays it as the Body of Christ in 1 Corinthians 12:12-26 and Ephesians 1:22-23. To what would you compare the Church? (Remember that the Church is not just a building. The people of faith—the family of God—are the living stones of the Church.)

Virtue – Understanding: A gift of the Holy Spirit that provides insight into the mysteries of faith and how to live them

Virtue Passage

Read page 62 from "Oh, no, Godfrey" through the first full paragraph on page 63 to "always has a hole in it."

Virtue Discussion

1. Discuss this passage. Can you recall any incidents from the lives of the saints that demonstrate this virtue?

2. Consider a time in your life when you or someone you know practiced this virtue. What was the effect of this action? Discuss at least two specific things you can do differently in your daily life to improve your practice of the virtue of understanding. Do them!

Chapter 8 – The Ruin in the Wood

Discussion Questions

1. "He thought of the promises, boyish promises, earnest, loving, whispered to the Lord Jesus." (page 68) Think of the promises you have made to Jesus, especially after receiving Him in Holy Communion. What can you do to help yourself follow through on these promises?

2. Stephen's heart was full of joy as he heard Gordon ask to receive the sacraments. Why did Stephen ask Gordon if he was now ready to suffer for God? (page 75)

Scripture References

1. Gordon escapes the fate of Absolom, the son of King David. (page 69) Read about this incident in 2 Samuel 18:9.

2. Stephen calls Godfrey "a devil with the oil of flattery upon his lips." (page 72) Read about flattery in Sirach 41:14-16.

Virtue – Faith: The theological virtue by which we believe in God and all that He has said and revealed to us

Virtue Passage

On pages 67-68, read how Gordon's faith is renewed as he recalls saying the rosary and receiving his First Holy Communion. Beginning with "Uncle Stephen" on the top of page 75, read to the end of the chapter to see how his faith impels him to receive the sacraments.

Virtue Discussion

1. Discuss this passage. Can you recall any incidents from the lives of the saints that demonstrate this virtue?

2. Consider a time in your life when you or someone you know practiced this virtue. What was the effect of this action? Discuss at least two specific things you can do differently in your daily life to improve your practice of the virtue of faith. Do them!

Chapter 9 – The Mercy of a Coward

Discussion Questions

1. "But sacraments have a strong effect on those who have as strong a faith in them as Gordon has." (pages 83-84) Do you think that the amount of grace we receive from the sacraments depends on the amount of faith we have?
2. Why do you think that Godfrey told Gordon, "Friar Douglas often binds the eyes of children whom he thinks too young to trust?" (page 85) What does this statement tell us about Godfrey's character?
3. What does "The Mercy of a Coward" mean?

Scripture References

1. "Wine, nothing but wine." (page 81) See Mark 14:22-25 and 1 Corinthians 11:23-26.
2. True to the prophecy of Stephen, Gordon begins to suffer for his faith when he is whipped by Uncle Roger. Read about St. Paul's sufferings in 2 Corinthians 11:24-27.

Virtue – Self-control (Continence): The act, power, or habit of having one's desires under the control of the will; a fruit of the Holy Spirit

Virtue Passage

Read about Roger's loss of self-control as contrasted with Gordon's perseverance beginning with "Sir Roger struck" on page 87 to "had the courage to take" on page 88.

Virtue Discussion

1. Discuss this passage. Can you recall any incidents from the lives of the saints that demonstrate self-control?
2. Consider a time in your life when you or someone you know practiced this virtue. What was the effect of this action? Discuss at least two specific things you can do differently in your daily life to improve your self-control. Do them!

Chapter 10 – Secret of the Fireplace

Discussion Questions

1. Betsy tells Gordon that shortly after Lady Margaret disappeared, Godfrey, who feeds the prisoners, "began to get two extra portions from the cook." (pages 90-91) For whom do you think the two extra portions were?
2. Name several ways that Lady Margaret prepared her son in the event of religious persecution and trial.

Scripture References

1. Like Gordon, the prophet Jeremiah was beaten and imprisoned. Read Jeremiah 37: 15-16.
2. Read and discuss Romans 8:35-37, 2 Timothy 3:12-15, and 1 Peter 2:19-23 on trials and persecution.

Virtue – Patience: A fruit of the Holy Spirit that enables us to endure the evils caused by another without sadness or resentment in conformity with the will of God; a form of fortitude

Virtue Passage

Re-read three paragraphs on page 92, beginning with "Shaken and weary," and ending with "knelt a long time with his head bowed on the old chair." In these paragraphs, we see how Gordon's sorrow and self-pity are transformed into patient tolerance for his sufferings.

Virtue Discussion

1. Discuss this passage. Can you recall any incidents from the lives of the saints that demonstrate patience?
2. Consider a time in your life when you or someone you know practiced this virtue. What was the effect of this action? Discuss at least two specific things you can do differently in your daily life to improve your practice of the virtue of patience. Do them!

Chapter 11 – Return of Lang-Sword

Discussion Questions

1. In what ways do you think the Church in Scotland served as a "great source of unity?" (page 104)
2. As she received our Lord in Holy Communion (page 106), what sacrifice did Lady Gordon offer to our Lord? What sacrifice can you offer to our Lord when you receive Him in the most Blessed Sacrament?
3. How can you apply Lady Gordon's cry, "No cause is lost while true hearts live!" (page 109) to your daily life?

Scripture References

1. "Ever since the Holy Three made blessed the home in Nazareth. . . ." (page 101) Read Matthew 2:19-23 and Luke 2:39-40.
2. Read the following Scripture passages on unity: 1 Corinthians 1:10-11, 2 Corinthians 13:11, Galatians 3:28, and Ephesians 4:3.

Virtue – Peace: A calm that accompanies the agreement of human wills upon which every well-ordered society rests; a fruit of the Holy Spirit; tranquility of order

Virtue Passage

Read the description of the disorder in Scotland on pages 103-104. Reflect on the role of Lang-Sword and King James V in restoring peace to this war-torn land.

Virtue Discussion

1. Discuss this passage. Can you recall any incidents from the lives of the saints that demonstrate this virtue?
2. Consider a time in your life when you or someone you know practiced this virtue. What was the effect of this action? Discuss at least two specific things you can do differently in your daily life to improve your practice of the virtue of peace. Do them!

Chapter 12 – Last Stand of the Old Earl

Discussion Questions

1. What does the phrase, "a martyr in fact if not in name" mean? (page 111) How can this idea also be applied to many of the saints?
2. The old Earl, as the godfather of the captain, implores him to reconsider his actions. (page 117) Discuss the godparents' duties to their godchildren.
3. What do you think motivates Bertrand's actions? What is *your* primary motivation?

Scripture References

1. "But the Master washed the feet of Judas and that same night was betrayed by him." (page 115) Read Matthew 26:14-16 and 47-50, and John 13:1-30.
2. Regarding the Precious Blood of Jesus, read 1 Peter 1:17-21.

Virtue – Fear of the Lord: The gift of the Holy Spirit that fills us with awe and reverence for God; protects us from offending Him by sin

Virtue Passage

Begin reading on page 117, "Captain John Brent" to "then he took his place"on the next page to see how this virtue causes Captain Brent to change from an attacker to a defender of the Lord and his people.

Virtue Discussion

1. Discuss this passage. Can you recall any incidents from the lives of the saints that demonstrate this virtue?
2. Consider a time in your life when you or someone you know practiced this virtue. What was the effect of this action? Discuss at least two specific things you can do differently in your daily life to improve your practice of the virtue of the fear of the Lord. Do them!

Chapter 13 – Guardians of the King

Discussion Questions

1. ". . .it is a sin to touch holy things." (page 124) Discuss the sin of sacrilege (desecration). What might you have done if you were in the situation of the four children?
2. "The trustful prayer of a child is an arrow that pierces the Heart of God." (page 132) Why are the prayers of children so powerful? (See Psalm 131.)
3. How are all Catholics called to be "Guardians of the King?"

Scripture References

1. ". . .but the angel Gabriel could scarcely have been more welcome than Benson." (page 133) Read the following Biblical references to the angel Gabriel: Daniel 8:15-27, Daniel 9:20-27, and Luke 1:10-38.
2. Regarding "the light of the joy that shines on those who have suffered for the Lord our God" (page 135), read Acts 6:8-15 in which the face of Stephen is described.

Virtue – Prudence: A moral (cardinal) virtue that helps us to discern the true good in every circumstance and to choose the right means of achieving it; sound judgment

Virtue Passage

Read two paragraphs beginning with "Stephen looked with trembling reverence" on page 124 to see this virtue in action.

Virtue Discussion

1. Discuss this passage. Can you recall any incidents from the lives of the saints that demonstrate prudence?
2. Consider a time in your life when you or someone you know practiced this virtue. What was the effect of this action? Discuss at least two specific things you can do differently in your daily life to improve your practice of the virtue of prudence. Do them!

Chapter 14 – Glory of the Bitter End

Discussion Questions

1. "A base nature cannot understand the kind of glory [the glory of dying for God] of which Sir Edward spoke." (page 140) Analyze this statement.
2. "No cause is dead while true hearts live" (page 142) and ". . .the will of a mob is the will of the wind." (pages 142-143) How can you apply the wisdom of these quotations?

Scripture References

1. ". . .she be nigh the gates that be made o' pearl" (page 138): Read of the New Jerusalem: Revelation 21:18-27.
2. "Would I were worthy to fall under the banner of the King of kings, worthy of my place in the red-robed army led by Stephen." (page 144) "Red-robed" usually refers to the clothing of martyrs. Read the story of the martyrdom of St. Stephen in Acts 7:51-60.

Virtue – Love (Charity): A theological virtue (and fruit of the Holy Spirit) by which we love God above all things for His own sake, and our neighbor as ourselves for the love of God

Virtue Passage

Read of Sir Angus' love of God in the second full paragraph on page 144 and his love of neighbor on page 145, beginning with "Allen," and ending with "my poor fellow."

Virtue Discussion

1. Discuss this passage. Can you recall any incidents from the lives of the saints that demonstrate charity?
2. Consider a time in your life when you or someone you know practiced this virtue. What was the effect of this action? Discuss at least two specific things you can do differently in your daily life to improve your practice of your love of neighbor. Do them!

Chapter 15 – Splinter of the Lang-Sword

Discussion Questions

1. Discuss the following quotation: "[Godfrey's] mind was too cunning to start a battle lost from the beginning." (page 150) What did Godfrey perceive about Gordon?
2. How might you feel if you believed you were suffering and near death? What might happen when you realized that death was not soon, but the pain was to continue? What tactics might you use to stand firm in your faith?

Scripture References

1. "His own battle horn was blowing." (pages 149-150) Read about the battle of Jericho in Joshua 6:1-20.
2. Gordon gained strength from the teaching of his mother (Deuteronomy 4:9), from those who had gone before him (Hebrews 13:7-8 and Psalm 78:5-7), from God's great love (Psalm 118:5-9), and from the sacred hearth-stone (1 Peter 2:4-7).

Virtue – Fortitude: A moral virtue that ensures firmness in difficulties and constancy in the pursuit of good; strengthens the resolve to resist temptations and enables one to overcome fear; courage; also a gift of the Holy Spirit

Virtue Passage

This entire chapter resounds of fortitude. Re-read especially the first full paragraph on page 150.

Virtue Discussion

1. Discuss this passage. Can you recall any incidents from the lives of the saints that demonstrate fortitude?
2. Consider a time in your life when you or someone you know practiced this virtue. What was the effect of this action? Discuss at least two specific things you can do differently in your daily life to improve your practice of the virtue of fortitude. Do them!

Chapter 16 – Escape

Discussion Questions

1. "This was a day on earth to win heaven—not heaven come down to earth." (page 154) Discuss the meaning of this statement.
2. What does Godfrey mean when he suggests, "Mend the folly with this [vial]"? (page 158)

Scripture References

1. Gordon hears the *Angelus* bells (page 153). Read about the Incarnation (which is what is celebrated in the *Angelus*) in Luke 1:26-38.
2. Gordon calls upon the Lord in his need. See Proverb 3:5, Mark 11:24, and Ephesians 6:10-18.

Virtue – Temperance: The moral virtue that moderates the attraction of pleasures and provides balance in the use of created goods; ensures the will's mastery over instincts and keeps desires within the limits of what is honorable

Virtue Passage

This chapter provides an illustration of what can happen when decisions are not governed by temperance. Begin reading at "The foolish child" on page 157 and read to the end of the chapter to see how Godfrey and Uncle Roger have let their greed and pride determine their course of action—rather than the virtue of temperance.

Virtue Discussion

1. Discuss this passage. Can you recall any incidents from the lives of the saints that demonstrate temperance?
2. Consider a time in your life when you or someone you know practiced this virtue. What was the effect of this action? Discuss at least two specific things you can do differently in your daily life to improve your practice of the virtue of temperance. Do them!

Chapter 17 – Secret Passages

Discussion Questions

1. "Ah, how sweet is God's own air!" (page 160) How often we forget to thank God for His many simple gifts. What gifts can you begin to thank God for each day?
2. Imagine being in the dark—lost, tired, and scared—and being grabbed by something or someone. How might you react? Speculate on who may have grabbed Gordon.

Scripture References

1. Regarding escape, read Psalm 124, Proverb 11:8, and Acts 9:23-25.
2. "I have been praying for a drop of water. Now the good Lord has given me a drop into it, instead of a drop of it." (page 160) Water is a gift from God. Read Isaiah 58:11, John 4:10-14, John 7:37-38, and Revelation 21:6.

Virtue – Knowledge: A gift of the Holy Spirit that enables us to see God reflected in all creation but to see all created things as nothing in themselves so we might desire God alone; perfects our faith; allows us to put creatures to their right use and to see God's care in all that happens to us

Virtue Passage

Gordon's faith allows him to see God in all creation. Find his exclamation of "God's own air" on page 160 and "God's good out-of-doors" on page 163.

Virtue Discussion

1. Discuss this passage. Can you recall any incidents from the lives of the saints that demonstrate this virtue?
2. Consider a time in your life when you or someone you know practiced this virtue. What was the effect of this action? Discuss at least two specific things you can do differently in your daily life to improve your practice of the virtue of knowledge. Do them!

Chapter 18 – Sir James of Gordon

Discussion Questions

1. What does Sir James' statement, "No brass in the ringing of that coin, boy!" on page 166 imply?
2. "Now, sweet Mother, you bring him to me." (page 168) "The Blessed Mother of God has watched over you." (page 169) Discuss what it means to entrust someone or something to our Lord's mother. Consider consecrating yourself and your family to the Blessed Virgin Mary.

Scripture References

1. Gordon's father rejoiced when he heard that Gordon was true to the Faith. (page 169) Read and discuss 2 Samuel 22:26-27, Psalm 89:2, and Colossians 1:21-23 on faithfulness.
2. Read about courage in Psalm 44:19-20 and about weariness in Isaiah 40:29-31.

Virtue – Generosity (Long-suffering or Longanimity): A fruit of the Holy Spirit; teaches us to consider the future good and to wait over an extended time with patience and constancy; includes restraint in demanding justice

Virtue Passage

Find examples of this virtue in the words and actions of Sir James on pages 171 and 174.

Virtue Discussion

1. Discuss this passage. Can you recall any incidents from the lives of the saints that demonstrate long-suffering?
2. Consider a time in your life when you or someone you know practiced this virtue. What was the effect of this action? Discuss at least two specific things you can do differently in your daily life to improve your practice of the virtue of generosity. Do them!

Chapter 19 – Muckle John

Discussion Questions

1. Muckle John is gentleness itself in his care for Gordon, "yet in his eyes was the coming fury." (page 180) What might this mean? What vow does he make to Clan Gordon to avenge Gordon's injuries? (page 181)
2. What plan does Godfrey contrive when confronted with members of Clan Gordon?

Scripture References

1. Muckle John says, "Keep the name o' God off that foul tongue o' yers!" (page 183) Read about God's name in these Scripture passages: Exodus 3:13-15, Psalm 113: 1-3, Isaiah 9:5, Jeremiah 10:6, and Philippians 2:5-11.
2. Persecuted for his faith, Gordon suffers injury and illness. Read about St. Paul, who also suffered for his faith: Acts 14:19-22, Acts 16:16-24, and Acts 21:27-32. What are you willing to suffer for the Faith?

Virtue – Gentleness (Mildness): Tenderness in disposition and behavior; a fruit of the Holy Spirit that perfects love and tempers justice by avoiding unnecessary action

Virtue Passage

Re-read Muckle John's gentleness with Gordon in the middle of page 180. Despite his gruff exterior, notice how Muckle John displays this virtue again later in the story.

Virtue Discussion

1. Discuss this passage. Can you recall any incidents from the lives of the saints that demonstrate gentleness?
2. Consider a time in your life when you or someone you know practiced this virtue. What was the effect of this action? Discuss at least two specific things you can do differently in your daily life to improve your practice of the virtue of gentleness. Do them!

Chapter 20 – Gordon for God and Our Lady

Discussion Questions

1. Many have "gone down with the evil tide." (page 192) Strong Christian friends and frequent reception of the sacraments are important aids in remaining true to the faith. How can you apply these ideas into your own life?

2. "Without priests and sacraments, the Faith must die among our children." (page 193) Consider what you can do to increase vocations in our country.

3. "Never to know Scotland more; never to smell the wind o' mornin' blowin' fresh fra' o'er the heath. . . ." (page 194) How hard would it be for you to move to a strange country in order to safely practice your faith?

Scripture References

1. Read Proverbs 13:20 and 22:24-25, Ecclesiastes 4:9-10, and Sirach 6:14-17 on Christian companionship.

2. Regarding revenge and vengeance, read Leviticus 19:17-18, Sirach 28:1-11, and Romans 12:17-21.

Virtue – Wisdom: A gift of the Holy Spirit that enables us to know the purpose and plan of God; allows us to see things as God sees them and to penetrate the truths of our faith

Virtue Passage

Read the plan proposed by Sir James on pages 193-194 to see this virtue in action. Begin with "I have a better plan."

Virtue Discussion

1. Discuss this passage. Can you recall any incidents from the lives of the saints that demonstrate wisdom?

2. Consider a time in your life when you or someone you know practiced this virtue. What was the effect of this action? Discuss at least two specific things you can do differently in your daily life to improve your practice of the virtue of wisdom. Do them!

Chapter 21 – Rock Raven No More

Discussion Questions

1. For what does Margaret ask forgiveness? (page 198)
2. Before receiving the sacrament of Holy Eucharist, Gordon desires confession (page 199)—even though he had participated in this sacrament only days prior. Are you as conscientious about the state of your soul before receiving the Holy Eucharist? Always remember Who it is that you are welcoming into your heart.
3. What is the "Bread of the strong?" (page 200) Why is it referred to in this way?

Scripture References

1. "And he was alone when he suffered." (page 198) Read Mark 15:34 and Philippians 2:26-27.
2. "Then Stephen anointed the boy." (page 200) Read about anointing, which confers a special blessing: 1 Samuel 16:13, Luke 4:16-21, John 12:3, and James 5:14-15.

Virtue – Charity: The theological virtue (and a fruit of the Holy Spirit) by which we love God above all things for His own sake, and our neighbor as ourselves for the love of God

Virtue Passage

Consider the charity exhibited in the life of Fr. Stephen. Re-read his actions in this chapter beginning with "A shadow" on page 199 and concluding at the end of the chapter.

Virtue Discussion

1. Discuss this passage. Can you recall any incidents from the lives of the saints that demonstrate this virtue?
2. Consider a time in your life when you or someone you know practiced this virtue. What was the effect of this action? Discuss at least two specific things you can do differently in your daily life to improve your practice of charity. Do them!

Chapter 22 – In the Hollow of God's Hand

Discussion Questions

1. Discuss the following quotation from page 205, "Pray more an' prate less." What does this mean? How can you apply the wisdom of this saying? How can you charitably help others apply this axiom to their lives as well?
2. What does it mean to be "more noble by nature than by blood?" (page 210)

Scripture References

1. Read Exodus 33:22 and Isaiah 49-15-16.
2. Read Luke 19:1-10 about someone else who climbed a tree to see some thing or some One.

Virtue – Counsel: The gift of the Holy Spirit that allows God's light to guide us in practical matters, enabling us to judge promptly and rightly, especially in difficult situations

Virtue Passage

Browse through this chapter paying special attention to the decisions made by Muckle John and Sir James. Find several passages that highlight this virtue and how it is practiced in the daily life of both these characters.

Virtue Discussion

1. Discuss this passage. Can you recall any incidents from the lives of the saints that demonstrate this virtue?
2. Consider a time in your life when you or someone you know practiced the virtue of counsel. What was the effect of this action? Discuss at least two specific things you can do differently in your daily life to improve your practice of this virtue. Do them!

Chapter 23 – Our Lady's Home

Discussion Questions

1. "Second rosary. . .for the eternal well-being and safe return of our George." (page 218) Remember that each prayer we say—each sacrifice we make—merits grace. Begin to offer this grace for a certain intention, just as the Abell family did in their rosary.

2. "Many times Daddy said, 'Thanks be to God and to His holy Mother!'" (page 221) Discuss how you and your family can help each other acquire the powerful holy habit of thanking God aloud.

Scripture References

1. Read John 17:9-21, Ephesians 1:15-17, 1 Thessalonians 1:2, and 2 Timothy 1:3 on remembering others in prayer.

2. Read Psalms 118:1, 118:28-29, 136:1-3, and 138; Philippians 4:6 and 1 Thessalonians 5:18 on giving thanks.

Virtue – Joy: The feeling aroused by the expectation or possession of a desired good; a fruit of the Holy Spirit; originates in the will while pleasure originates in the senses

Virtue Passage

Imagine Gordon's joy in the knowledge that help has arrived for the shipwrecked clan members. Consider the joy of Clan Gordon as they establish themselves safely in Mary's Land to practice their faith without persecution.

Virtue Discussion

1. Discuss this passage. Can you recall any incidents from the lives of the saints that demonstrate true joy?

2. Consider a time in your life when you or someone you know practiced this virtue. What was the effect of this action? Discuss at least two specific things you can do differently in your daily life to improve your practice of the virtue of joy. Do them!

Epilogue

Discussion Questions

1. ". . .jottings of God's finger on the shifting dunes of time." (page 223) Discuss the meaning of this phrase.
2. Edwin suggests that Roger had a conversion (page 223) in "the last dread hour." (page 202) Review Roger's attitude toward Jesus' Precious Blood on pages 80-81. Discuss how easy it is to come under the influence of power, prestige, and money—especially when friends reinforce those attitudes. What can you do to avoid this pitfall and keep focused on eternity?

Scripture References

1. Read and discuss the following Biblical passages that relate to time: Job 16:22, Psalm 39:5-7, Psalm 90:4, Ecclesiastes 1:4, James 4:13-15, and 2 Peter 3:8-9.
2. Read about worldliness: Matthew 24:36-44, Luke 16:13, Romans 8:5-9, Romans 12:2, and Titus 2:11-13.

Virtue – Hope: Virtue by which we desire the Kingdom of Heaven and eternal life as our happiness, placing our trust in Christ's promises and relying not on our own strength but the grace of the Holy Spirit; a gift of the Holy Spirit

Virtue Passage

Re-read page 223. God loves all His children. We must always trust in Him and His greatest attribute of mercy.

Virtue Discussion

1. Discuss this passage. Can you recall any incidents from the lives of the saints that demonstrate hope?
2. Consider a time in your life when you or someone you know practiced this virtue. What was the effect of this action? Discuss at least two specific things you can do differently in your daily life to improve your practice of the virtue of hope. Do them!

Works of Mercy and the Beatitudes

While the virtues and the gifts and fruits of the Holy Spirit help us to understand what type of personality traits Jesus wants us to develop, the corporal and spiritual works of mercy, and the Beatitudes help us to put our faith into action. The works of mercy are "charitable actions by which we come to the aid of our neighbor in his spiritual and bodily necessities" (*Catechism of the Catholic Church* ¶2447)— good deeds done for others. According to the *Compendium* of the *Catechism of the Catholic Church*, the Beatitudes "depict the very countenance of Jesus" and "characterize authentic Christian life" (¶360). They are the perfection of the Christian life.

Below are three matching exercises, one each for the spiritual works of mercy, the corporal works of mercy, and the Beatitudes. Read the page from *Outlaws of Ravenhurst* listed on the left. Find an action from that page that corresponds with an appropriate work of mercy or Beatitude on the right. Draw a line to connect them. Possible answers are provided on pages 255-257, but keep in mind that other answers may be defensible.

Additional (blank) charts are included so that readers may begin to track their own practice of the Beatitudes and works of mercy in their daily lives.

(As the *Catechism of the Catholic Church* speaks only generally of the works of mercy, the fourteen works of mercy listed below are the Church's traditional works of mercy as provided in *The Baltimore Catechism* of 1891. The Beatitudes are from Matthew 5:3-11 in the *New American* translation.)

Corporal Works of Mercy in *Outlaws*

page 194	Visit the imprisoned
page 2	Bury the dead
page 170	Feed the hungry
page 145	Shelter the homeless
page 16	Visit the sick
page 199	Give drink to the thirsty
page 178	Clothe the naked

Spiritual Works of Mercy in *Outlaws*

page 198	Counsel the doubtful
page 62	Pray for the living and the dead
page 192	Comfort the sorrowful
page 17	Admonish the sinner
page 73	Instruct the ignorant
page 196	Bear wrongs patiently
page 171	Forgive all injuries

Beatitudes in *Outlaws*

page 203	Blessed are the clean of heart
page 142	Blessed are the poor in spirit
page 19	Blessed are the merciful
page 132	Blessed are they who hunger and thirst for righteousness
page 145	Blessed are the peacemakers
page 47	Blessed are they who mourn (over injustice)
page 193	Blessed are the meek

Optional exercise: Choose a character and write an essay using incidents from the book to illustrate how this character models the virtues, gifts and fruits of the Holy Spirit, works of mercy, and Beatitudes. Use direct quotations of their conversations and cite specific actions to strengthen your character analysis. You may also choose a character who is weak in these Christ-like characteristics. In your essay, discuss how different his/her life would be if he/she practiced these virtues.

Answer Key for Matching Exercises

Corporal Works of Mercy Answer Key

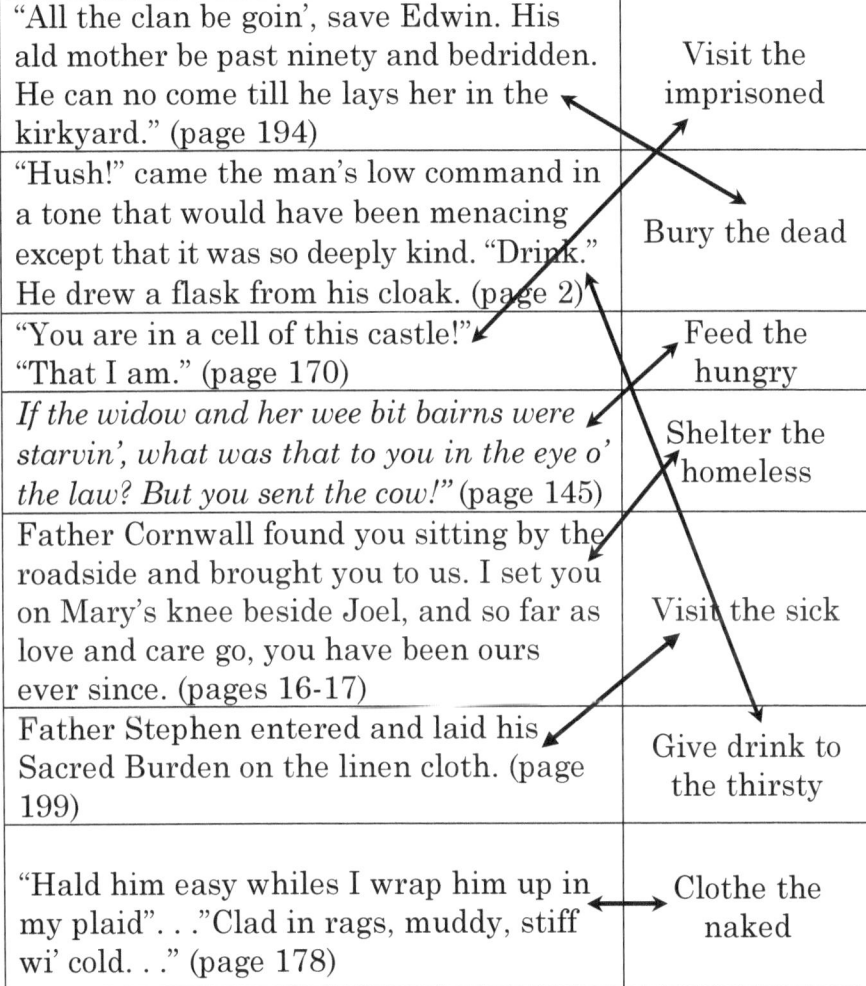

"All the clan be goin', save Edwin. His ald mother be past ninety and bedridden. He can no come till he lays her in the kirkyard." (page 194)	Visit the imprisoned
"Hush!" came the man's low command in a tone that would have been menacing except that it was so deeply kind. "Drink." He drew a flask from his cloak. (page 2)	Bury the dead
"You are in a cell of this castle!" "That I am." (page 170)	Feed the hungry
If the widow and her wee bit bairns were starvin', what was that to you in the eye o' the law? But you sent the cow! (page 145)	Shelter the homeless
Father Cornwall found you sitting by the roadside and brought you to us. I set you on Mary's knee beside Joel, and so far as love and care go, you have been ours ever since. (pages 16-17)	Visit the sick
Father Stephen entered and laid his Sacred Burden on the linen cloth. (page 199)	Give drink to the thirsty
"Hald him easy whiles I wrap him up in my plaid". . ."Clad in rags, muddy, stiff wi' cold. . ." (page 178)	Clothe the naked

These are only a few illustrations of the corporal works of mercy in action. Challenge yourself to find others in the story.

Spiritual Works of Mercy Answer Key

"No, no! We can hope! We must hope still! (page 198)	Counsel the doubtful
"Oh, no, Godfrey! Are the oaks dead because the leaves have fallen? Neither is the Church of God dead!" (page 62)	Pray for the living and the dead
"Do not judge poor Roger overhard. . .Poor fellow, he has gone down with the evil tide." (page 192)	Comfort the sorrowful
"We'll say the beads every day till we know that you are safe." (page 17)	Admonish the sinner
Never allow anyone to come between you and your mother, or between you and your God. These two friends are true." (page 73)	Instruct the ignorant
"Vengeance is sin, Muckle John. . .Because Roger has wounded the heart of Christ by sin, need you sin also?" (page 196)	Bear wrongs patiently
"When a man faces life imprisonment in a doorless pit thirty feet below the land where God's sun is shining, he has the choice of three things. . ." (page 171)	Forgive all injuries

These are only a few illustrations of the spiritual works of mercy in action. Challenge yourself to find others in the story.

The Beatitudes Answer Key

Quote	Beatitude
". . .No lives were lost. Only our treasured goods and our chest of gold are gone. God's Mother will provide." (page 203)	Blessed are the clean of heart
"When I am Earl, I shall take up the battle where my grandfather lays it down!" (page 142)	Blessed are the poor in spirit
"Do as you are bid". . ."Yes, Mother." (page 19)	Blessed are the merciful
The trustful prayer of a child is an arrow that pierces the Heart of God. (page 132)	Blessed are they who hunger and thirst for righteousness
". . .the sin of this lies on the judge, not upon the executioner. You will be merely doing your duty according to law." (page 145)	Blessed are the peacemakers
Margaret was not weeping; she had borne her pain too long for that. (page 47)	Blessed are they who mourn
"Erecting a fortress means the beginning of a feud and the end of that we all know." (page 193)	Blessed are the meek

My Practice of the Corporal Works of Mercy

Action and Date	Work of Mercy
	Visit the imprisoned
	Bury the dead
	Feed the hungry
	Shelter the homeless
	Visit the sick
	Give drink to the thirsty
	Clothe the naked

My Practice of the Spiritual Works of Mercy

Action and Date	Work of Mercy
	Counsel the doubtful
	Pray for the living and the dead
	Comfort the sorrowful
	Admonish the sinner
	Instruct the ignorant
	Bear wrongs patiently
	Forgive all injuries

My Practice of the Beatitudes

Action and Date	Beatitude
	Blessed are the clean of heart
	Blessed are the poor in spirit
	Blessed are the merciful
	Blessed are they who hunger and thirst for righteous
	Blessed are the peacemakers
	Blessed are they who mourn (for injustice)
	Blessed are the meek
	Blessed are the merciful

Other RACE for Heaven Products

RACE for Heaven study guides use Mary Fabyan Windeatt's saint biographies to teach the Catholic faith to all members of your family. Written with your family's various learning levels in mind, these flexible study guides succeed as stand-alone unit studies or supplements to your regular curriculum. Thirty to sixty minutes per day will allow your family to experience:

- ☑ The spirituality and holy habits of the saints
- ☑ Lively family discussions on important faith topics
- ☑ Increased critical thinking and reading comprehension skills
- ☑ Quality read-aloud time with Catholic "living books"
- ☑ Enhanced knowledge of Catholic doctrine and the Bible
- ☑ History and geography incorporated into saintly literature
- ☑ Writing projects based on secular and Catholic historical events and characters

Grades 3-4: *St. Thomas Aquinas, The Story of the "Dumb Ox"; St. Catherine of Siena, The Girl Who Saw Saints in the Sky; Patron Saint of First Communicants, The Story of Blessed Imelda Lambertini;* and *The Miraculous Medal, The Story of Our Lady's Appearances to St. Catherine Labouré*

Grade 5: *St. Rose, First Canonized Saint of the Americas; St. Martin de Porres, The Story of the Little Doctor of Lima, Peru; King David and His Songs, A Story of the Psalms;* and *Blessed Marie of New France, The Story of the First Missionary Sisters in Canada*

Grade 6: *St. Dominic, Preacher of the Rosary and Founder of the Dominicans; St. Benedict, The Story of the Father of the Western Monks; The Children of Fatima and*

Our Lady's Message to the World; and *St. John Masias, Marvelous Dominican Gatekeeper of Lima, Peru*

Grade 7: *The Little Flower, The Story of St. Therese of the Child Jesus; St. Hyacinth, The Story of the Apostle of the North; Curé of Ars, The Story of St. John Vianney, Patron Saint of Parish Priests;* and *St. Louis de Montfort, The Story of Our Lady's Slave*

Grade 8: *Pauline Jaricot, Foundress of the Living Rosary and the Society for the Propagation of Faith; St. Francis Solano, Wonder-Worker of the New World and Apostle of Argentina and Peru; St. Paul the Apostle, The Story of the Apostle to the Gentiles;* and *St. Margaret Mary, Apostle of the Sacred Heart*

The Windeatt Dictionary: Pre-Vatican II Terms and Catholic Words from Mary Fabyan Windeatt's Saint Biographies explains over 450 Catholic terms and expressions used in this popular saint biography series. Indispensable in expanding knowledge and practice of the Catholic faith, this book provides a ready access for the Catholic vocabulary words used in the RACE for Heaven Windeatt study guides. This dictionary also includes a Catholic book report resource that contains suggestions for forty-five Catholic book reports: fourteen writing projects, ten book report activities, and twenty-one topics for saint biographies.

Graced Encounters with Mary Fabyan Windeatt's Saints: 344 Ways to Imitate the Holy Habits of the Saints is a compilation of the "Growing in Holiness" sections of RACE for Heaven's Catholic study guides for the Windeatt saint biography series and presents 344 examples of saintly behavior, one for nearly every chapter in each of these twenty biographies. Enhance your encounter with the saints by practicing the models of devotion, service, penance, prayer, and virtue offered in this guide.

Communion with the Saints: A Family Preparation Program for First Communion and Beyond in the Spirit of St. Therese utilizes three of the Windeatt biographies (*The Patron Saint of First Communicants, The Little Flower, and The Children of Fatima*), *The King of the Golden City*, and St. Therese's autobiography to prepare the entire family over a period of sixty-nine days for the Sacrament of Holy Eucharist. Uses journal entries, read-aloud lessons, meditational readings, weekend family projects, Scripture readings, and review of the catechism.

My First Communion Journal in Imitation of Saint Therese of the Child Jesus provides a lasting keepsake of a child's First Holy Communion. Saint Therese of the Child Jesus and her family studied and prayed for sixty-nine days prior to Therese's First Holy Communion. This journal imitates that family model of preparation for the reception of the Most Holy Eucharist. Each daily entry contains a stanza of a poem composed by Saint Therese, a quotation from Saint Faustina Kowalska's diary (*Divine Mercy in My Soul*), or a Scripture quotation. Two weekly themes—a floral theme in imitation of Saint Therese and a battle theme molded from the teachings of Saint Paul—are offered with accompanying weekly passages from Scripture suitable for memorization. This journal may be completed in conjunction with the *Communion with the Saints* pro-gram or used separately.

The King of the Golden City Study Edition is a new edition of a book that was originally published in 1921. This treasure of a book was written in response to a student's appeal for instructions along with "little stories" to help her prepare for Holy Communion. To fulfill this request, Mother Loyola of the Bar Convent in York, England, wrote a simple story that illustrates Jesus' desire to share an intimate relationship with each one of His children. This new edition contains some updated language but, quite deliberately, does not contain any pictures. Readers, as they progress through this story, will form a mental image of their King, one as unique and personal as their own relationship with Him. The study sections assist with the allegory, connect to the Bible as well as to the catechism, and explore the art of prayer in the spirit of the three Carmelite Doctors of the Church. Although written over eighty-five years ago for a young child, this book remains a timeless masterpiece of Catholic literature suitable for all ages.

Reading the Saints: Lists of Catholic Books for Children Plus Book Collecting Tips for the Home and School Library lists over 800 individual titles of books—both in print and out of print —listed by series name, author, century, and geographical setting with each book's reading level noted. Information on obtaining both in-print and out-of-print Catholic books—as well as caring for books—is included.

Alternative Book Reports for Catholic Students contains forty-five book report ideas to encourage critical thinking for ages seven to fourteen. These ideas are intended to provoke a reflection on those themes and topics that support and encourage Catholic living as well as some that may conflict with our Faith. Many report topics require an examination of our personal faith life and prompt us to take a lesson from the book to strengthen our own faith in God. The suggested activities vary from written exercises to creative art projects and include twenty-one topics specifically designed for saint biographies. Other activities can be used within a group or family.

To Order: Email race4hvn@hughes.net or place an order from RaceforHeaven.com. MasterCard, VISA, Discover, American Express, Paypal, checks, and money orders are accepted.